THE BECKONING

Absolute silence. Standing just outside the salon, Vita feels a growing tingle down her spine. Coldness engulfs her as suddenly as a tidal wave.

Ring

Vita's throat constricts as she sees the reflection on the polished panels of the library's sliding doors: a wan blue glimmer swiftly spreading in the salon's farthest corner. This time the column forms more rapidly as the figure slowly advances on her. A heavy scent clogs her lungs. Still half-way across the salon, the spirit grows steadily clearer. A frizzed mat of white hair. Grotesquely protrusive eyes. Closer and ever closer, unsubstantial arms eagerly out-stretched to fold her in their clasp...

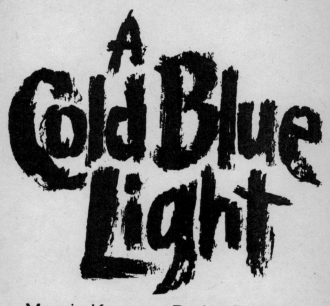

A Cold Blue Light

Marvin Kaye and **Parke Godwin**

CHARTER BOOKS, NEW YORK

A COLD BLUE LIGHT

A Charter Book / published by arrangement with
the authors

PRINTING HISTORY
Charter Original / September 1983

ISBN: 0-441-11503-9

Charter Books are published by The Berkley Publishing Group,
200 Madison Avenue, New York, N.Y. 10016.
PRINTED IN THE UNITED STATES OF AMERICA

ACKNOWLEDGMENTS

The authors are indebted to the research and writings of several anthropologists, philosophers, psychic investigators, psychologists and sociologists. Of particular importance in the creation of this fiction were the following four books and one article:

FOX, Oliver, *Astral Projection, A Record of Out-of-Body Experiences*, University Books, Inc., 1962.

HUGHES, Pennethorne, *Witchcraft*, Pelican Books, 1965.

LEWIS, I. M., *Ecstatic Religion*, Pelican Books, 1971.

MURRAY, Dr. Margaret A., *The God of the Witches*, Oxford University Press, 1973.

SCHACHTER, Daniel L., "The Hypnagogic State: A Critical Review of the Literature," in *Psychological Bulletin*, Vol. 83, No. 3, 1976.

We are indebted for vital medical data and suggestions—and the time spent providing them—by the late Gottlieb Helpern, M.D.

CONTENTS

■

For Westerners, subjective experience is no confirmation of anything. It is only when instruments can provide numbers, when measurements can be taken to provide objective verification that the existence of a phenomenon is proved.

—*Sweet Spot in Time*
JOHN JEROME

MERLYN'S CHOICES

■

Aubrey House is empty now. No one visits, no one wants to buy it. And yet it's such a lovely place . . . not a gloomy Gothic pile reeking with predictable atmosphere but a large, sunlit white frame house in rural Pennsylvania, not far from Doylestown, northeast of Philadelphia.

Built a little more than a century ago before white frame was replaced as a status symbol by agonized Tudor and fieldstone, Aubrey House is an antique collector's dream: filled with chair rails, dark plank floors, stuffed and forgotten cupboard closets (one of them sealed off), mahogany stairs, smelling of seasoned wood and shrouded with expensive old rugs fading out their years in dusty sunlight. Notice the wainscoting in the parlor and the bas-relief cherubs, potbellied and puerile, on the mantelpiece. Cherubs were a favorite subject then. The Gilded Age was not subtle, and the Aubrey fortune greatly exceeded Aubrey taste.

Packed away in various rooms are shaving cups, porcelain bowls and pitchers, dust-sheeted Empire sofas, original razor strops, even a built-in barber's chair. There are marble washstands and ball-and-claw tubs in the vast bathrooms. One chamber on the third floor contains a stereoscope with boxes and boxes of views as well as albums with thick cardboard pages—family photos mounted on heavy backing, pictures of children swaddled and shapeless in summery white, their stiff expressions as solemn as the stern men and austere women by their sides . . . wait: *that* picture . . . beautiful, wasn't she? Charlotte Aubrey, late grandmother of Merlyn Aubrey. Charlotte seems as exquisite as an agate doll, with eyes as difficult to fathom.

Close the old album, brush the fine dust from your hands, descend one flight and walk slowly down the second floor hall until—

Stop. You've reached it.

3

There's something else in Aubrey House besides antiques. Charles Singleton simply calls it "the Aubrey effect," but in 1935, an investigator named Falzer described it as "a cold blue light that nothing drives away or brings closer. It's just there, a constant." But Drew Beltane will disagree with this characterization; he will perceive it as something altogether different.

In late summer of last year, three men and two women came to Aubrey House, each seeking something intensely personal. Five separate houses, if you will, all of them haunted.

They're at dinner now in the Aubrey dining room—tentative, cautious, feeling their way with one another and the house.

Interesting group. Look them over, try to see them plain.

That forceful-looking, somewhat reserved gentleman with eyes less aloof than his manner is Richard Creighton, a philosophy teacher with an imposing number of books on interdisciplinary convergence, metaphysics and epistemology to his credit. He has a reputation for uncompromising pragmatism, but the analysis is too pat. An artistic or emotional woman like Vita would see him as a vital man in his forties with "interesting" angles and shadows in his face. He can't be all logic and no heart, can he? See how judiciously he enjoys his food and wine.

Creighton is haunted by the recent accidental death of his wife and young daughter, a tragedy he is afraid he might have prevented. His mind won't entirely accept the guilt, his heart won't let it go.

On Creighton's left is Vita Henry, a woman whose type you've seen at a hundred social functions and as a member of countless civic and church groups: eagerness apotheosized even as she doubts the springs of her own zeal, a person anxious to find her own definition, yet praying some handsome stranger will liberate her from the need to do so. Vita is tremulously ready to please without any clear notion of how to go about doing it; there is a curiously *unused* quality about her. And yet, look closer . . . see how her hair, if she let it fall, would curve around a rather fine caste of features. Her mouth is full, her jaw well shaped, her skin clear and smooth. Creighton's senior by a few years, Vita still fits into a size 9 dress, but not without some hint of the shape of things to come. Lately she's taken to dressing younger.

Vita laments (with propriety) her dead husband of twenty-five years, a man as sexually dormant as she. His infrequent needs left her feeling clumsy, unattractive and too embarrassed to return his advances. There was once a right time and a right man, but her conservative family bullied her out of it, and now she has nothing left but the shriveled remains of their common sense. Yet Vita is still vital, if only someone cared to notice.

The candlelight, at least, is kind to her.

Across the table from Vita is a round, animated little man named Charles Singleton. He's fifty-three, a dangerous age for a person with his weight and blood pressure. He eats rapidly, nervously, tries to be on everyone's frequency at once, often is on no one's. A dependent man but quick to cover up his need to identify with someone stronger. He smiles tolerantly at those who haven't his experience, but is all too aware of the precariousness of his own authority and characteristically masks it with a kind of jocular pomposity.

The analytical Creighton tends to slough off Singleton, but though the little man may be bewildered and self-deluding, his brown eyes still lend a certain canniness to his flushed clown face, and there is a sensitivity in the way his lips are set: not a creator but a man with some capacity to shape what is already there.

To his left sits the enigmatic Drew Beltane, in some respects Creighton's twin and in others his opposite number. Drew's twisted, pain-wracked body is kept functioning only by the deliberate effort of his own iron will. Life is an unending series of choices that Drew must make in spite of never-absent agony.

Vita has heard the common rumors amongst paranormal "savants" that Drew is a man of many lifetimes and places. She finds him terribly attractive; his eyes, she thinks, have witnessed too much, have read cosmic secrets in suffering and silence.

The last member of the party sits at the head of the table, her place by right. One tends to think of Merlyn Aubrey as a girl, though her Philadelphia Main Line debut took place twelve years ago. Since then, she attended Bryn Mawr and made an abortive stab at postgraduate studies at Columbia. Her blonde hair frames exquisite features. She seems fawn-shy and fragile as a piece of Sandwich glass; her complexion is as delicately tinted. It shows off well in the candlelight, a circumstance she carefully arranged.

Five years ago, Merlyn's child-woman attitude was winsome though a little cloying. But now, at twenty-eight, it is no longer a chic cocktail party neurosis; it is a lethal battle between the warring factions of her personality. She recently left a rest home and sees her therapist two or three times a week, but Merlyn is a desperately confused person. Her few affairs have always been with older men, men initially flattered by her way of placing power over her into their hands, men ultimately puzzled and sometimes shattered when she ruthlessly snatched it back.

It's beginning again. See how carefully she listens to Creighton? How openly, how trustingly she smiles at him? Yet isn't it peculiar how often her gaze strays to the far end of the dining room and the portrait hanging there of her grandmother, Charlotte Aubrey?

Richard Creighton. Vita Henry. Charles Singleton. Drew Beltane. Merlyn Aubrey.

Interesting group.

Five very different people, each with his or her own private ghosts. An unlikely quintet. Why are they sharing dinner together in a seldom-tenanted old home in rural Pennsylvania? What brought them to Aubrey House?

What do they hope to find?

death and the shattering impact of his daughter's head into the windshield told him he was dreaming again because he wasn't there when the accident happened, though now he'd always be there even though it was doubly dead, interred in the casket of the past, and he could only experience it in the recurrent nightmare when the headlights blinded him and he pressed the floorboard in sympathetic response to Lana pedaling the brake gently at first then harder and faster as she realized the brakes weren't working and her foot went clear to the floor while the big diesel truck rolled from warning to danger to

The pattern broke. Reshifted. The sense of remoteness faded. The dream was over.

—Now I'm there. Really.

Sure about that?

—Yes.

Why?

—Dreams not this complex.

Define. Elucidate.

—Dimensionality of objects perceived. Thousands of details: dew on the dashboard in intricate patterns; familiar patina of dust where Lana forgot to wipe it clean.

Blaming Lana?

—No. Merely an observation. *I* could have kept it dusted.

Yes. And as for your reasons: unconvincing. Dream related to hyperesthesia. Detailing common to hypnagogic state.

Slow motion. Huge truck hurtling. Too slow. Inconsiderate of time being wasted.

busy Creighton time valuable

But at last the diesel crumpled the driver's side like a

7

Styrofoam cup wadded for disposal, pinning Lana between the door and the twisted steering shaft. Her blood gushed but didn't puddle because she once covered the seats with Scotchgard. Next to her, the spider web of shatter waves veined the windshield with abstract and beautiful patterns where his daughter's head smashed into it.

And then they got out of the car. Walked to him, wife and daughter. Lana and Marla. Spotless. No mark. No wound. No blood. Charade of death. On Lana's face he saw the old disapproval, the familiar lip quirk, the unspoken accusation in her green eyes: *you never had enough time for us, Rich, not for us.* But Marla had no reprimand, only merriment. Love. One day short of her seventh birthday when it happened, saying *daddy* arms outstretched *daddy pick me up daddy carry me home I don't like it here*

—Where?

so he cradled her in his arms because she was afraid of piggyback *too high daddy* and he wanted to comfort her, crooning and rocking her in the security of his love that was inadequate to protect her from the big diesel truck that rolled from warning to danger to death and the

—No.

shattering impact created a spi

—No!

der web of abstract and beauti

—*No!*

ful patterns where her head smashed into the windshie

—NO!

And Richard Creighton wakes.

He immediately senses the different atmosphere, reality versus false waking.

Sure about that?

His red-rimmed eyes try to focus, racing over the too-familiar bedroom walls, the textured wallpaper, the molding running just below the pale ceiling, wallpaper again down to the crumpled bed as the dream flickers and ebbs on the periphery of his mind.

Light blue wallpaper. Pale moonlight. A ticking clock. His own breath in the dark, not the gentle aspiration of his wife. No faint sound down the hall, Marla turning over in sleep.

Nothing.

Fighting the dead weight of loneliness, Creighton pushes back the covers, slides his legs over the bed and sits up.

—Waking worse than dreaming.

Why?

—In the dream: the illusion they're still alive. Frozen. Not final. It's better.

Sure about that?

His mouth tastes rancid with the dark sourness welling up from his stomach. A cigarette will only make it worse, but he lights one anyway, hunching on the edge of the bed, head hanging over his knees.

The digital clock in the FM glows: 3:52. He switches on the radio. WNYC. Spritely flute-chamber orchestra composition, preclassical, inanely cheerful for the hour and his mood.

—Let it play. Music = musicians. Living people.

Invalid premise. When recorded? Half the musicians might be dead. Consort of ghosts.

—Ghosts? Define.

Nothing.

Springing to his feet, Creighton paces the confines of his bedroom, 19 by 17, pads over the thick deep shag carpet. The dining room windows are already open to catch sounds from 89th Street, but now Creighton pushes up the bedroom windows, too.

The apartment was always too big for the three of them. Nine rent-controlled rooms. The way it was laid out, he could feel totally isolated even with Lana busy in the kitchen and Marla raising hell on her trike in the wide entrance hall, and when mother and daughter argued, he didn't hear because that was the plan: *don't bother daddy he's working*— so they fought in whispers, and he never heard, or at least pretended not to. That much of them wasted.

—Loving one another but spending too much time together. Nothing now but the empty suite of rooms, silent except for the music and the shuffling noises Creighton deliberately makes to remind himself he still must function in a peopled world, not a vacuum. Turning up the radio, he lurches into the hall, stumbles down it.

In the kitchen, he pours out a glass of V-8, adds vodka, pepper, worcestershire, tabasco, lemon juice, celery salt. Mixes it. Sips. Then wanders with the drink, snapping on lights and leaving them burning.

Why?

—Illusion of life.

He straggles into the study, drink already half-consumed, begins to turn on the TV, remembers the FM is still playing. Sinks into the worn black leatherette recliner, stares at his desk as though he'd never before set eyes on it or the things it holds: dictionary, covered typewriter, unfinished syllabus for spring term intro course.

> PHILOSOPHY I. BASIC PRINCIPLES OF LOGIC:
> (or) INTRODUCTION AND SURVEY OF
> ORDERED THOUGHT.
> (or) RATIONALISM FOR SIMIANS.

Next to the syllabus are the insurance forms.

> CAUSE: Faulty brake drum.

—But the brakes worked.
Sure about that?

The day before it happened, on the George Washington Bridge, he jockeyed his foot on the brake, knowing its feel as well as his hands knew the wheel. He felt a slight but palpable difference in pressure, a bit of give to the pedal, not much, but he thought he'd better have it looked at soon, maybe in two or three days, because first he had his lecture and a full teaching load the following afternoon and he couldn't take the time.

busy Creighton time valuable

Later he had a spat with Lana and they didn't speak to one another that night. In the morning, he avoided her until she went out to take Marla to school and

and

Pushing out of the chair, he paces the study, 12 by 15, finishes his drink, knows he can't keep doing it to himself, three weeks of sleeping out of habit on the same side of the big bed, dragging through each day, letting dishes pile up. Insurance forms not done. Unsigned. The damned syllabus silhouetted with dust on the dark mahogany desktop. Just basic phil, he ought to be able to polish it off in half an hour, copying one of the old catalog entries.

Only he couldn't start. Couldn't drop the needle on the world again and let it play.

—But I've got to do something.

False. Sartre, Camus: existence arbitrary, no fixed final meanings.

—Sure about that?

Licking pepper from the crusted glass rim, wanting another cigarette but the pack is empty and the carton is in the bedroom, Creighton fishes a sizable butt from the desk ashtray, finds a crumpled matchbook, lights up. Far down below in the dark, a car horn honks on 89th Street.

—It matters what I do with myself. I want it to matter.

Sure about that?

—Shut up.

Thoroughly sick of his own inner dialogue, Richard Creighton decides to decide.

—A philosopher may be able to afford to sit in his underwear at four in the morning and ponder the futility of pulling on his pants, but a human being has to go on living.

?

—Yes.

Rising, he approaches the desk, turns over papers, studies the syllabus, rejects it. Examines the insurance forms, discards them. Turns over a letter, a pale blue envelope, tosses it aside. Pauses. Picks it up again.

damn silly letter

Inside the envelope, matching stationery slightly scented with Nina Ricci. He examines the precise but flowery hand, the studied femininity of the generous loops and inconsistently flattened capitals.

My Dear Mr. Creighton,

I read your guest review of *Beyond Clinical Death* in the Sunday *Times* and since that book is the subject of our Tuesday evening talk at the ESP Forum (First Universalist, 76th & Central Park West), we would be honored to have you address the meeting on your views. It may be of interest to know that Charles Singleton will be present. Perhaps you have read some of his articles on the occult? That is Tuesday, September 14, 8 p.m. Please let me know as soon as possible if this is as convenient to you as it is exciting to us! My personal telephone number is 555–0816.

Sincerely,

(Mrs.) Vita Henry

Creighton imagines the room peopled with the ESP Forum of the First Universalist Church at 76th Street and Central Park West. Bright, expectant, eager, all eyes riveted on him.

"My view of death, friends? All in all, I'd rather be in Philadelphia."

He chuckles. The old W. C. Fields quip suddenly seems disproportionately funny. The sound of his laughter wells out in a great flood that turns harsh as he discovers he's really crying.

Creighton reaches for the phone.

—Yes, my dear weird (Mrs.) Vita Henry. Though I've met you and can't say I like you very much, I will consent to address your inane group.

Why?

—Because I feel like seeing other people and listening to another sound besides a ticking clock turning over meaningless minutes. I'll tell them about the impossibility of objectifying the out-of-body experience and the delusion of rationalist methodology in investigating the afterlife *and* the necessity of rationalist methodology in investigating the afterlife and the idiots won't get to first base trying to figure out what the hell I said.

And

—Because I'm beginning to count trivialities like subway cars and letters in billboards and the number of steps in flights of stairs.

And

—Because I forgot to buy a new bulb for Marla's night light, so she sobbed herself to sleep the night before she died.

And

—Because I'm afraid to go to bed and afraid to wake up.

And

—WILL YOU PLEASE ANSWER YOUR FUCKING PHONE, (MRS.) VITA HENRY?

Angled midnight. Cobwebs, slants and shafts. Flashes of iridescent pain glowing in the dark wet ground as the hot drops splash the plain, plain Vita. Waterwall down plastering thin down nightgowndown damp can't earth rise. Michael clinging rainplastered mama nightgown beasts rainfingers buttocks skinstirringblood.

Faces. Michaelmama? It? He?

Before been it's here coming coming here it's been before It? He? *coming* Ithe?

Cupping beasts, nipples pointing mute*myth*sacrifice to Him? It? floodwarm change *me*her rising water = slivers slicing nipples, rainrip, muscles drop, arms, bones steelstrip bloodflowarmsbeaststhighspulsefastpain trickling faststrippleasure

Ring

No!

Ring

Notyet

Ring

What a strange man, Vita Henry thought, replacing the receiver. Her cup still sat by the bed. She picked it up and sipped tepid rose hip tea, thinking about Richard Creighton actually calling at 4:15 a.m. to say he'd address her group. Well, she was just as glad he'd wakened her, she never slept well now without tablets, but they made her dream.

She took another sip and tried to remember how he sounded. His voice was a good one, a bit strained but forceful, vibrant, masculine. She wanted to rest on its comforting male sound, wrap it round her like a warm robe.

I met him once, but he probably doesn't remember.

And why should he? They say young girls are silly, but surely, thought Vita, there's something pathetic about a

14

forty-seven-year-old woman sitting up in the middle of the night with a drowsy, disapproving cat on her lap, still squeezing the last ounce of contact from a man's voice over the telephone. *But loneliness is another planet.*

She was not a New Yorker, did not appreciate its alleged charisma. She came to Manhattan fifteen years earlier when Walter took the ministry at St. Anne's Episcopal. Now that he was dead, nothing kept her from moving away except inertia. Most of her acquaintances were in a tight quadrangle from 86th south to 59th, east from Riverside Drive to Central Park West. But though West End Avenue was beginning to resemble a row of mausoleums, there was nothing left to return to in Steubenville, Ohio.

Vita gently shooed the cat off her lap and took the cup to the kitchen sink. She debated going back to sleep against remaining awake. It really didn't matter, of course, what she did, and that was horrible. Horrible.

Why would he call me so late?

Back home, the telephone ringing after midnight could only mean death or fire or some other emergency. But people did it casually in New York.

Perhaps he remembers me?

There was a special quality to isolation in New York, a crushing anonymity, a nakedness. Like the Single Again meetings at First Universalist, the consciousness-raising rap groups where people found thousands of different ways of crying "I'm lonely" without ever really saying it at all. Vita went twice. She couldn't stand it any more after that. Women over forty, over fifty, dressing too young *like me* trained to be wives and nothing else, glib with Friedan and Steinem and Jong but still desperate behind the set expression of their eyes, wanting the men they said they despised.

And the men. Just as lost, just as pathetic, trying to be sauve, as if it didn't matter whether they found someone or went home alone for the hundredth time, men no longer married, required to hunt and confront as human beings those women they'd always taken for granted but eventually grew to need like narcotics, terrified of their dependency, helpless to fight it, most of the time unable to satisfy it. A few of the men at the group were different, they'd never married, never would: frightened, aging boy-men walled up in their own egos and empty lives, as comfortably numb in their solitude as if freezing to death.

After Walter was gone, Vita went to bed with men on two widely spaced and unfortunate occasions. The men were as awkward as she, embarrassed and perfunctory, pretending passion while keeping it safely at arm's length, too eager to get dressed and go home to a desolate bed that was at least familiar.

Dear God.

Though St. Anne's was "her church," Vita preferred going to First Universalist because there were more singles of her own age, and there were discussion groups on different lifestyles. It was a more "now" church, she felt, and the mixers were only part of it, there was also her ESP Forum.

Charles Singleton's ESP Forum.

Vita was certain she had the potential to be a mental medium. When she was in her twenties *after Michael was gone*, she felt vulnerable and very open, and there were times late at night when another woman's voice came from her mouth . . . a person she never knew and wouldn't *want* to know, a coarse, greedy cat in heat. A woman who died young and angry and who inexplicably picked Vita to speak through. *Defiling! Degrading!*

But she often spoke of that experience. It was her validation in psychic discussion circles—though she had to invent many of the details because she could never repeat or describe the actual things the little slut said with her own mouth.

Vita Henry went to the wall telephone just inside the kitchen door and scribbled a note on the pad hung next to it.

Call Merlyn about Richard Creighton

Merlyn was the closest thing Vita had to a friend, despite their great difference in age. They met under unusual circumstances and Merlyn eventually told her about the cold blue light at Aubrey House. Which enabled Vita to speak of her mediumship when she was Merlyn's age, and they each sensed the other's loneliness, *though it must be different at twenty-eight, because by instinct Merlyn looks forward while I look back.*

Well, at least they were both in the world again and coping, whatever that meant. Little Merlyn, fragile as crystal, just as lost as Vita, though she had no trouble attracting men. But it was strange how the good, viable choices seemed to slip by her, the young men. Merlyn always gravitated to men considerably older than she, but her choices never lasted long.

Merlyn Aubrey. Blonde beauty, delicacy enhanced by soft light and subtle makeup. Only her hands belied the china-doll impression: big, long-fingered and capable, a sculptor's hands. Merlyn hated them. Yet they seemed so very strong and expressive when she used them to hide her face in a curious, self-destructive clawing motion at her cheek whenever she became agitated.

Vita's mouth tasted terrible. She walked into the bathroom, brushed and rinsed. Out of habit, she surveyed the status quo in the mirror. The image gratified her . . . the dark opposite of Merlyn, eyes clear and sleep-washed, lids drooping with a hint of sensuality. Her hair falling softly over the shoulders of the wine robe. She leaned closer. Even in the brutal 5 a.m. bathroom light, the gray barely showed. The whole survey would be richer for sleep, but *Merlyn says sometimes I look so bitter* at least there were no wrinkles yet, no real wrinkles, she could still call them character lines without actually lying, and thank God none of those blurrings of the upper lip line, no puckering vertical lines, not yet. Still full and straight.

Useless Beauty: a story she'd read once. About a man so afraid of his wife's beauty that he kept her pregnant for years. *If only—*

But Walter didn't.

Her fist knotted on the smooth tile of the sink. Forty-seven. No man. No children. A church and a spayed cat. Ticking clock in the living room. Rows of Walter's books with the yellow-edged, unfinished manuscript ("Promise me you'll try to finish it, Vita") of his essay on St. Paul jutting between Gibbon and Renan, seen from the same tiresome angle from her reading chair. Sunday mornings as a kind of respected dowager queen at St. Anne's: Wife of the Late; Chairperson of the Flower Committee; hushed and trivial conferences, dry as pew velvet, in the vestry.

Dear God.

She didn't like the way she felt, but *it's nothing,* she reasoned to the cat. A bad time of day to be awake, everything is worse before the sun comes up *weakness and bad dreams*.

Vita stroked her cat, resisted the urge to hammer at the innocent animal. She remembered her mother *fat spayed bitch* like the cat . . .

> *Are you ready? Will you come with me?*
> *Michael, yes, yes. Yes! I told mother.*

Only she never did. She never said anything. Not then, at any rate. Only later. Now: to the wall, to the cat, but not then, when it mattered. Then she just hung up the phone and let it ring. And ring. Three times.

And Michael married an Australian girl. By now he would be fifty-five less thirteen days, if he was still alive. He surely had children, perhaps grandchildren.

And I have a cat and a spayed church.

The clock ticked spitefully.

"Say it, Merlyn."

Dr. Samuel Lichinsky kept his voice low as he leaned forward in his chair and gently urged his patient on. After a few months of working through Merlyn Aubrey's peculiarly cyclic behavior, he could recognize certain signs. At this moment, the slight blonde sitting on the edge of his couch looked pathetic, collapsed in on herself. A familiar stage—and whether she admitted it or not, it *was* staged: expensive clothes that would look better on a teenager, hair very carefully careless, a wistful expression that was suspiciously naive for twenty-eight. He wondered what she'd been like before entering Bayview. He'd seen the reports, but they were inadequate; he wondered how much help they'd really given her.

"Go on," he repeated. "Say it."

"But I've said it before." Small-voiced and pitiful. "What good does it do?"

"It's a step. Go on."

With a sigh, Merlyn twisted her head around to the closed venetian blinds, then back. "I don't want to grow up. I want to stay a little girl."

"Part of you does. Only part of you."

"At *my* age?"

He recognized the edge of irritation. The change was coming, he knew. First the irritation, then anger, then Merlyn would get up and stride the room, a completely different person. She even changed physically.

"Your age doesn't matter, Merlyn . . . some people never make it. But twenty-eight already has its own built-in problems. In your case, they're obviously complicated by other factors. Still, part of you knows it has to grow up."

"Then why can't I just do it?"

Lichinsky smiled. "You are. That's what frightens the

little girl so much that she hangs on tighter. Because she knows it's a losing battle."

"What makes you so damn sure?" she asked with cold superiority. The doctor knew that tone, too. "Maybe the child will win. I can go back to Bayview and play with dolls."

"Is that really what you want, Merlyn?"

She ignored the question. "I know I should have started growing up long ago, but I was afraid of—" She let the half-born sentence die, frowned at her hands.

"Of what, Merlyn?"

A long silence.

"Of your family?"

"Of . . . of everything." Small voice again.

Deliberate pendulum swing the other way. Lichinsky made a quick note. "Precisely what are you saying, Merlyn? Are you obliquely suggesting that poor little rich girls have expensive breakdowns because they're raised to afford them? To expect them?"

Her large, capable hands clawed at her cheek, raking the unbound hair back in an angry movement. "Hell, I don't have that much money any longer, Sam. After Bayview, I can hardly afford you. There's only about eighteen thousand a year and the house, and the taxes would eat that up if I didn't rent it out most of the year. Which isn't always easy, either."

"Is it rented now?"

"No, but some people from Philly think they might want it through New Year's, so I have to go down there soon. Twenty-five rooms full of Belle Époque charm. Charming until they get the fuel bill."

"How do you feel about going back there?" This was the crux, the thing he always sensed she held back on. Something unspoken.

"You always ask me that," she said, irritation mounting again. "I told you before, I don't know how I feel. When I'm away, I suppose I miss it. When I'm there, I hate her."

"Who?"

"It. I meant to say 'it.' I can't get away from there fast enough." Abruptly, she hurled herself off the couch and began to pace.

Here it comes. Until the last few sessions, Lichinsky didn't realize it was the house itself that triggered Merlyn. Logic connected it to causal persons, yes, but logic struck only so deep. Beneath there was something else, had to be.

"That damned house." She spat it bitterly. "Everything bad began there, Sam. You probably think, 'Oh, but she's been so fortunate.'" Her voice was deepening, changing from a thin lyric to a *mezzo*. "Wealthy family. Private school. Bryn Mawr. A useless degree, Sam, and I couldn't hack it at Columbia or keep a job or hold onto a man—"

"Because you never wanted to," he gently reminded her.

"But they were all useless adolescents."

"*Adolescents*, Merlyn?"

"I'm not talking calendar age. I always throw myself at dumb old farts like my father."

"Describe how they're similar."

"Christ, *again?* They're all assholes. Decorations. Like daddy. Like me, Sam—a wiz at failure. A genius at expensive breakdowns. So now isn't it about time to ask me how I feel about being out of Bayview?"

He ignored the cutting edge. "Yes? How *do* you feel?"

"The same, Sam, *the same*. I want to run back inside, but I hate it there, too. And I want a man, sure, but nobody I can't play, that I can't control. A comfortable over-forty type who's got a fantasy about humping little girls. Then I can feel like daddy's precious baby again—until the woman part of me gets fed up and dumps the poor bewildered old prick."

"Which means what?"

"Yes, yes, it means I'm really rejecting daddy. He was a goddamned porcelain Blue Boy, Sam, and I'm no better, and I hate the whole fucking waste of—" She stopped abruptly.

"Of what, Merlyn? Of *what?*" But he knew it was too late to prod any further. She'd shunted her secret aside once more, hidden something behind her pretended hatred for her father.

And now the change came quickly, as usual. Her squared shoulders perceptibly slumped, her head bowed. She rose from the sofa a woman, returned to it a child. Hands clenched, small feet in their expensive Gucci shoes angled slightly toward each other. Always at this moment, Merlyn reminded Lichinsky of Mrs. Lanier in Parker's *The Custard Heart*. Wistfulness cubed.

"Oh, Sam, I'm really sorry," she murmured, profoundly embarrassed.

"Why?"

"I used such awful language."

"It helped release your anger. The woman part is getting stronger, Merlyn. When she finally makes it, I think she's going to be a winner."

She did not respond to his encouragement. Lichinsky looked at his watch. *A few more minutes, good.* There was a question he wanted to ask while she was open and flowing.

"Your grandmother, Merlyn. Charlotte Aubrey. Sometimes you allude to her, but you never seem to talk about her."

"What's there to talk about?" she asked, her voice strange.

"Well, it's just that you've indirectly mentioned her more often than even your mother, but then you drop the subject. Why?"

Merlyn fluttered her hands (almost stagily, he noted). "Sam . . . isn't my time about up?"

"Not quite. You still have a couple of minutes."

Silence.

"Well?"

No reply.

"Feel a block, Merlyn?"

"I guess." She rose again, as demure now as her rage had been feral. She slipped into her coat. "I've really got to go, Sam. I have a dinner date with Vita Henry, then we're going to a meeting afterwards."

Dr. Lichinsky said nothing.

Merlyn sighed. "All right—yes, *yes,* I do feel a block on Charlotte. A nothing."

He waited.

"So should we get together once more this week before I go down to Pennsylvania?"

Lichinsky riffled through his appointment book. "Friday at four?"

"I'll be here. I'll even be on time."

"Fine. What kind of meeting are you going to tonight? Or shouldn't I ask?"

"No, I don't mind. It's the ESP Forum at First Universalist Church." Merlyn caught the wry smile that flitted across Lichinsky's warm, wizened monkey face. "I know you don't believe."

"About as much as dream books and horoscopes. Maybe the senses they talk about are there, but if they are, they certainly are not 'extra.' We just haven't charted them yet."

Merlyn buttoned her coat. "And do you have an opinion on survival?"

"After death?" He shrugged dubiously, then wished he hadn't. She'd asked it casually, too casually. She evidently had strong feelings on the subject.

"Sam, have you ever read about the Aubrey effect?"

"The Aubrey effect?"

"Sometimes called the Aubrey Constant."

He furrowed his forehead. "That sounds familiar, I think I—*wait!*" It suddenly connected, all the tantalizing bits and references in previous sessions, things that meant nothing came into focus. *Oh, my God!* "That's the place you've been talking about all this time? Aubrey House?" *Oh, my God!*

"Yes, Sam."

Merlyn Aubrey from Doylestown—for Christ's sake!

"I'm sorry," he stammered. "I never added it up." A textbook case come to life, springing off the dry dead page of print.

"Well," she told him, "it's there..."

"The Aubrey Constant?" *The cold blue light?*

"Yes. It's been there as long as I can remember. Every medium claims to sense it. The physical ones say they see a blue glow—always in the same spot in the second-floor hall. I really ought to charge admission."

"I remember now," Lichinsky nodded. "You brought me an article by . . . by that man you know."

"Charles Singleton. I think he's sort of gay, but he's a sweet old thing."

At the time, Lichinsky thought Merlyn just wanted to validate her interest in the paranormal with him. She could have no idea, of course, that he'd read the identical article quite a while earlier when Singleton himself gave him a copy. The piece, though not uninteresting, was written in a style bordered with violets, and Lichinsky did not subject himself to it a second time. Thus he missed its actual significance to Merlyn Aubrey.

"Singleton's article, as I recall, claimed this—uh—'constant' never tries to contact or touch anyone."

Merlyn rose abruptly. "I'll . . . I'll see you Friday, Sam." And she was quickly gone.

The doctor pivoted in his chair, flicked on his Dictaphone and spoke into the mouthpiece. "Merlyn Aubrey. Progress. My suspicion is now a certainty. Beyond the love-hate relationship with her father, behind the unexpressed but ill-concealed loathing for her grandmother is the house itself, *the* Aubrey House of *psi* fame. Note to look up literature on the subject, especially article in the Charles Singleton file. This house seems to hold a rather complex symbolism for the patient."

He went on to describe Merlyn's physical transformation from girl to woman and back again, then shut off the machine and wondered whether she would keep her appointment on Friday. He hoped she wouldn't cancel, yet felt almost positive that she would. *Damn!* Of all times for her to go to Pennsylvania, this had to be the worst. He needed to probe the ominous significance Aubrey House held for her. Whatever it did to his patient, it was surely too soon after her discharge from Bayview for her to undergo it again. She was too vulnerable.

On reflection, Lichinsky decided that "vulnerable" was the wrong word to describe her present mental condition. At the moment, Merlyn Aubrey was a walking psychic time bomb.

And ticking.

First Universalist Church was practically empty when Drew Beltane arrived half an hour early. He'd planned it that way. Whenever possible, he came to public meetings ahead of time in order to avoid the tortuous progress from door to seat and the embarrassment of inching by people's legs and feet, hating the excessive politeness that masked their impatience with him, reading the thought in their minds: *he moves like a squirrel.* His paralysis had been with him since childhood, a rare form that he had to battle every moment of his waking life, commanding each separate movement with conscious and painful effort. Discipline and exercise worked him down to one cane, but the need for constant muscular control gave his actions the start-freeze-start appearance of a stop-action film.

He settled into the middle seat of a row of pews toward the rear of the vestry and watched the people file in a few at a time. *Typical fuzzy-headed acolytes,* he judged, scanning their faces vainly for signs of intelligence. *Coming to have at the iconoclast.* Only from what he'd heard of Richard Creighton, Drew suspected it was going to be the other way around.

As for the frail target of Creighton's lance, William Perry's book, *Beyond Clinical Death,* Drew privately subtitled it *Beneath Critical Contempt.* A slapdash compilation of deathbed commentary, it leaned heavily on the high incidence of similar "experiences" reported by those who were declared clinically dead, yet survived: heart failure patients, drowning victims, operating table near-casualties. Perry placed great significance on the white lights and shining faces and progresses through tunnels to far rivers that he'd recorded from the lips of several hundred men, women and children who, for a little while, registered no pulse or breath or heartbeat.

26

Populist preaching to the converted. The book's lugubrious comforts sold close to a million copies. *So much for objectivity,* Drew shrugged mentally. The author's trusting solemnity provoked Drew to comment in his own review, written for the Falzer *Proceedings:*

> *Perry accepts these preconditioned experiences with the naiveté of a child taking sweets from a pederast.*

Perry's wounded yelp of a reply scored Drew for irreverent flippancy. Drew's italicized codicil at the bottom of the printed authorial response simply asked, "And why not laughter? Man being the only animal with the conscious assurance of his own death, he'd damn well better be able to laugh."

A buzz of nervous anticipation. Drew watched the vestry begin to fill up with a deluded synod of sheep eager to tilt at the dragon Creighton, apprehensive lest he prove too fierce to slay. *As if they had the intellectual tools to meet him on his own turf.*

Yes, Mr. Perry, Drew thought, quite right: death *is* a serious subject, altogether too somber to treat with anything other than irony. An elusive thing, too. One would think, being so close to it so often, he himself might once reach escape velocity. But no: always back, dragged up through layers of the mind by some irrelevant visceral wish to live. Back to existence and all its foolish questions, back in spite of the low but constant ache in his spine and limbs. *Death is not so easy to find.*

Drew's hand twitched on the head of his cane. In a series of short, spasmodic motions, he turned a yearning eye to the coffee wagon wheeled in and positioned near a wall outlet by a not unattractive middle-aged woman in red. *Bit more cleavage than one usually sees in church.* He fervently hoped that one of the urns held tea.

Looking around the room, Drew saw Merlyn Aubrey, recognizing her from the photograph he'd gone to great trouble and some expense to secure. *Fragile type. Looks as if her petals are about to shatter.*

When Drew queried Merlyn by mail about researching Aubrey House, he received a response from her agents: "The property rents for a thousand per summer week, six hundred after Labor Day." An outrageous reply, Drew felt. The price would decimate his carefully hoarded sabbatical money and then some. Yet he *had* to find a way to read Aubrey House because, damn it, there never was such a thing as a psychic constant.

But when Falzer wrote his report in 1935, no one had ever died at Aubrey House. If that were true, how could there be a stagnant pool, so to speak, of psychic energy on the second floor? The first death was Charlotte Aubrey in 1964. Shortly afterward, the dreadful incident of the Burtons took place, but few *psi* investigators knew about that swiftly hushed-up matter. It made no sense to Drew. The so-called constant simply had to catalyze or manifest or move or dispel under some circumstance so far overlooked.

There must be a way for a good, shrewd Scot to pass through that thousand-dollar door.

The conversational murmur in the vestry died down as a balding, paunchy, impeccably dressed little man with lips sucked in as if tasting a prune or sucking the marrow of an egg rose and called the ESP Forum to order.

Beltane studied Charles Percy Singleton III. He knew some of his writings, purple patches infrequently leavened with flickers of intellect like far-off lightning. *Nibbling crumbs on the nearer shingle of darkness*.

Singleton delivered an animated and mildly pompous recap of the contents of "Perry's remarkable book on survival after death," rhapsodizing on the tome's ingenuous reassurances. Drew endured twenty minutes of inanity. At length, the speaker brought up "the inevitable critical backlash to Perry's important work by the scientific and academic establishment," then turned the meeting over to "our own dear Vita Henry, who made all the necessary arrangements for the appearance of tonight's guest speaker."

The woman in red whom Drew had seen wheel in the coffee wagon stepped forward, blushing slightly. She mumbled through Richard Creighton's weighty credentials, then yielded place to the scholar, who walked to the podium to a smattering of unenthusiastic applause.

Undaunted by the chilly reception or perhaps oblivious to it, Creighton began dissecting Perry's flimsy tract with the emotional precision of a medical student cutting tissue samples from a dead thing. Drew immediately liked the man: a bit polemic perhaps, but a stainless-steel thinker; not overly impressed with himself, either. *Rare virtues in psychic research*, Drew thought, *a field where one mostly treads a fine line between observed fact and subjective bullshit*.

Beltane decided he wanted to meet Creighton later.

Merlyn Aubrey stared hard at the speaker's gray-tinged temples. *So very sure of yourself, Dr. Richard Creighton, but I wonder how you'd behave at my house?*

More to the point, she wondered whether she would like to sleep with him.

"—inescapable," says Creighton. "So, to summarize, no matter how much one may admire Perry's documentation of the so-called 'out-of-body experience' at the moment of death, I must raise several critical objections to what he optimistically terms his 'findings.'"

Dramatic pause prior to peroration.

—Not the sole reason for stopping. Throat hurts. Slogging through a Manhattan monsoon without umbrella or overshoes.

Humbug.

—It takes one to catch one.

Pouring water into a Styrofoam cup, he sips as he surveys the First Universalist's vestry, its high leaded windows and long loose pews cushioned in the inevitable red velvet, the seats arranged three-sided with the podium centered on the missing fourth border of the square. Coffee on the wagon near the door to 76th Street. Stacked tower of Styrofoam cups like the one he holds in his hand. Easy to wad up and dispose of *like the way the driver's seat folded in*

—Don't!

Creighton carefully sets down the cup, stares, darts his gaze about the corners of the room, looking for something, perhaps an architectural detail to arrest his attention and divert his thoughts.

—The room. A paradox in dimensions. Vaulting ceiling. Excellent acoustics. Cramped floor space. Arbitrarily diminished. Enclosed with folding partitions. Loose pews in rows, velvety red cushioned seats

redder than blood that wouldn't puddle because the car's upholstery is Scotchgarded

—Faces. Study the faces of Singleton's flock. Dull eyes, a respectable lunatic fringe, well-dressed, "with it," no Village types in dungarees, but maybe one artist with a showing in SoHo. Singleton in the first row, mother hen coddling chicks.

chicks = children

At least ten people here, maybe more, who have unfinished novels in attics or dusty drawers, cellars, cedar chests. Effete spirits with nothing to say or recall, but they would claim the world got in the way and someday when they retire or the kids are grown

Marla won't grow up

—DON'T!

A low murmur. The sheep stir. Why is Creighton taking so long to sum up? Singleton in the front row appears to be mildly concerned.

—Then he must have read about the accident. He has that certain look.

Spare us the sympathy of simps.

And then, in the back of the vestry, Creighton notices another face, that of a young blonde, her eyes focused intently on his.

—Exquisite. She actually looks intelligent.

Creighton clears his throat and begins to speak again, but from time to time his eyes return to the girl's face.

As soon as she knew the speaker was about to summarize, Vita rose and took her position next to the coffee wagon, poised to conduct the question-and-answer session as soon as the talk was over.

Creighton fascinated her. She admired the interesting angles and shadows of his features, was especially taken by the way his eyes darted about the room, searching every face, hers included, seeking something, she wished she knew what. Unconsciously, Vita primped her already bouffant hairdo.

His trouble, she decided abruptly, *is he's too closed off.* But from what? Nothing she could name or describe in a word or even a phrase. For no logical reason in the world, Walter's unfinished essay on St. Paul suddenly came to mind.

Vita checked her watch. Plenty of time for the debate, and she supposed Charles, dear Charles, must be bursting to refute, but still she hoped the discussion wouldn't become too protracted. She *so* wanted Richard Creighton to accept her invitation to the small reception she was giving afterward in her West End Avenue apartment.

So this is Richard Creighton, Singleton sadly reflected. *His sorrow palpably heavies him.*

Tall; imperially slim like another Richard; angular New England bones: jaw like Ethan Frome; full lips reminiscent of Tiberian coin portraiture. A sensualist by heredity but psychologically an ascetic. By choice or necessity?

Odd how the man shattered things held dear without once suggesting the iconoclast. *He doesn't seem much concerned with what he's saying.* Singleton imagined the contradiction was due to the tragedy of his wife and daughter. He felt disposed to comfort rather than argue with him. *The death of a child is a terrible thing.*

"Specifically," Creighton said, "I have three principal objections, all of them interrelated."

Wiggling his butt forward on the pew, Singleton stretched the folds of his neck in an effort to bring himself physically closer to the pith of Creighton's analysis. Without realizing it, he wore a smile on his face as the speaker's logic unfolded.

"My first point," Creighton stated, "is that Perry is extremely timorous or perhaps just incapable of exploring other possibilities than those commonly advanced by orthodox religion and traditional occultism. If, for instance, he compared his data with ongoing work in psychology labs, he would discover that in the crucial sleep/waking phase known as the hypnagogic state, subjects sometimes manifest visual and/or auditory hallucinations suspiciously similar to the phenomenology of what mystics like to call astral projection or out-of-body experiences, or merely OBEs.

"My second point extends the first. Perry's book is weighted by its very organization along thoroughly orthodox lines. Even subjects of other faiths report postmortem episodes laded with Christian symbolism. Why? Is it because they share traditional myth patterns for want of correspondent structural legendry in their own cultures? Or might it be because Perry is so unfamiliar with other mythic silhouettes that he unwittingly guided or forced these subjects' testimony into the Procrustean bed of Catholic-Protestant cosmology?"

Interesting point, Singleton admitted. *The psyche, too, abhors a vacuum.*

"Most of Perry's subjects," said Creighton, "have been unwittingly and subconsciously programmed by church and family and even the media for the very terminal visions they seemed to experience after they were clinically dead. These episodes, I suggest, may be variations of a basic Occidental or at least American cultural hallucination. Some of you look skeptical, but I assure you I am not advancing some glib untested theory. As far back as 1897, in a book published by Scribner's entitled *Sleep: Its Physiology, Pathology, Hygiene, and Psychology,* an investigator named de Manaceine noted that one-third of her subjects had an unusual propensity for undergoing hypnagogic phenomena. This third happened to be composed entirely of Finns. Let me quote the author in part: 'I think we have here a national propensity . . . explained by the fact that among the natives of Finland it is nearly impossible to find a person of sanguine temperament.' Today, we might note, Finland still seems to be the most economically backward of the Scandinavian nations. Its people may have good reason to be morose. As for America . . ." Creighton shrugged. "At any rate, I view this cultural hallucination thesis as a logical offshoot of the old psychiatric truism that Freud's patients tend to have Freudian dreams while Jung's patients have Jungian dreams."

A moment of silence. Singleton sensed the growing depression shrouding the room.

"My final objection," Creighton went on, "is mechanistic, but it should be considered in connection with what I have just said. Perry's subjects passed beyond clinical death, but what does that mean? Only that they were not breathing, that their hearts were not functioning. However, the blood in their skulls was not totally dysfunctional. Or, if you will, there was oxygen flowing across their brain cells. Their minds were still alive and therefore presumably susceptible to those vivid hallucinations that children frequently experience and remember but adults rarely recall."

Another lengthy pause. When Creighton spoke again, his voice sounded curiously hushed to Singleton.

"Death is a complicated process that we still have a great deal to learn about. But we do know this much—there is an enormous difference between 'clinical death,', a sometimes treatable condition of pulmonary-respiratory failure, and biological death, which involves the irreversible breakdown of the body's cells."

Creighton put down the last of his 4 by 7 note cards.

"Any questions?"

Drew was sourly amused by the ensuing silence. At length, Mrs. Henry prompted Charles Singleton to begin the discussion. The rotund little man slowly rose—*probably wondering how to snatch the chestnuts from the fire*—and thanked the speaker for his "cogent commentary." Then, pursing his lips, Singleton continued: "I must admit my confidence in Mr. Perry's book has been severely tried, but before I rush to condemn him, I fully intend to reread *Beyond Clinical*

Death in the light of tonight's lecture. I do not plan to make up my mind until I have weighed all the evidence over some period of time, and I invite you all to do the same. Meanwhile, let us remember that what we have been discussing is merely the work of one man. Whether it proves valid or no, it can in no way dim the luster of such pioneers in psychic study as the great Dr. Rhine or the late Harry Price. The work goes on, and even the beckoning byways of error have their purpose in the eventual enlightenment that we in this room are fervently and gloriously helping to bring about."

Neatly executed bit of false rhetoric worthy of Callicles, Drew observed sardonically as Singleton sat down to a swell of approval: the speaker acknowledged, even as his irrefutable logic was politely but determinedly shunted aside; the worshipers both praised and reassured that though Perry might prove a false prophet, yet theirs unquestionably was The One True Faith.

No one had any questions. Mrs. Henry in the low-cut red gown therefore announced the end of the formal portion of the program. *With some alacrity,* Drew noted.

The forum members streamed for the coffee wagon.

Dear Merlyn, Singleton chuckled to himself with avuncular malice, watching her commandeer Creighton immediately after Vita broke the meeting. *She always chases authority figures.*

His attention was diverted from Merlyn Aubrey by an interesting-looking young man with a cane barely able to navigate through the press of people to the refreshment wagon. *Nice bearded face, thirty-two or thirty-three, badly handicapped. Polio?* Singleton studied his slow stop-start progress, then decided to intercept him as if by accident.

"Going for coffee?"

"Hopefully for a spot of tea."

"Bit of a crowd." Always an Anglophile, ever an actor manqué, he clipped his speech in deference. "I'm Charles Singleton."

"Indeed." The other's hand shot out to shake his in a

spastic movement. "Drew Beltane, University of Edinburgh."

Charles stifled his surprise. *The* Drew Beltane? Rumors of his mediumistic forays had certainly come to his ears. Besides, he'd read one or two of his columns in *Proceedings*. Quite a cutting edge to them, he seemed to recall.

Pretending the name meant nothing to him, Charles took in the Scot's trim whiskers, canny, wide-set blue eyes and humorous curl of mouth. Singleton prided himself on his actor's ear for dialect. Though Edinburgh may have educated Beltane, it couldn't disguise his slurred brogue's Ayrshire roots.

"Born rather west of Edinburgh, I should imagine?"

"Yes," Drew admitted. "Ardrossan. You've been?"

"I travel now and then. May I bring you some tea?"

"Yes, thanks, Mr. Singleton."

"Please call me Charles."

"Right. No milk."

Seems a decent chap, if a bit of a nance, Drew told himself while he waited for Singleton to return with a cup of dark brown tea. He thanked him for it and tried to swallow a nondescript mouthful. Drew frowned into the cup. He should have waited till the urn was nearly empty. It would have more character then.

"Are you in psychic research?" Charles asked innocently.

"Privately. I teach Celtic history and literature."

"Ah." The other smiled. "Yes. They do join, don't they?"

"Perhaps." Drew sighed inwardly. Another romantic. If they find out you're a Celt, they assume ipso facto that you were born with second sight. *Which might have been better than my own dubious gifts.* Well, no need to disabuse him.

"Charles, by any chance do you happen to know Miss Aubrey?"

"Merlee? Oh, Lord, yes."

"I've attempted to get in touch with her, not with any success. Would you mind awfully introducing me?"

"Not at all." Singleton touched his arm, adding with a

bit of a feline purr, "That is, if we can tear her away temporarily from her legitimate prey."

"You make her sound predatory."

"Oh, Merlyn's a charmer," Singleton beamed. "I love her dearly. Are you in the States for long?"

"Six-month visa," Drew replied—but got no further. Mrs. Henry descended on them.

"Charles! I didn't have time to do the hors d'oeuvres for the party. You've *got* to help me set up before they all arrive."

Drew watched Singleton give her a dry peck on the cheek. "Of course I shall, darling. Have you met our visitor from Scotland?"

Vita was too preoccupied with her party to pay more than token attention to the newcomer. She shook his hand politely then immediately returned to Singleton.

"Charles, you must remind Merlyn that I'll need her help beforehand, too."

"Certainly. I'll try to prize her away from Dr. Creighton." He smiled apologetically to Drew. "I'm afraid there might not be time to introduce you to Merlyn. Unless..." Singleton turned to Vita. "Do you think perhaps Mr. Beltane might come along, too?"

"Why, of course!" Vita was effusive. "Mr. Belting, you simply *must* join us, it's going to be such fun. Dr. Creighton has consented to come, *do* say you will, too!"

"Love to," Drew lied, sure the party would be a lugubrious bore, Creighton's presence notwithstanding. However, it would give him more time to cultivate Merlyn Aubrey's acquaintance. "Where is it being held?"

Vita suddenly noticed his physical infirmity. "Oh ...perhaps you might be able to share a cab with Dr. Creighton. He has the address."

"That would be fine." Drew nodded. "I'll ask him myself."

Nudging his way to the coffee wagon, Creighton ponders his motive for agreeing to attend (Mrs.) Vita Henry's tedious soirée.

—Refusing would have meant walking through the rain, lingering at windows of closed shops on Broadway, more abominable coffee at an all-night restaurant before facing the empty apartment. Hell, even a Dullsville party's better than going back to that silence. And there's also Merlyn.

First-name basis already?

—I suppose she's the main reason I accepted the insipid invitation.

You suppose?

—All right. I know she's the cause of it. I caught the green-light signals she was giving off, and they flattered me.

But her subtext's confused.

—True. Come close go away. Maybe she just gets off on the foreplay dance. But there's only one way to find out.

O most wicked speed to post with such dexterity—

"One needs wicked swiftness to meet someone here."

Creighton starts at the voice, sees at his elbow a delicately built young man leaning on a cane, a heavy dark gray fisherman's sweater thickening his frail bulk. "Sorry," says Creighton, "afraid I was wrapped in thought."

"Dr. Creighton, I'm Drew Beltane. I enjoyed your lecture. Some of the most intelligent words I've heard on the subject in years."

Flushing with sudden appreciation, Creighton shrugs. "Well, Perry's pretty easy to shoot down."

"Agreed. Written strictly for the gallery seats."

The scholar nods, his brows drawn down in an effort to fit an elusive definition to a familiar term. "Beltane...I think I've heard of you."

"Perhaps in the Falzer journal, *Proceedings?*"

Creighton's brows reverse direction. "Of course! You wrote an excellent paper on—let me think of it—personality and telepathic interchange."

"Yes. *Aspects of Personality in Deep Mind Projection.*"

"That's the one," Creighton nods. "Some brilliant work there."

"'My blushes, Watson,'" Drew objects.

Creighton grasps the other's thin hand. "The name's

Richard, but call me Rich. Glad to meet someone who approaches *psi* research with a slide rule instead of a tambourine."

"Well, Rich, if a botanist sets out to observe roses, he won't get far at the outset by calling them orchids, will he now?"

An ironic lip twist of agreement, then Creighton notices Beltane's cane and the empty cup in his free hand. "Look, can I get you something?"

"Indeed, yes. Another tea, please."

Opening the spout, Creighton lets the stygian liquid flow into the cup. "It's pretty strong, Drew."

"Not to worry. *Now* it's tea." He sips it beatifically. "I understand there's a party at Mrs. Henry's."

"Afraid so, Drew. Have you been invited?"

"Afraid so. Care to share a cab?"

"Glad to. Let it be my treat."

"Thanks. I shan't argue... sabbatical purse strings and all that."

"Then it's settled," says Creighton, patting Drew's shoulder. "Better finish your tea. Vita just left with Singleton and Merlyn Aubrey. It's what Matheson would call 'Brontean weather.' We're going to have quite a job finding a taxi tonight. Why are you smiling?"

"Your mention of Matheson. You've read *Hell House?*"

"Yes. Why?"

The Scot samples his tea. "Marvelous. Though it could have steeped longer." A grin. "Somehow, Rich, you don't impress me as the sort who spends his leisure hours perusing occult fiction."

busy Creighton time valuable

"Oh, I dabble. Fairy tales for grownups. *Hell House* was ghoulish fun. Which obliquely reminds me of something." Creighton twirls a finger, attempting to recall another fact about Drew Beltane from the dusty library stacks of memory. "You wrote another piece for Falzer... what was it?... had to do with psychic energy. Kind of a 'ghostometer.'"

Drew laughs at Creighton's characterization. "Well, yes, I suppose you could call it that. You're referring to an article I did quite some time ago. I described a process for measuring variable levels of psychic activity. Mostly just theory, though, none too accurate yet. Very hard to be when one's own body is the gauge."

"Yes, I remember it now."

"And judging from your expression, you took exception to something therein?"

Creighton shrugs. "Just the de facto assumption that there's something to measure. You unquestioningly believe in holdovers of psychic energy?"

Draining the villainous contents of his cup with a sigh of pleasure, Drew counters, "Tell me this, Rich—do you unquestionably believe in Grand Central Station?"

In one of those cramped kitchens typical of a whole generation of Manhattan architects ignorant of the minimal space needed to prepare cuisine, Vita cracked ice from plastic trays into an aluminum bucket. She was glad for the drone of voices from the living room. *A house needs human sounds.*

She was beginning to dislike her furniture almost as much as her kitchen. *Ample but not comfortable.* Her only decorative touch since Walter died was a painting that Merlyn laughingly called an act of rebellion. One weekend, tired of staring at Greco's *Repentant Peter,* she took it down from its hallowed spot over the mantel and shoved it face to wall behind a breakfront. Then she went out and bought a replacement, a well-executed but rather liberal nude figure of a young woman. Vita's other houseguests never commented on the substitution, but the first time Merlyn saw it, she said, "The trouble with us, Vita, is we're both horny, but there's not a cock in sight."

Merlyn could suddenly be as earthy as she normally was demure, and lately seemed to be growing worse. She upset Vita when she talked that way. That very night, arriving home early from the forum in Merlyn's and Charles' company, Vita noticed her friend once more contemplating the nude.

"Yes, that's us," the blonde declared. "Muffs to rent, but no tenants."

Vita felt compelled to defend her artistic taste. "Merlyn," she protested, "this picture represents the spiritual me. Surely you understand what I mean by 'spirit'?"

"Uh huh. You need a spirited fuck."

"*Miss* Aubrey, bite your tongue," Singleton chided with mock severity, "or I shall be forced to rinse your mouth with Veuve Cliquot." He handed each woman a superbly

40

arranged plate of cheese, caviar and smoked salmon as the intercom buzzed, signaling the arrival of the first guests.

Drew stood underneath an awning for ten minutes before Creighton managed to hail a taxi. His new friend opened the door and helped him get seated before joining him in the back seat. Rain and heavy traffic turned it into a longish ride, but neither minded the chance for private conversation.

Creighton began it. "So what in hell are you doing on this side of the Atlantic attending a postmortem for a silly paperback book?"

"I'm on sabbatical, Rich. Saved my pennies to have a go at a pet project."

"Which is?"

"Ever heard of Aubrey House?"

Creighton shrugged. "Read about it a long while ago. Isn't it in Pennsylvania?"

"Yes. Near a place called Doylestown."

"Then it's not too far from Philadelphia. Allegedly haunted, as I recall. But—" Suddenly he made the connection. *"Aubrey?* As in Merlyn?"

"The same. I wanted to meet her tonight, but she was talking with you, and then they whisked her away." Drew nodded at his cane. "I'm not quite a rocket for speed."

"I'm remembering it a little. Didn't Falzer himself once investigate the place?"

"Yes. He was the second. An Olive Masconi reported a perceptible aura as far back as 1920, but Falzer localized the phenomenon to the second floor and called it a 'constant.'"

"You sound dubious."

"You look skeptical," Beltane countered.

"True. Whatever they thought they felt or saw is probably part subjective reaction, part wishful thinking. Is that what you had in mind?"

"No, though what you say certainly contributes to the mystical haze around most hauntings. People's heads are filled with old films or books or fables of 'past lives.'

Though not Falzer. He's about as stolid an investigator as I've ever known. But Aubrey is not your classic haunted house. It's an enigma." Drew stared out of the cab window and the parked cars sliding behind them. "There's none of the usual lurid tales attached to it. Just that so-called constant that offends every one of my instincts."

"Why?"

A slight lift of the shoulders. "No idea, Rich. It's just wrong. Perhaps it's a personality, though the facts would seem to preclude it."

"By that, I assume you mean a ghost, as usually defined?"

"Yes, or a fragment of one. I tend to that theory at the moment. But that's not the entire puzzle. There are quite ordinary things about Aubrey House that smell wrong to me. Such as Charlotte's nurse, a woman named Shipperton."

"You've certainly researched it."

"I have. I uncovered data that few ever found. Were you aware, for instance, that there's an entire book about the house?"

"No. But I never dug into the subject."

"Even if you had, you might well have overlooked *Aubrey House, Home of the Spirits.*"

"Who wrote it?"

"Some friends of Merlyn's grandmother. A couple named the Burtons."

"Never heard of them."

"Not surprising. Psychic dabblers from suburban Philadelphia. Amateurs, really—the title tells one that. A small Bucks County publisher printed their book, much to the clan's displeasure. Merlyn's grandmother bought up and destroyed most of the printing. Fortunately, a few copies escaped. One of my students took a trip to see friends in Pennsylvania, and I prevailed on him to visit Bucks County and do some on-the-spot investigating. One of the tidbits he turned up was the existence of the Burtons' little tome."

"But how on earth did you track down a copy in Scotland?"

Just then the cab pulled up in front of Vita's building. Drew was grateful. He would have been ashamed to admit he'd bribed his pupil to steal a copy from the Doylestown Public Library.

Joanna Larson bubbled in with her stolid, out-of-place mate, Burt, who streaked to the comprehensible rye bottle. Jack Barsho brought his testy cousin Steffy, and some boy from where was it showed up for Charles. Charles always invited dim adolescents with evasive eyes, embryos who mercifully faded from memory when they went home.

Now Richard was here, and so was the curious man with the cane, but the party kept Vita from talking to them, which she regretted. Though she liked the church people, she was also faintly bored with their petty prejudices and venalities. She realized that her life had gone as far as it could in the interim track between Walter's death and whatever was to follow. Dear God, let something follow.

More people arrived. Vita entered the living room, basking in the lively chatter that rose above the FM music, sentimental oldies from WPAT. Merlyn hailed her. At the church, Vita watched with some apprehension as her friend determinedly appropriated Richard, but now Merlyn was pointedly ignoring him. Perched on the sofa, knees and feet demurely together, drink held to her lips with both hands, she was talking over its rim to the Scot. Odd Merlyn. Odder Mr. Belting: so wispy, having such trouble just reaching for the drink Vita offered him, though he covered his difficulty with an elfin grin.

"No problem," he told her. "I just have to plan it before I do it."

A nice young man, really—attractive in a way a woman could appreciate without quite pinning down why. Not as handsome as Richard, but in both she sensed a strength and sureness that was terribly exciting, though Mr. Belting seemed warmer. The smile in his eyes went deep before brushing against something else—what? A weariness? No. A sense of great age? Closer, but still wrong.

Agelessness. That was it.

And where Creighton was guarded, possibly holding something that hurt at arm's length, the little Scot was open. He was a person more interested in others than himself: deftly able to shift conversation away from his own history to that of his companions of the moment. He did not appear to require any of that deference that most men automatically elicited from Vita.

Vita watched him lift his drink ever so carefully to his lips. She hoped he wouldn't spill it. For his sake, not the sofa's.

Managing the feat, he smiled at her. "Merlyn has been telling me you've had some unusual paranormal episodes in your life. I'd like to hear about them."

Vita blushed, gratified. It had been a long time since she'd had the opportunity to tell someone new about the séances she'd attended (especially one in particular). She also mentioned the devastating possession that happened to her shortly after Michael passed out of her life forever.

"And did that young woman ever come back?" Drew asked.

"No, she finally faded away."

"I see." He nodded soberly, sipped, said nothing more.

Vita excused herself, feeling it her duty to keep mingling. The Scot returned to his conversation with Merlyn.

A few moments later, Vita drew Singleton aside.

"Charles, have you spoken with Mr. Belting? He is an extremely—"

"Bel*ting?*" Singleton interrupted, laughing. "Precious woman, you don't mean to say you've been talking to him all this time without even knowing who he is?"

"Charles, I don't understand."

"My dear Vita, your Mr. 'Belting' happens to be Drew Bel*tane* of Edinburgh. *The* Drew Beltane."

"Oh, dear." Her face flushed deep crimson. "I had no idea. I hope I haven't offended him."

"He doesn't strike me as having a delicate vanity."

"Charles," she suddenly exclaimed, "our ESP Forum must be famous!"

"Much as I'd like to agree with you," Singleton said, pausing for a bite of Gjetost and cracker, "I suspect he is far more interested in our little Merlee."

"You really think so?"

Singleton nibbled crumbs from the tips of his fingers. "Well, to be more specific, in our friend's house in Pennsylvania. He appears to know quite a bit about it."

"Do you think he wants to investigate Aubrey House?"

"That's why he's here, I'd guess. But I'm afraid he's in for quite a disappointment. Look how often you and I have hinted to her about it without results."

"Yes." She looked speculatively at the Scot. "So that's *the* Drew Beltane. I just wonder, don't you, whether half the things they say about him are true."

"Second cousin to the Wandering Jew and so forth? Assuredly not." Singleton sliced another transparent wafer of caramel-colored cheese and decorously worried at it like a mouse tutored by Emily Post. "But he is without doubt one of the finest mediums in the field. Did you by any chance ever read that article of his I gave you last year?"

"Yes, certainly, Charles, I was enormously impressed by it." It was a lie. She'd tried to get into it but gave up after a few paragraphs, put off by Beltane's dry, clinical style. "Drew Beltane," she repeated, tasting the sound. "It's rather a lovely name, isn't it?"

Singleton nodded. "In Gaelic, it means 'sacred fire.'"

While Drew rambled on about early Aubrey history, Merlyn watched Richard from the corner of her eye. She was puzzled and a bit annoyed. She knew he'd responded earlier, but now he appeared to be doing everything possible to ignore her. She didn't mind so much his paying attention to Joanna, not with her cloddish husband close by, but Merlyn thought he'd been talking all too long now with Steffy, a slender, thirty-fivish brunette with slogans in her head instead of thoughts of her own.

Maybe, Merlyn thought, he's one of those aloof types who expect the woman to make the first move. Well, she could do that, yet there was something about him from which she shrank. *Dry ice empiricals where his heart ought to be.*

But just then, though still engaged in conversation with Steffy, Creighton glanced questioningly over at Merlyn, and she knew he was fixed. She pretended not to notice.

You'll just have to wait a wee bit longer, Dr. C.

Laughter and the tinkle of glassware all around, but Creighton feels like an uninhabited island in a sea of humanity. He suffers a familiar apocalyptic moment, one he often has at large social gatherings: seeing the crowd with double vision—as they are, as they will be. Silent mounds of grass set off by grave markers.

Shuddering, he excuses himself from the tiresome brunette and goes to the bar for a refill of Glenfiddich. At least Vita Henry's taste in scotch can't be faulted.

—By now, I've gone through the expected motions. Polite with Steffy. Steinem eating her gray cells like dry rot. Civil with that vacuous newlywed, Joanna. Sure there's an afterlife because she just read it in McCall's. Still believes in Rosa Kuleshova, Uri Geller, Margery Crandall. Her husband's got more common sense. No manners, though, just about comes out and says his wife's group's made up of fags and lunatics. The cretin's "into cars."

A distasteful topic to Dr. Creighton.

—Hell, Beltane's the only one here with his deck shuffled—

More or less

—and Merlyn's bending his ear like she did mine at the church. All that spiritualistic bullshit about haunted houses.

Correction: one haunted house. Hers.

—Exception. She owns a house. Maybe she's haunted.

Floundering for something to divert his thoughts, Creighton examines Vita's bookshelf. A wilderness of Gothics, occults, devotionals, soft-focus self-help guides, turgid fairy tales of love and power amongst the wealthy, pseudo-intellectual soap operas. Here and there a bolder work of erotica made marginally respectable by the quoted opinion of some critic with a weakness for softcore pornography.

—Coming was a mistake. Thought I could get out of prison for a while.

Surprise. You brought it with you.

—Might as well go home.

Turning away from the books, he nearly bumps into Merlyn, who is suddenly standing close. He stares down at her gazing up at him with a wistful sincerity.

"Richard, hi!" A sparkling smile. "Thought you forgot me."

—Incredible crust.

"Hardly. You're the elusive one, Merlyn."

"But I've been sitting right here for the past half hour."

"Yes, deeply preoccupied. And I've been standing on the other side of the room, and you knew it." He cuts off further protest with an upraised palm. "Look, Merlyn, I'm too old for games. Once the teaching year begins, I don't get out much. Will you have dinner with me one night soon?"

"Such urgency," she says drily, lifting her Jack Daniels to her lips, little-girl fashion, with both hands. "Wife on vacation, due back next week?"

"No."

"Be honest, Richard. Are you married?"

"No."

She shrugs. "They always say that."

"Look," he tells her coldly, "I said I'm not married. I don't lie."

The severity of his tone makes her change expression instantly. Creighton is reminded of a naughty child afraid she's pushed authority too far.

"All right, I'm sorry, I really am, I *was* fresh. Dinner would be lovely, but not till I get back from Doylestown."

"When are you going?"

"Day after tomorrow."

"Then how about tomorrow evening?"

"You *are* in a hurry." A tentative smile. "Maybe. Call me in the afternoon?"

"Fine." The ritual accomplished, Creighton feels better, lighter, able to change the subject. "I notice you and Drew had a chance to become acquainted."

"Yes. I swear he knows more about my house than I do." They both glance at the object of their conversation. Still sitting on the sofa, Drew talks easily with Singleton. "You know," Merlyn says, "he came all the way from Scotland just to see that old barn of mine in Pennsylvania. I remember now, my attorneys showed me his letter, but I just couldn't let the place go for less than a certain amount."

—Poor little rich girl.

"Merlyn, he can't afford your prices."

"Oh, I don't know, Richard, I suspect Mr. Beltane keeps very close company with his pennies. He's been hinting for me to take him along when I drive down Thursday, but I don't think it'd be proper. Though he does seem harmless enough."

"I don't see anything wrong with helping him."

Merlyn shakes her head dubiously. "I hardly know him. Of course, it's not as if he'd be keeping a paying tenant from using the place . . . I have to go, anyway. But it wouldn't look right." She gives Richard a sudden coquettish smile. "I don't suppose you'd consider coming, would you?"

"What? You're kidding."

"No, I'm not. I'd feel a whole lot better if you came."

"Two men more respectable than one?"

She touches his arm. "That's not really it, Richard. It's just that I hate being alone in that house. If you say yes, I'll ask Drew. In fact, the more the merrier."

Not catching the import of her last remark, Creighton considers the proposition. The idea of a trip with Merlyn Aubrey is hardly repugnant, but he still feels uneasy about accepting her offer.

—Why?

Simple. Old-fashioned guilt over Lana, Marla.

—No.

?

—All right; yes. But something else, too. The way she

looks when she mentions the house.

Merlyn pretends to pout. "Thought you'd like the invitation to spend a few days alone with me, Richard."

"I'm tempted."

"Only what?"

"I don't know why not."

"Then say yes, you'll really be doing me a favor. Drew, too. And as long as you're there, if you want to, you could square off your logic against the Aubrey constant."

"Well . . . all right."

An impulsive kiss on his cheek, then, before he can change his mind, Merlyn darts over to the sofa where Drew and Singleton are chatting. She interrupts, talks to them both, then returns to Creighton.

"It's all arranged. Day after tomorrow. You and me and Drew and Charles."

"Charles?"

—A few days "alone" with you, Merlyn?

What's the rush? Lana coming back?

"I had to ask him, Richard. As long as I've known Charles, he's wanted to investigate my house. Don't you see? He'd be terribly hurt if I invited two comparative strangers but not him." A quick squeeze of Creighton's arm. "Say you understand."

"Of course."

And she leaves him again, hurrying to find Vita.

—I understand better than you think, Merlyn. I crowded you on the dinner invitation, now you're giving yourself room. A group outing keeps me at a distance.

She's entitled. She just met you.

—So? We want each other—simple as that. I don't share Merlyn's illusion that time has no end.

A quick sip of scotch. Another.

—So now there's four in the traveling sideshow. Charles Singleton with his lavender-valentine notion of the afterlife. Head stuffed with God's plan, revealed word. Mind blocked off by sentimentalism, subjectivity. Probably still thinks Houdini returned to his wife. Reads all the debunkings yet swallows the lozenge whole like a little kid who won't admit Santa Claus is really daddy with a pillow underneath the red suit.

From the FM, Paul Simon's voice emerges in ironic counterpoint to Creighton's thoughts: ". . . a man hears what he wants to hear . . ."

—And disregards the rest.

When Merlyn barged into their conversation to tell Drew of his good fortune, the Scot immediately caught Singleton's crestfallen look.

"I'm jealous," the other moaned. "I've wanted to hold a séance there for years."

Merlyn kissed his bald head. "So come with us, silly."

"You mean it, Merlee? Honestly?"

"Charles, have I ever said anything I don't mean?"

"Frequently, darling."

"Only to my lovers. You can't pass the physical. Are you free to go Thursday?"

"Positively!"

"All right, then. Nine a.m. at my place. Bring your camera and your blood pressure pills and a note pad. Knowing you, you'll get an article out of it."

"An article?" Singleton expanded. "Surely nothing short of a book! I'll start my agent working on a contract first thing in the morning."

Laughing, the two friends excused themselves, Merlyn briefly returning to Creighton, Singleton hurrying away to find Vita and tell her of his spur-of-the-minute expedition to Aubrey House. Drew stared after them, caught up in his own dizzy swirl of planning.

Creighton, abandoned by Merlyn, strolled over and sat down beside Drew. "Congratulations, Mr. Beltane. Looks like you've achieved your goal."

"With a little help from you, I suspect. Merlyn was anything but encouraging, then she walked away and spoke to you, and next thing I know, I'm to be ready Thursday morning. Whatever you said that turned the trick, Rich, I'm in your debt."

Creighton shook his head. "I didn't do much. The mood just struck her."

"Then she's certainly impulsive."

Staring through the doorway into the next room where Merlyn and Charles talked animatedly with Vita Henry, Creighton shook his head. "Not impulsive. I think 'frightened' is a better word. Whenever she mentions the house, she looks like she's making an effort not to cringe."

They discussed Merlyn a while longer, passed on to Singleton and then Vita. Drew told Creighton what he'd heard of her *psi* experiences, but neither was very impressed.

"Well, Drew? What happens Thursday? How do you intend to proceed?"

"At Aubrey? I'm going to try to define the 'constant,' see what it really is."

"*If* it is."

"Yes. Well." Drew gave his new friend a peculiar twist of a smile: at once open and yet remote. "Do be tactful in your skepticism, Rich. Remember, Singleton will be there too."

"Hardly likely to forget it."

"Yes, but he's a precondition," said Drew, with a jerky nod in Merlyn's direction, "and should we perform a tracheotomy on a gift horse?"

Merlyn waited till the taxi pulled up in front of her 69th Street walkup before informing Creighton that Vita also was coming on their Pennsylvania junket.

He said nothing, but she knew he wasn't pleased. "She's a good person, Richard, and my closest friend. A little old-fashioned and hung up, but aren't we all?"

"Drew told me she had a breakdown once at a séance. She spent weeks at Bayview Sanitarium."

"Yes, I know." She unlatched the cab door. "That's where she and I met."

"You were visiting Bayview?"

Merlyn shook her head. "But when you pay what I did for a private room and therapy, they call you a guest, not a patient." She pushed the door open and slid one leg out.

"So, Dr. Creighton, love me, love my friends. See you soon."

—Well, you try to systematize life, but it ends up a simple roll of the dice. Random sequence.

Sure about that?

—Sure about nothing. Only that a set of faulty brakes tore off my future like the end of a paper towel.

As the taxi wends its way back up West End toward 89th, Richard Creighton muses over his new acquaintances: a Scottish elf, a fussy homosexual, a middle-aged woman as desperately adrift as himself, and an enticing but inconsistent girl who might or might not let him take her to bed.

—Sooner or later, I suppose.

Four strangers. Cyphers.

—So what? Till the terms begins, I'm in limbo. Might as well play out the dice roll.

"—persists in accusing his family for alleged mistakes of upbringing committed some fifty years ago. This obsession with the past stultifies Singleton's ability to cope with the present and is surely contributory to his pattern of setting unrealistic future goals. When he does not achieve them, patient ultimately blames his parents for his failures."

Dr. Sam Lichinsky switched off his Dictaphone. He was finished with his notes on the final patient of the day. Wednesday was always grueling: there was the clinic in the morning and a full office schedule in the afternoon. He glanced at his watch. Six p.m. Time to call his wife and start home.

The phone rang. He considered letting the answering service take it, but as usual, picked it up before the third ring. It was Merlyn Aubrey.

"Sam, I'm truly sorry, but I'm going to have to cancel Friday's session. I'm going to Pennsylvania tomorrow."

"I see. Could you hold the line for just one moment?" Lichinsky swiftly flipped his appointment book to Thursday's page. "Merlyn, I could fit you in early tomorrow morning. It doesn't need to be a full session."

"I'm afraid not, Sam. I have to pick up some people first thing for my trip."

"Then you're not going alone?"

"No, I'm taking Charles Singleton, Vita Henry and two others."

Lichinsky was not greatly reassured by her choice of traveling companions. Probably all a gaggle of ESP freaks. "Merlyn," he persisted, "it's important for us to discuss the house. Have you any time this evening?"

"I wish I did, but I've got a dinner date. I promise I'll be in touch as soon as I'm back in town."

He sighed. "Please do. Meanwhile, if you want to talk

53

for any reason, don't hesitate to call me no matter what the time, day or night. Do you still have my home phone number?"

"It's in my purse. Thanks a lot, Sam. Talk to you soon."

She hung up.

Lichinsky muttered an oath. He'd been sure she was going to cancel, recognized all the usual symptoms, but hoped he'd misread the situation. *I shouldn't have pressed her so hard about her grandmother*. It was a topic that upset her enough to run all the way to Pennsylvania. To the one place where she could not avoid considering it.

Wednesday evening: 9:40 p.m.

Charles Singleton unlatched his front door from the inside and politely but firmly ushered his young friend into the hall. The would-be actor—dressed in the faded dungarees and hallucinative tie-dyed T-shirt considered obligatory garb in certain parts of the East Village—turned around to argue again with the older man.

"I just don't see why I've gotta go. You're not using your pad for a whole week. I could keep the place clean for you, answer your phone and take messages, pick up your mail—"

"No, no," Singleton interrupted, the furrows of his high forehead creased, his lips puckered into a disapproving moue. "You cannot stay here while I'm away, it's positively out of the question."

"Why not?" the other pouted. "You don't trust me, that's why. Isn't it?"

"How can you even begin to imagine that?" Charles was a study in outraged innocence. Leaning through the portal, he spoke to his friend reassuringly. "You see, I only have your interest at heart. I'm trying to protect you."

"From what?"

"From Angelo. I'm afraid to leave you alone here with him."

A dark suspicious scowl. "Who the hell is Angelo?"

"Shh!" Charles glanced apprehensively over his shoulder, then stepped out into the corridor and lowered his voice. "Angelo was a charming lad I once knew. He slit his throat in my bathroom."

"Omigod! *Why?*"

"Out of sheer jealousy." He paused to let it sink in.

"Then you mean he's a ghost?" the youth whispered.

Charles gravely inclined his head. "Ever since he passed over, he's refused to leave me. Of course he's come to understand he can no longer fulfill all my needs for companionship. He's grown much more understanding about that. But I'm afraid he regards the apartment as predominately his domain. I could never allow you to remain here in my absence. I have no idea what Angelo might do. I hope you understand?"

The young man nodded. He looked a little pale.

"I *knew* you'd see I'm only trying to protect you," Charles smiled, patting the other's shoulder affectionately. Removing two fifty-dollar bills from his wallet, he tucked them into the youth's shirt pocket. "Be good till I get back."

"Right on! Ciao!"

The boy turned and hurried off to the elevators. Charles shook his head. *Calls himself an actor, but he can't even manage to play out the scene. Not even a thank you.*

All in all, though, he'd gotten off cheaply. Singleton knew if he'd given in to the transparent little schemer, he would have come back to a ransacked apartment.

But the Angelo story worked every time.

Resting in his host's black leatherette den chair, Drew Beltane sipped Hennessy and read the introduction to one of Creighton's best-known books, *Towards Castalia*, a discussion of interdisciplinary convergence that postulated Herman Hesse's fanciful glass bead game as a viable role model for the university of the future.

"Hesse's game," the introduction stated, "is probably the most famous literary treatment of a post-Renaissance concept—that all information must be combined to properly redefine the nature of life, god and the universe."

Interesting, Drew judged. In his own field, he'd already personally noted remarkable similarities between the hypnotic state, Yoga meditation, the psychic trance condition and his personal method of inducing out-of-body events. Each of these systems required pulse-monitored rhythmic breathing, muscular relaxation, the channeling of consciousness into one thin-focused filament of—

SLAM.

The loud report broke Drew's concentration. He shut the book, surprised that his friend was back so soon. All afternoon, Rich had been looking forward to his dinner date with Merlyn Aubrey, had gone to the barber's for a trim, shine and manicure, had shaved and showered and donned a flattering lightweight tan leisure suit—yet here he was home early and, if the force with which he banged the hall door shut was any indicator, in a rather foul mood.

Beltane listened to the clink of bottles. After a moment, Creighton strode into the den with a highball glass in hand. He nodded curtly at Drew, carelessly shed his jacket on the floor, dropped onto the lounge seat and swallowed an ounce of scotch before kicking off his shoes and leaning back.

"I presume Miss Aubrey was not thoroughly charming," Drew remarked with one brow cocked.

"The bitch didn't even show up. I waited at Shelter for her at least an hour and a half."

"Are you hungry?"

"No. I finally ordered dinner. It was embarrassing, tying up a table all that time when I could have been a lot less conspicuous at the bar. But she told me to wait for her in the dining room." Creighton scowled. "If I were you, Drew, I wouldn't count too heavily on Merlyn keeping her word tomorrow morning."

"Oh, I intend to see her house one way or another, even if I have to hobble all the way to Doylestown on my cane." Drew smiled crookedly. "But have you changed your mind about coming?"

"I'm definitely wavering."

"I understand your ire. However, if you'll permit me a

self-indulgence, Rich, my invitation is contingent on your being a member of the party."

"Yes, but that was before she decided also to include Singleton and Vita Henry. I wouldn't worry—"

The telephone cut him off.

"That's her," Drew said.

"Probably."

"No, I'm certain it's Merlyn."

Creighton ignored the premonition. "Well, in case it is, do me a favor and answer it. I don't feel like hearing a honey-coated apology."

Another ring.

"If you prefer," Drew said. "Best hand it to me, though. If I reach for it, I'll be an hour." He took the proffered phone and spoke into it. Drew nodded, assuring Creighton that it was indeed Merlyn Aubrey on the other end.

"No, it's Drew Beltane, Miss Aubrey...well, Rich offered me hospitality, so we can both be ready when you come tomorrow...we *are* still going, aren't we?" A brief silence. Drew frowned, put his hand over the receiver and addressed his friend. "She wants to speak to you, or the trip's off."

"What the hell does she want?"

"She claims she waited for you at Shelter, but you never arrived."

"What?" Creighton banged down his glass on the side-table. "Give me that damned phone!"

Drew did so, then decided it would be impolitic to over-hear the wrangle. He tactfully rose and though it was a great effort, passed along the hallway and into the kitchen, where he poured himself another ounce of Hennessy. He sipped at it, added a mite more, then returned to the den. The process was lengthy enough to allow the argument to run its course. By the time he reentered, the phone once more rested on its hook. He looked quizzically at the other man.

"Well? Had I better unpack my things?"

"Relax, she's taking you." Creighton shook his head. "Merlyn claims she waited for me near the entrance of

Shelter. I was sitting at the opposite end. That put a fifty-foot bar jammed with the usual singles crowd between us, not counting an additional ten feet of restaurant. No wonder we couldn't spot each other."

"But why didn't she meet you in the dining area? Isn't that where she told you to be?"

Creighton nodded. "Only it appears that our Merlyn's a claustrophobe. The crowd upset her. She couldn't run a fifty-foot gamut of wall-to-wall bodies. So she sat near the door and hoped I'm somehow materialize."

"Which you didn't."

"I stayed put where I was supposed to meet her. When I finally left, I went out the side door. *I* didn't feel like getting shoved and trampled, either."

"If she dislikes people en masse, why in blazes did she pick that restaurant in the first place?"

"Merlyn claims she usually only goes there for lunch. It's never very crowded then."

Drew eased himself back into the leatherette chair. "Well, what's the upshot? Are the two of you again on amicable terms?"

"More or less. She apologized profusely at the end. Practically groveled." Creighton frowned into his glass. "Drew, what's your candid opinion of Merlyn?"

The Scot shrugged. "She does seem to be tuned to her own frequency. However, as I'm to be her guest at table, I don't plan to set myself at cross-purposes to anything she says or does." He sipped a mouthful of cognac, savored it before swallowing. "More to the point, Rich, what do you think of her?"

"Frankly, I'm still trying to decide."

"Perhaps the best way is to observe her in her native habitat. Will you come with us tomorrow?"

"To Aubrey House?" Creighton drained the rest of his scotch and set down the tumbler. "Yes. There's nothing left for me here."

It was nearly midnight. Merlyn couldn't sleep. She sat propped up in bed, the reading lamp silhouetting her face starkly in shadow and light. She never slept in total darkness.

Merlyn felt guilty for lying to Richard. The crowd at Shelter hadn't bothered her, *he* did. No sooner had she walked through the front door than her legs locked together and she could not stir a step in his direction. The almighty professor irritated her. What right had he to affect her so powerfully?

Beads of sweat flecked Merlyn's forehead and cheeks. Her air conditioner was off; her last electric bill totaled $93. Perspiration pooled under her arms and knees, in her crotch, but in spite of the dreadful summer heat, she shivered. She watched the sweep hand of her electric clock slice seconds off the night like a miniature sickle of Death.

A thin smile faintly touched her lips.

At least tomorrow I'll be home.

THE MIDNIGHT CALLER

■

Drifting up from sleep, Vita felt a vague sense of loss. For once, she'd been having a pleasant dream—but what was it? She closed her eyes again and tried to remember.

1950. Yes. That was it. The evening before, she'd been thinking back to that time of wonderful possibilities, and her fantasy continued into sleep.

Picking up her wristwatch from the nightstand, she squinted to see the small numerals and was disappointed that it was only 5:30 Thursday morning. Vita was anxious to begin her grand adventure with Richard Creighton and Drew Beltane and dear Charles and Merlyn. And Aubrey House.

Goodness knows she'd been to haunted houses before and participated in séances (one of them personally disastrous), but the coming days were going to be altogether different, Vita was positive she was right.

Dear God, let me be right.

A promise of new beginnings. Yes. That was it. The house and the people were all so very special.

Vita turned over, and the smooth cool silk of her pajama top stealthily slid across her already erect nipples. Sometimes at night her body tuned itself to sensuality without bothering to consult her about it first. On these occasions, she silently had to admit that her friend Merlyn was not altogether wrong: she indeed needed a man to seek out all those secret corners of her spirit that Walter never found. *And Christ knows, I don't have much inspiration along those lines during the day*.

As soon as the thought came into her mind—and even though she was alone in the seclusion of her darkened bedchamber—Vita blushed at her silent irreverency, conjoining the savior's name with fleshly considerations.

Suddenly she remembered a time when one of Walter's

most intractable parishioners played a dreadful prank on him by lending him "an obscure religious poem" by Pushkin. After reading it, Walter was so upset that he could barely keep from destroying the pernicious volume. He refused to let his wife see it, but Vita waited till he was at church, and stole into his study and read it. She, too, was shocked by its Godless premise: that before the Virgin Mary conceived, she coupled with the Deity, the Devil and the Archangel Gabriel all in a single day, thus calling into question the paternity of her Blessed Child.

Strange how vividly Vita remembered that colossal blasphemy when her memory of Walter had since become so dim.

1950.

She had no difficulty in recalling that evening in late spring when she and Michael almost "did it." They'd gone to the drive-in to see Betty Grable and Victor Mature in *Wabash Avenue,* and Vita was certain Betty had made another movie just like it back during the war, and on the way home they heard "When April Comes Again" on the radio, and they parked in their usual place.

For a year before that night, they'd crept up on sex like two children peeking into a parent's bedroom, talking about it in a guarded, solemn way, and if she were going to do it with any boy, it would surely be Michael. All that year he kissed and groped and writhed against her while she tried to make up her mind why she didn't just let him do it, Michael was so sweet and gentle. But all the same she faced a towering mountain of fear.

Mama, of course. Fat Mama, who actively loathed any bodily process other than eating. Vita never could imagine her parents in bed, not even to conceive her. *He must have sent it by mail.* Her mother would never discuss anything remotely associated with sex or the female body. She considered bathroom hygiene a disgusting topic, and nakedness was something that nice young girls ought never to dwell upon. The only effort she ever made on behalf of her daughter's needs was to hand her a brief pamphlet on the topic of menstruation that she'd removed from a box of sanitary napkins, and even that minimal gesture was accompanied by tight-lipped disapproval. *My fault I wasn't a boy*.

A dozen times Vita and Michael were almost ready, nearly dared to make love. For months he carried a nervously purchased packet of contraceptives. "Tonight's the night" became a titillating yet uneasy joke between them. While they were kissing, and when he cupped and squeezed her, Vita was eager enough, but as soon as Michael's fingertips brushed between her legs, she went cold with fear. He never forced her beyond that point, unsure as he was of anything other than his own need.

Then, on that beautiful warm night in 1950, even though she made him stop at the usual moment, he suddenly clutched her tight and kissed her with an urgency that confused her and made her feel giddy and glad all at once. Afterwards, she realized he'd come without even entering her, and though Michael was embarrassed about it, Vita was ecstatic to think that just being near her excited him so much.

Oh, it all could have been so easy, even his clumsiness was dear and tender. But always they had to try in cramped, chilly cars, and they never knew if the police might come along and shine flashlights in the windows. In 1950 in Steubenville, Ohio, you couldn't even ask your best friend to use her house because she was just as confused as you, and it'd be all over gym class the next day.

That night Michael asked Vita to marry him.

"I should have," she murmured into her pillow, then turned over and stared at the pale morning light edging her windows. "I should have said yes."

Over the years, it became a familiar litany.

Drew dressed himself in a thin yellow short-sleeve shirt and white slacks. He ate a largish breakfast, packed toothbrush and razor and lotion, and took the elevator down to the lobby with Richard. The weatherman predicted temperatures in the nineties, but as they emerged from the building and walked to the curb, Drew pleasurably observed that the balmy morning, at least, had shaped up nicely.

"If you say so," Creighton grunted. "My metabolism doesn't punch in till noon." He set down a single suitcase on the sidewalk. His only other gear was a portable cassette recorder which Drew regarded with wry interest.

"Are you planning to tape the alleged crackle of psychic energy?"

Creighton smiled sardonically. "No, I just want to make notes of things as they occur. If they occur."

Drew returned the smile. "Doubtless an effort to keep me and Charles honest."

"Just objective." Creighton offered Drew a cigarette, but the Scotsman declined. "Care to bet on how late Merlyn's going to be?" He took a long drag of smoke into his lungs. "Or whether she'll even bother showing up at all?"

"Methinks you wrong milady, Rich. If I'm not mistaken, she's at the helm of yon looming battleship." He flicked his cane in the direction of West End's north traffic lane. Creighton turned and gaped.

The Scot reflected on the vagaries of those born rich. At Vita's party, Merlyn went on so about being so absolutely impoverished and how sorry she was he couldn't rent the house for less than the exorbitant advertised rate that he gleaned an impression of grinding Dickensian poverty. He hardly expected her to drive up to the curb in a rented livery Rolls Royce complete with power seats, brakes and steering, air conditioning, stereo, and a bank of unnamed controls that might serve one dinner, draw a bath or, for all he knew, bomb Berlin. He suspected she had no idea of budget whatever. The money would either be there or gone, and that was it.

Drew remembered his mother's narrow, hospital-neat little guest house on Arran Place in Ardrossan where a net profit of thirty-five pounds in a week was considered a windfall. How odd this life, giving back with one stroke what it takes with another. If not for his physical problem, he might have gone to work in the shipyards instead of turning to books. The books led him to thought, the short-comings of his tortured frame helped him discover the unique power of mind—and his peculiar psychic gift. The Ardrossan slips were idle now, the town a backwater. People commuted to work in Glasgow or idled out their days over darts and beer in Nichols' Pub, but fragile Drew Beltane flourished, a dynamo in a frail armature, turning all his energy inward to explore and formulate his controversial theories of existence and psychic survival.

To Drew, existence was linear, but how much of its line one perceived at a given time was quite variable. He regarded personality as vertical, and in survival as in life, it was capable of fragmentation. Thus, to see what people like Charles or Vita called a ghost, it was necessary to read what was there linearly, but with a vertical harmonic element as well, all parts having a separate rate of emitted *psi* power. These emissions, he contended, might eventually be reduced to formulae with enough work along the right path and enough money to cover the research. Not catch as catch can stuff like a single week in a "live" house like Aubrey. He had to make the most of it, though.

Merlyn's mammoth auto purred to the curb and Singleton got out of the back where he'd been sitting with Vita. He assisted Drew with his luggage, chattering on eagerly about the "great things in store for them" at the end of their journey. Creighton was invited in front, while Drew settled onto the wide, soft rear seat next to Vita. She sat in the middle, between the men.

"There's chilled champagne in the compartment," Merlyn told him, "and croissants, too. Help yourself. Richard?"

Creighton declined, still suffering the morning with scant grace.

They drove down West End till it became 11th Avenue and continued southward. The Lincoln Tunnel entrance loomed just below 42nd Street. Merlyn turned left into it, and a few moments later the vehicle emerged into the bright sunlight on the New Jersey side of the Hudson River.

Singleton, professing great interest in his colleague's way

of working, was eager to talk strategy, but Drew chose not to discuss his technique for investigating Aubrey House in other than polite generalities. He suspected Charles knew a great deal more about his methods than he'd let out when they met at First Universalist and was now delicately baiting him. Besides, there was Vita to consider. Drew rather liked the lady, saw no reason to disturb her with his personal theories; she'd probably find them too cerebral, maybe even verging on the profane. The question of survival after death was very likely intimately intertwined in her mind (Charles' too, for that matter) with the promise of Holy Mother Church. But when you lived every day with a body like a wrecked car, never wholly divorced from pain, the enigma of existence became about as spiritual as a hangover.

In Doylestown, when Merlyn stopped to grocery shop, Vita was appalled at the way her friend rapidly filled two carts without bothering to look at the prices.

"Merlyn, dear, we can't eat all that meat! Get a good-sized roast, and I'll make hash leftovers."

"I hate hash," Merlyn declared shortly, pushing her prime steaks to the checkout register, which rang a total close to $100. Merlyn spent another $70 or $80 at their next stop, the state liquor store. She bought scotch for Richard, Drew and Vita; cream sherry for Charles; Jack Daniels for herself, and a general assortment of after-dinner drinks.

As the huge silver-gray Rolls turned out of Doylestown onto Route 611, Merlyn proudly announced she would save "heaps of money" buying their eggs, milk and butter from a local farmer she'd known all her life. Vita glanced at Drew and caught the guarded gleam of amusement in his pale blue eyes. A smile began to crinkle her lips, but she brought it under control. Not before Drew had noticed, though.

They rode through gorgeous rolling country prematurely touched with the first amber flames of Pennsylvania autumn. Farmland swelled and dipped, cresting in russet and green stands of black walnut, shagbark, chestnut oak, needle-bearing hemlock. While Merlyn prattled on about the delicious fresh local produce and "all the marvelous manufacturers' outlets in Reading" some forty-five miles west, Vita obliviously looked out the windshield, enchanted by the gentle curve of the land and the bittersweet hues of the dying leaves. Manhattan was a cramped vertical clump of concrete-and-brick exclamation marks, a high-rise fortress without a horizon.

"Magnificent country, isn't it?" Drew remarked.

"Yes," she whispered, feeling a kind of harmony with their surroundings. "Pennsylvania is so gloriously linear." Then Vita leaned forward to tap Merlyn's shoulder. "Is it much farther to the house?"

"No, we're almost there. In fact, you'll see it as soon as we get around the next turn."

The car followed the swerving road, and then, far across dun fields and rolling lawn and sparkling water, the white frame enormity of Aubrey House shimmered in September heat.

"Oh, yes!" Singleton suddenly exclaimed.

Creighton half-turned in his seat. "'Oh, yes' what?"

"The house," Charles replied. "A definite aura."

Vita did not miss the arch glance that Drew exchanged with Richard.

As Merlyn pulled into the driveway, Vita was amused by an odd thought that popped into her mind: *I'm home*.

Well, here I am, Aubrey, Drew thought when the great house loomed up in the distance. *I know you and I don't.* He'd scanned its blueprints, memorized its plans and old letters and accounts, and still it was a new experience to see it for the first time, like a play often read in manuscript but never witnessed on stage.

The front of Aubrey House bayed out in two towerlike structures that ended short of the third floor in a railed widow's walk. A wide veranda ran half the circumference of the ground floor. The place had been planned with a patrician disregard for space or the tired legs of harried servants. Its axis was northeast-southwest so that the morning sun would wash the breakfast room, but the high-windowed salon living room would catch the afternoon daylight.

Merlyn tossed a question to the back seat. "Well, Charlie, is it everything you hoped?"

"Yes, indeed! Lovely old place. I suppose that garage was once a stable?"

Drew automatically nodded with Merlyn. She said, "For four overfed hackneys, a groom, stableboy, groundskeeper and assistant."

"Glorious, Merlee!" Charles crowed. "Your ancestral home makes me think of long summer days with lemonade and croquet on the lawn."

Vita agreed effusively, but the blonde shook her head and said softly, "I've got other memories."

"That lawn goes on forever," Vita observed. "And didn't I see water, too, not far away?"

"Yes. The lake." Merlyn shifted into second as the tires crunched over the rutted driveway. "The near shore's within my property line. There's a rowboat."

"Punting on the lake," Charles giggled. Turning to Drew,

he opened his mouth to ask a question, then thought better of it and looked back at the house.

Drew was amused. *Yes, Mr. Singleton, it would be a bit gauche to ask whether I'd ever poled along Thames.*

Vita impulsively squeezed Drew's arm. "Don't you just love it here?"

"Well," he admitted, relishing the feel of her warm fingers, "it does have more visible charm than I'd anticipated."

"It does," she nodded. "I almost remember it."

Charles' eyes shone. "Vita . . . are you experiencing *déjà vu?*"

"Yes. No. Not exactly."

Merlyn braked the car in front of the wide steps and switched off the motor. "Well, here we are. I admit the old place looks romantic from out here, but wait. Inside there's asthmatic plumbing, acres of dust, tons of old junk upstairs and clammy air in rooms that haven't been opened in decades. To me, the place is bleak."

"Well, if it's that bad," Creighton asked, "how come you never sold it?"

Drew saw Merlyn stiffen and Vita cringe. *Apparently one doesn't ask Miss Aubrey that.* But nothing happened. Merlyn shrugged and said something about her warped sense of family loyalty. Then suddenly she turned to the back seat and held out a ring of heavy keys.

"Charles, would you take these and open up? The long one's for the front door."

Nodding, Singleton clutched the key ring and opened his door. Drew said he wouldn't mind stretching his legs, too, so Charles came around to his side and helped him out. Though there was considerable room in the auto, it still felt good to straighten up.

"As long as you're going in," Merlyn called, "would one of you open a few windows to let the place air? And find out whether or not they've turned on the phone yet."

"You'd best wrestle with the windows and leave me to tackle the telephone," Drew said wryly as he cane-pegged toward the wide front steps. At the car, Vita struggled a grocery bag out of the back seat while Merlyn went to the trunk.

Singleton inserted the indicated key in the front door lock. It rasped and resisted, so he used both hands to turn it the rest of the way. It uttered a metallic groan and capitulated.

"Well," Charles said, "whatever's inside certainly knows we're here now." He paused melodramatically, hand on knob. "After all these years . . . Aubrey House!"

He pushed the door open and stepped through. Drew followed. They found themselves in a great entrance hall paneled in dark, somber wood. The corridor ran the length of the house, dividing the downstairs into left and right lobes; at its further end was a portal to the pantry. Drew knew that the single door opening off the hall on its right side led to a banquet-sized dining room. Immediately to their right was a cloak and storage room that would easily have served as a bachelor's bedroom in Manhattan. Straight ahead but still on the right side of the main hall, they saw a heavy, graceless staircase to the second floor.

There were three openings on the left of the central corridor: the one farthest back was for the kitchen, the middle door led to the library, the nearest, almost opposite the cloakroom, was a broad arch that formed the entrance to the huge formal living room-salon. Drew recalled it was connected by sliding doors with the library.

Charles stepped to the archway, stopped and spoke in a low voice. "Oh, yes. Can't you feel it waiting? As if something was holding its breath."

Drew did not comment. Not as theatrically sensitive as his companion, his first impression was of nothing more dramatic than the flat air of a house shut up for months. Silence. Dust motes in the sudden sunlight.

Charles entered the room and began wrestling with the fastener of an out-opening bay window. Drew approached the arch and scanned the contents of the salon. It was a massive compromise between Victorian and modern furniture. Over the fireplace was a stern painting of . . . *yes*,

Drew decided, *that would be Derek Aubrey, Merlyn's grandfather*. Probably painted about 1910, when American artists mostly tried to emulate the styles of Whistler or Sargent.

Derek's features were handsome and open behind the bluff mustache. A hale, athletic man, almost as arrestingly comely as Charlotte Aubrey, his wife. But he went toward overweight in his middle years and was dead in his Philadelphia office by the age of forty-five. A heart attack took him in 1920.

"That's Merlee's grandfather," Singleton puffed, doing his best to wrench the second bay window open.

"I know, I've seen his photograph. The artist firmed up his mouth."

In the wide alcove formed by one of the two-story bays stood a nine-foot Chickering grand piano covered with a faded blue brocade scarf. On it rested a black cradle telephone.

"Here's my assignment," Drew said, lifting the receiver.

"Is it working, Drew?"

"No. The line's dead."

"Tch. Merlyn will be furious." Singleton lowered his voice. "You'd best gird your loins. Mam'selle Aubrey has been known to utter imprecations."

"So warned," said Drew. "Shall we take in the library?"

The Scot had a warm affection for any room set aside for displaying and storing books. As a scholar, he'd spent some of his happiest hours in the hushed atmosphere of reading rooms in his native land as well as London and several British university towns. But the Aubrey library felt unused, unlived-in. The love seat, a blatant contradiction in terms, dared anyone to tarry on it, singly or together. Behind the glass doors stood leather-bound books with spines still bright with gold lettering, hardly ever handled. He drew closer and saw the volumes of the matched sets were occasionally out of sequence. Some were even upside down. *Purchased by some effete Victorian interior decorator, no doubt.*

Charles picked up on it too. "It feels more like a stage set than a room, wouldn't you say?"

Drew agreed.

"Yes," the little bald man said with head-wagging certainty. "A typical Barrie setting. Act One...Lord Plushwood's study. Neatly arranged, glassed-in books planned for the visual unanimity of their exteriors. Enclosed to prevent frivolous misuse, such as reading of their contents. They are attended at the wake by a quartet of hunting and gamebird prints, a gargantuan world globe in a teakwood tripod, a preposterously incommodious cherrywood desk and a Third Empire love seat that would quash the libido of Lothario himself."

Drew laughed at the unexpected whimsy. Singleton had his amiable facets. Leaving the little man to contemplate the cheerless study, the Scot returned through the salon to the main hall, where he glanced through the still-open front door. Merlyn was swearing at the trunk of the car, which appeared to be stuck. Rich was doing what he could to assist, while Vita valiantly hefted another bulky bag of groceries. Drew wished he could help, but nature had left him unfit for either chore.

Turning away from the outside, he followed the main hall to the last left-hand portal and stepped through into the kitchen. It was a restaurant-sized facility entirely free from the garishness of Victorian design: completely modern, with a new Westinghouse refrigerator and deep freeze, an electric stove, microwave wall oven, a breakfast grill and a long butcher-block island over which dangled an impressive array of cutlery and gourmet instruments for the preparation of food.

The south wall contained an archway into a characterless sewing room that formed an unbroken partition between itself and the library. The kitchen also had a single door in its northerly face. Passing through it, Drew found himself in a dim rectangular chamber whose two small high windows begrudgingly admitted a few feeble beams of sunlight. He saw a stone floor, exposed wall piping and rough sturdy ceiling beams half hidden in the gloom. Left of the entryway stood three clothes washers and a pair of heavy-load dryers.

The right half of the room was fitted with several rows of lofty wooden shelves laden with earthen jugs and wide-mouthed glass jars whose spidery inscriptions identified pre-served peaches, plums, cherries, pears, persimmon, pickled melon, tomatoes in aspic, apple sauce with brown sugar and cinnamon. But the lids were blanketed with gray dust, the labels were worm-streaked by the rusty tears of many harsh Pennsylvania winters. Through the glass of some con-tainers Drew saw pale green layers of fungus lewdly inter-laced with the foodstuffs; others wore coconut-white caps of mold. One handled jug's corked neck slowly oozed bub-bles that smelled pungent in the chilly air. He made a mental note to caution Merlyn about it.

Drew wondered why it suddenly felt cold, then guessed where the breeze must be coming from. He rounded the last right-hand aisle. Set in the laundry's east wall was a plain wooden door gently swinging in a whisper of air from its other side. *Has to be the servants' stairs*. He walked to it and looked up a narrow, steep shaft ascending into darkness. He squinted and strained his eyes, but could see only the first few risers.

Singleton, he supposed, would claim the place reeked with atmosphere, but it was nothing but an unlighted stair-case at the back of the house. Dilettante psychics were always anxious to find meaning in every damp cellar and dusty garret and—

Drew froze.

A delicate tingling. A fluctuating current, tiny rushings like the singing of blood in his ear . . . and beneath, a deep subaudible *thrum* of power like the pedal tone of some monstrous pipe organ.

Beltane never probed a suspected site till he got the feel of it, but this sensation was coming to him unbidden. *What am I reading? The famous Aubrey effect?* But it was sup-posed to be anchored to a spot on the second floor. Could it be so strong he was picking it up this far away? Puzzled, Drew cautiously measures the ripples and shivers on his skin.

No, not up the stairs. On them.

Resisting the temptation to open further or start up the flight—*either's risky*—he stares into the darkness where the steps vanish. The power builds. *Moving closer. Practically in front of me now.* He probes gingerly at the essence, then pulls back. *Remember the Burtons.*

As soon as Drew recoils, he feels a corresponding riptide in the waves pulsing along his pores. As if the thing had just noticed *him*.

A long, uncertain moment, then it moves off, going back up the stairs. The power ebbs.

Drew exhales raggedly, startled at how shaken he is from brushing against such intense power. *If that's a glancing contact, what the hell is its full potential?*

Drew is convinced of one thing: the hallowed tradition of Aubrey's unmoving cold blue light is nonsense. *The power's constant, yes, but whatever sustains it is hardly still.* The restless movement was as palpable as the thing's untapped reserves of energy. And yet—how could the Falzer team have been *so* far off?

But that was a question for later. At the moment, it would be better to rejoin the others. *Music coming from the parlor.*

Vita wrestled the last grocery bag as far as the front entrance, then went back for her overnight case. Richard was still battling the recalcitrant trunk of the Rolls. Vita picked up her luggage, carried it to the archway of the salon and put it down.

"Drew?"

No answer.

She looked around the living room, feeling an excitement she could not in the least comprehend, but did not want to go away. *How can Merlyn hate this place?* It was so friendly and inviting, and the hall bannister was perfect for children to slide down, and at Christmas it could be festooned with

garlands and holly and tinsel. The scent of old wood seasoned through a century of hot summers, chilled through
as many winters, made her head giddy with its vintage
aroma.

"Drew? Are you upstairs?"

Receiving no reply, she stepped into the drowsy quiet
and mellow light of the salon. She instantly saw its splendid
possibilities.

*Crisp autumn, with a sturdy fire on the hearth. Fer-
mented cider laced with nutmeg. A few good friends engaged
in witty conversation. Through the arch a maid sidles in.
"Miss Vita, will you be wanting another tray of hors
d'oeuvres before dinner?" "I don't think so, Alice, but have
the butler decant the wine . . ."*

The dream faded. Vita frowned at herself. *Bourgeois
ideas of respectability!* Which she bitterly blamed on the
lack of creature comforts in her father's dreary rectory in
Steubenville, Ohio. A place excellently designed to wither
souls in the paradoxical profession of preserving them. Yes,
there were better things to pretend. She and Michael might
have lived in a house like this. Not right away, of course.
Michael wasn't wealthy, but over the years it could have
happened.

Could have.

As the fantasy spun itself out in Vita's mind, she approached the piano. There was an open song resting on the
music rack, and she idly fingered the keys, sounding out
the familiar melody.

Suddenly she stopped. Picked up the sheet music, turned
to the title page.

"When April Comes Again."

Odd. The same Jo Stafford-Paul Weston song that was
playing in Michael's old Ford that wonderful night in 1950
when he proposed to her.

And then Vita hears the telephone ring.

"Well, we finally got the dumb thing open!" Merlyn
dropped her grip in the hall and peered through the archway.

Behind her, Creighton picked up a double armful of groceries where Vita had set them.

"Where's the kitchen?" he asked.

"Go up the hall to the last door on your left," said Merlyn. "Vita, where are Charles and Drew?"

Vita tried a few chords on the piano. "Looking around, I suppose. Mind if I play?"

"It's out of tune, but help yourself." She followed Creighton to the kitchen as Vita sat down at the bench and began "When April Comes Again" in earnest. When the song ended, she heard applause from Singleton, who was now sitting across from her in a tall armchair. His face looked rather florid.

"Charles," she worried, "you haven't been trying to carry any of the suitcases, have you?"

"No," he puffed, "I was in the library examining the Aubrey book collection. Leaves all uncut, of course. The air's rather close in there. I suddenly felt a great weight pressing on my chest."

"Well, you'd better stay put till your color comes back. Did you bring your pills?"

"I never travel without them. Too much of this, Horatio. You never told me you play."

She ran a few stiff arpeggios. "I don't really any more."

"You put a great deal of feeling into what I heard. False modesty, Vita." He smiled. "Which is the only kind I trust. Would you favor me with another selection?"

Rising, she curtsied playfully, then rummaged through the choices stored in the piano bench. "Oh, here, Charles . . . you'll love this. A Noel Coward songbook."

He clapped his hands enthusiastically, reminding Vita of a pudgy oversized child. She plunged into "Mad Dogs and Englishmen" as Drew hobbled into the room. When the song was over, she asked Drew where he'd been.

"Poking about." His voice was subdued.

"Well, I just can't wait to see the rest of the house," Vita replied. "I think it's marvelous."

"It does have possibilities," Singleton agreed, now

breathing more normally. "One can feel so many things. I'm going to try a séance right after dinner."

The frail Scot fixed him with a level stare. "That would be quite foolish."

The other man's jaw tilted up. "I *beg* your pardon?"

"No offense intended. I merely meant that we're all rather tired from motoring and it'd be better to conserve our energies and get a fresh start tomorrow."

"Well, perhaps you're right," Singleton admitted, still sounding ruffled.

Merlyn appeared in the archway. "Richard's got the fridge plugged in, and all the groceries have been stowed. Charles, could you be persuaded to whip up one of your famous light snacks? We can all eat in the breakfast nook next to the pantry before we go upstairs."

"I suppose I could manage something," said Singleton, rising. As he left the room, he pointedly ignored Beltane.

"Oh, Drew," the hostess asked, "did you or Charles check on whether they've turned on the telephone yet?"

Before he could answer, Vita spoke. "I just heard it ring a few moments ago."

"Yes?" Merlyn asked. "Who was it?"

Vita shrugged. "It only rang once and stopped. I didn't bother picking it up."

The blonde stepped over to the instrument, held the receiver to her ear, then slammed it back on its cradle. "Oh, shit! Those damned incompetents."

"Still no dial tone?" Drew asked.

"No." Merlyn waved away the annoyance. "Screw it. Let's go have lunch."

Most of the food needed refrigeration, but Charles selected cheese and eggs, buttered a quantity of noodles and washed some greens that Merlyn picked up at a roadside stand. The ale was cold from the supermarket, and the woman chose an indifferently chilled Riesling, but the cook restricted himself to milk.

"This is splendid," Drew said, forking a mouthful of fondue. "What's the secret?"

"Oh, just a recipe I picked up a long time ago in the unlikeliest of places."

"Where?"

"A mystery novel by the late Anthony Boucher. The trick's in the mixing. The cheese and eggs blend together till it's impossible to say where one leaves off and the other begins."

"Well, it's first-rate," Drew reaffirmed.

Singleton silently forgave the Scot his earlier gaffe.

After lunch, Merlyn pushed away her plate and said, "I'd like to rest for a few hours. Who's for seeing the upstairs?"

Everyone said yes, so she rose and suggested they all follow her. Charles began to clear away the dishes, but Merlyn stopped him. "Don't worry about cleaning up. They can sit for a while."

Singleton nevertheless put the plates in the sink and gave them a light rinse before falling in behind Vita. Merlyn led them through the hall and up the front steps.

The second-floor hall of Aubrey House ran the whole length of the building, paralleling the downstairs corridor. A double row of bronze guardian angels and tubby cherubs erupting from the wainscoting at intervals heavied the passage with a ponderousness little relieved by the electric sconces. Charles generally relished the excesses of the Gilded Age, but this was a bit overdone even for him.

Merlyn paused at the second-floor stair landing and pointed to a door directly opposite. "That's my bedroom. There are ten others on this floor, some of them bigger, a few of them smaller. Not all of them have sheets, but you can help yourselves from the linen closet at the back of the hall. You're welcome to whichever room you fancy."

Now that he was actually on the famous second floor of Aubrey House, Charles was almost reluctant to explore, and from the general hush, he suspected the others were feeling the same. The grimness of the dim hall seemed to intimidate all but Merlyn, who took her luggage into her room and shut the door. Creighton, recovering first, chose the chamber directly to the right of his host's. Drew took a step into the corridor, then paused, eyes closed, leaning on his cane in what Charles thought a gratuitously histrionic attitude. Vita, suddenly fired with the spirit of adventure, began opening doors along the left of the passage, peeking in like Alice lost in a wonderland of portals.

Charles arbitrarily settled on the room to the left of Merlyn's abode. It was the only remaining door on that side of the hall, and as he walked toward it, he mentally oriented himself. *This is at the front of the house,* he calculated, *so the room must be directly over the salon.* He turned the knob and pushed, and the door swung open on a spacious bedchamber richly hung with tapestries and fitted with an ensemble of polished walnut furniture: an armoire, an escritoire, two matching night tables and a mammoth four-poster shrouded in deep velvet and covered with a quilt of matching burgundy hue. He clapped his hands at the magnificence of his new quarters.

Hearing him, Drew and Vita curiously wandered over. "Oh, my," she said, looking in, "this must have been the master bedroom."

"It was," Drew said positively.

"You know," Charles confessed to them, "I've always harbored a vulgar desire to sleep in a canopied four-poster."

Drew winked. "After reading Le Fanu by a guttering candle."

"Yes!" Charles laughed. "And on the stroke of midnight, an immense Dickensian spectre booms out, 'But touch my gown, lad!'"

"Well, should the atmosphere grow too thick, boyo, I'll be directly across the hall." Drew departed, and Vita went off to continue her exploration of the other rooms.

Charles poked into the closets and crannies of his accommodations, but soon tiring, removed his shoes and turned down the quilt only to discover a bare mattress. Just then, there was a rap at his door.

"Entrez."

Vita peered in. "Charles, I took the room next to Drew, but there's no linen. Where did Merlyn say to get it?"

"At the rear of the hall. I'll go with you, I need some, too." He padded stocking-footed into the carpeted corridor and saw Drew standing at the farther end. "Apparently we're all in the same boat." But as he walked with Vita toward the back of the house, Charles realized Drew was not searching for the linen closet, but stood staring at a large gilt-edged glass picture frame suspended on the easterly wall a yard or two from the end of the hall.

"Oh—my!" Vita exclaimed as they joined Drew and looked up at the picture.

Charles' breath caught as he beheld an elegant sepia photograph of a stunningly attractive woman of a bygone era.

"That," said Drew, "is Charlotte Aubrey at age twenty. Taken about 1900."

Beltane was beginning to irritate Charles slightly with his encyclopedic command of Aubrey history and geography. *As if he holds an exclusive franchise on the subject.*

"Charles, isn't she exquisite?" Vita asked. "And back then, women never wore much makeup."

Charles disagreed. "Oh, they did too, Vita."

"Well, not nice women, and Merlyn's grandmother must have been nice. Look how beautiful she was!"

"Beautiful?" Drew echoed. "But is she really?"

"How can you doubt it?" Charles was incredulous. "Look

at the symmetry of those features, the perfect high cheek-bones!"

"Oh, she was handsome to behold, I grant you," Beltane said seriously, "but I don't think 'beautiful' is the best word to characterize her. I've seen a smaller version of this same photo, and it bothered me, and now the original disturbs me even more."

"Perhaps you'd care to enlighten us as to why?" Singleton asked with ironic politeness.

"I can't precisely. But there's a disparity between her glamour and her expression, a—a wrongness. You won't find it in her other photos. I mean, even here Charlotte's face is perfectly and fashionably posed, but for the second that the shutter tripped, something else seems to have looked out of her eyes. I can't put a name to it."

Charles examined the picture more closely and at length reluctantly nodded. "Well, there *is* something that snags a loose end of truth, as it were."

"Whatever it is," Drew judged.

"At any rate," Singleton said, "she's a match for Derek. Did you see his portrait in the salon, Vita?"

"Yes."

Charles smirked. "He and Charlotte must have had a busy little boudoir."

Drew shook his head. "I doubt that very much."

The Scot's quietly superior attitude was definitely getting on Singleton's nerves. Charles opened his mouth to say something rather tart when he was distracted by the sound of an opening door.

"I thought I heard voices," Merlyn said, entering the corridor and walking toward them. "So you've already found it."

"No," Charles disagreed, "our grand quest for the Aubrey linen closet was somewhat diverted by speculations on your granny's visage."

"That's not what I'm talking about, Charlie," the blonde merrily replied. "You don't mean that none of you picked up on it?"

"Picked up on what?" Vita asked, perplexed.

Singleton suddenly understood. It startled him, for truthfully, he hadn't noticed a blessed thing...though he was damned if he'd admit it in front of Beltane. Luckily, Vita's question gave him a precious second to order his thoughts and reply in his best wise-uncle fashion.

"Why, Vita, this is where it is. Didn't you know?"

"Where what is?"

"The Aubrey effect. The cold blue light." Charles glanced at Merlyn, who confirmed it with a nod of her head. Then he turned to bait Drew with honeyed malice. "Of course, you read it right away, too, didn't you?" The Scot, he saw with disdainful amusement, had suddenly busied himself with a door at the very end of the hallway. Turning, the most ingenuous of blank expressions on his trimly bearded face, Drew said, "Excuse me, Charlie—did you ask me something?"

"I wondered whether you noticed the Aubrey effect here beneath Charlotte's picture."

"Yes, but actually, I find the power stronger over by this door."

Charles' lips tightened at Beltane's one-upmanship. "Indeed? Perhaps you're suggesting the linen closet is haunted?" He'd already decided where the sheets and pillowcases must be stored.

But Merlyn shook her head. "That isn't the linen closet. It's the servants' staircase."

click

"Testing. One. Two. Three. Four."

click

"Testing. One. Two. Three. Four."

click

Creighton settles back into a commodious armchair and holds the microphone just below his chin.

click

"Thursday, 5 p.m., first afternoon in Aubrey House, Doylestown R.D. 1, Pennsylvania. Initial impressions.

"I'm in a tastelessly overdecorated bedroom on the second floor, next to Merlyn's room. There's a connecting door between us, but it's locked. I know because Merlyn was in my room earlier, and when she left, I heard her turn the key. More about that in a minute. First, let me try to describe my surroundings. This is a big room, at least twenty feet square. Bare wooden floor, polished to a high gloss. The furniture is late Victorian or maybe early Edwardian, I'm no expert, but despite her bitching, Merlyn doesn't change anything. It all reminds me of the Podsnap establishment in *Our Mutual Friend*—characterized by hideous solidity. I've got a brass monstrosity of a bed. Never could understand the brass bed mystique, this one is typical of the breed: squat, wide and ugly. There's a nightstand with a chimney lamp that actually burns fuel. It has to, there aren't any sockets in this room. This tape machine's running on batteries."

Creighton glances around. "What else? There's a massive cabinet, I forget what it's called, there's a French name for it—combination bureau and clothes closet. Two big doors right and left open on an interior partially fitted with drawers, partly with a rod for hangers. Right now, I'm sitting next to the bed in an armchair that sucks you in like quicksand. The wallpaper's right out of Charlotte Perkins Gilman, yellow and tan pattern so busy it tires the eye."

The tape uncurls and winds. Creighton silently muses on the absurdity of his presence at Aubrey House.

—Waste of time.

Because Merlyn locked her door?

—Making sure I heard. Deliberate insult.

Maybe only a statement of policy.

Creighton fishes a pack of cigarettes from his shirt pocket, lights up, inhales, then addresses the microphone again. "Except for a pleasant, sunny breakfast nook and functional kitchen, the rest of this place is equally dense. Luxury without the leaven of refinement. Might paraphrase Shaw— it's a pity wealth is wasted on the rich.

"Drew visited me earlier. Says he picked up quote a strong residue unquote on the servants' staircase. I read an article of his once that described a system for calibrating psychic energy through tactile sensations on the skin of the forearms and other parts of the body. I'd assumed it to be an ingenious speculation, kind of a 'ghostometer,' but it turns out Drew claims he was born with the ability. He strikes me as scrupulously honest, so I'm willing to believe he indeed felt something on the rear staircase, though that's all I'm prepared to accept at this point. However, with a characteristic rush to interpret, Drew insists that what he experienced was a huge outpouring of *psi* force.

"I tried to get him to describe his sensations minutely, but he took it wrong. Told me that psychic research is neither as darkly romantic as Singleton supposes nor as slide ruled— I'm quoting again—as I'd have it. He left then, and I didn't try to stop him or argue. No point. Like other allegedly open-minded researchers, Drew's got a few blind spots when it comes to *a priori* examination of the bases of his theory. But we all write our own scenarios, and if Drew needs to cast me as Ye Compleat Skeptic in order to deal with me, that's his privilege. It doesn't bother me.

"After Drew left, I napped nearly two hours. Shoes off, clothes on. Best rest in weeks, no nightmares. Though I had one bad moment when I woke—an irrational feeling that Lana was in the room watching me. Told myself it's just the Aubrey atmosphere infiltrating my imagination, but when I opened my eyes, there *was* a woman in the chair where I'm sitting now. I think my heart literally stopped for a few seconds.

"It was Merlyn, of course. Said she'd knocked, but there was no answer. She came in because she was sure I wouldn't mind. When she saw I was asleep, she didn't want to wake me, so she sat down and waited.

"Merlyn asked whether I'd do her a favor and pick out an appropriate burgundy for dinner. A chore calculated to boost the male ego, I suppose, but I said yes. She explained how to find the Aubrey wine cellar, then returned to her own room through the connecting door, making sure to close it behind her. Almost immediately, I heard her turn the key in the lock. She must've had it in her hand before the door was even half shut."

Mulling it over once more, Creighton stubs out his cigarette and lights another. It worries him how much he's been smoking lately, but he nevertheless exhales pleasurably, his lids slit so he sees nothing but a garish sliver of wallpaper.

"Ashamed to admit the wine cellar jangled me a bit. Merlyn said to take a flashlight. I went downstairs through the breakfast room where the lunch dishes were still piled in the sink, caked with bits of egg and dried cheese. On the outside of the nook there's a step down into a mud room, and in the far corner of that place is a flight of wooden stairs to the basement. There's no light switch, so I groped my way to the bottom with the aid of the flash, then swept the beam around till I found, suspended from the ceiling, the 150-watt bulb Merlyn told me to look for. I pulled its cord and saw a largish room with stone walls covered with cobwebs, a cracked cement floor and no windows. Possibly originally intended as a root cellar. The air is cold and musty and damp. The sudden light sent water bugs scurrying for dark corners.

"I wandered among rack after rack of bottles, most of them containing wine too old to drink. Practically a vintner's mortuary. I guess I was still logy from my nap. Yawning a lot. I rested my forehead against the side of one of the racks and closed my eyes. Then all of a sudden, I was wide awake. I . . . I thought I'd heard something . . ."

daddy I don't like it here

"Waited to hear it again, but of course I didn't. Auditory hallucination. Common in sleep/waking state, and I'd evidently dozed. Shook myself out of it and went on with the wine search." He swallows with the difficulty of shifting emotional gears. "Pretty soon, I lucked on a cache of '70 Pommard. Amazing how Merlyn or some other Aubrey got hold of so much, it's scarce. Chose three bottles, couldn't manage them all in one trip, so I stuck my flash in my back pocket and lugged two bottles upstairs to the kitchen."

A longish pause. The recorder rotates with a gentle hiss. Gray ash silently falls to the polished floor planks. Creighton continues in a more subdued tone.

"I started back for the last bottle of Pommard. Got as far as the top of the cellar steps, automatically reached for my flashlight because it was pitch black down there. Then I stopped dead. I'd left the bulb burning in the basement, but now it was no longer lit. Tried to convince myself that I must've absentmindedly yanked its cord on my way upstairs, but both my hands were busy hefting the bottles and I couldn't have worked the flashlight, so it would have been ridiculous for me to turn off the overhead light.

"I stood at the top of the steps for at least a minute. I wanted to go down and I didn't." Creighton smiles sourly. "Drew's Compleat Skeptic on the brink of Singletonian dark romanticism. I let it go, finally, walked away and came up to my room. Logically, of course, the bulb must have burned out while I was in the kitchen, but—"

Creighton stops. There is a sudden tap on the door between his room and Merlyn's. He looks up.

"Yes?"

"May I come in?"

—Differentially polite, isn't she?

"Yes."

The key turns and Merlyn opens the door a crack, peeps in. "Richard, could you lend a hand? I've got a drawer that's stuck."

"First the car trunk, now a drawer? I'm getting to be a specialist." Creighton rises, pressing the Stop button on the recorder as he does.

click

Merlyn's west-facing room gleams with late sun. She leads Creighton to a heavy oak dresser with an old-fashioned basin and pitcher on top. Fresh air blows from the windows but can't completely mask a cloying sweetness underneath.

"Perfume," Merlyn says scornfully. "Decades of it. This was my grandmother's dressing room."

"Oh?" A politely noncommittal sound while he wrestles with the stubborn drawer and Merlyn's unpredictability.

—So why would she pick this room for herself if she can't stand Grandma? Can't be a one-time whim, not with the college pictures on the wall, Bryn Mawr yearbooks on the table, old dresses in that closet. She must use this room every time she comes here.

Another tug. The drawer finally groans open, wafting more sweetness from cedar depths.

"Lavender," says Merlyn. "All the drawers reek of it, even the wallpaper. I keep hoping it'll fade, but it never does."

"Is that Charlotte Aubrey?" Creighton asks, pointing to a framed photograph of a sixtyish woman laughing over a brandy glass from a patio chair.

"No. My mother." She drops the word like something cold and dead. "She lives with a musician in Cannes. We never write. I wouldn't have bothered to put it up, except she sent it already framed. Charlotte's on display in the hall and the dining room."

"Your dad still alive?"

"No. He died in 1972."

"How old was he?"

"Sixty-two. Bad heart like *his* daddy. Runs in the family, at least among the men." She sits on the edge of her bed, her feet primly together, her hands clasped about her knees.

"You don't seem to have much affection for your folks," Creighton observes, sitting next to her.

"There wasn't much love in this house, Richard." A ghastly parody of a smile. "My grandmother only kissed me once."

"I'm curious about her."

"You are? Why?"

"It's not hard to see she wasn't one of your favorite people. Yet you use her room. Any special reason?"

"Ask my analyst. That's what I overpay him for."

"Maybe you've got more feeling for her than you care to admit."

"You know, Richard," she says in a tone suddenly deeper and harsher, "I wasn't aware that you number psychiatry among your many intellectual accomplishments."

"Sorry, I didn't mean to step over any boundary lines."

"Well, you certainly did."

"I'm really sorry, Merlyn."

"Better try another tack. The way to my beaver's not through my psyche."

Creighton's back stiffens. "What's that supposed to mean?"

"Oh, come off it, Richard . . . you older men have your bullshit just like the younger ones, it's just smoother. You don't give a fuck about my problems. You're just going through the motions, aren't you, doctor?"

"That's the second time you've practically called me a liar, Merlyn. I'm getting damn sick of it. I didn't force myself on you, I wasn't even that anxious to come here. You led me to believe that you needed me close by."

The severity of his tone has its effect. Her head droops, her feet turn inward, her voice loses its cutting edge.

"Richard, I'm sorry. I'm a bitch, I know it."

He says nothing.

"It's just that you confuse me. You sound so together but very distant too, very guarded. You don't come on to a girl with an obvious line. I can only guess how you work the trick. I mean, everybody's got a theme song, but I can't decide what yours is."

Her childishness touches Creighton. He puts his hand over hers. "I don't have the energy or the patience any more for games, Merlyn. Life's brutal enough without making it worse with lies. What you think you see is exactly what I am. I don't have a lot of warmth to give right now. I'm in limbo...at the end of one thing, not sure I'm ready to begin again."

"A recent divorce?"

"No." A lengthy silence. "Divorce might have come eventually. Lana—my wife—knew a lot of words, too. We used them to keep away from each other. You've got to know how to touch as well as talk, and we couldn't do it very well. We tried. Don't know whether we would've made it eventually or just split."

"Richard, what happened?"

"She and my daughter were killed last month in a car crash."

"Oh, God! Oh, no!"

He squeezes his temples, puzzled. "Was it last month? I don't remember for sure. I've got a lousy memory, mostly by design. The past is equidistantly dead."

Her large hand sweeps a few strands of blonde hair from her face with a curious clawing motion. "And I thought you were married and pretending you weren't. But you look married."

A wordless shrug.

"I mean, I like older men, Richard, it's my weakness. Most of them *are* married." She brings one of his hands to her cheek, rests against it. "Can you forgive me?"

"It's all right, you couldn't have known. I've been telling myself to get back on the track and go on living. A week in Pennsylvania with you seemed like it might work for me. If I've got a line, Merlyn, that's it. And if you've been worried about locking that door, you needn't be."

"I know. I'm just fucked up. Scared of everything. Especially myself."

"The feeling's familiar. Nice to have company."

She puts her head on his shoulder. His arm circles hers with the easy authority of a father comforting his daughter. They sit quietly together and only the breeze moves stealthily through the old room still redolent of lavender.

After a while, Merlyn murmurs, "I wonder whether Vita is really a good cook?"

It strikes Creighton funny. A disproportionate wave of mirth drains off a little of the tension he's kept inside for weeks.

"What's so amusing?" She sounds hurt.

"Nothing personal. Here we are in Charlotte's slightly spooky dressing room doing Chayefsky dialogue, and suddenly you wonder about tonight's dinner."

"That's not personal?"

"No, not at all, Merlyn. It's the Life Force Triumphant, as Shaw would say—and I needed to hear it."

Her tight mouth eases into a lopsided and very youthful grin. "Well, I can't help it, I'm hungry. Did you find a decent wine?"

"Uh huh. Someone in your family evidently knew his or her vintages."

She frowns again. "Daddy was an expert on anything in a bottle."

—Talking to her is like waltzing on eggs.

"Oh, incidentally, Merlyn, I ought to mention, I think the basement bulb burned out."

"Oh, Lord," she laughs. "I forgot to tell you! You didn't get caught in the dark, did you?"

"Not quite. Why?"

"There was a couple who rented the house once and left the thing burning for weeks. Maybe they figured it was easier to keep it on than buy a flashlight. Anyway, they ran up my electric bill, so I had the bulb put on a timer so it'd switch off after ten minutes whether the string is pulled or not."

—And that ends the mystery.

Disappointed?

—Irrelevant.

"Hey," Merlyn says, placing finger and thumb at the edges of his mouth, forcing them upward, "why the long face? I thought we were beginning to enjoy each other, remember?"

"Yes." His smile turns real. "And you were hungry."

"I still am. But you're also beginning to look good to me, lover..." Drawing close to him, she covers his mouth with hers. Creighton grips her, tightly at first, then tenderly.

When their lips part, her breath is warm and sweet against his cheek. "About that door, Rich...let me decide."

They kiss again, a healthy joining that goes on and on.

By five-thirty, Vita's east-facing room was already fairly cool. Though it was one of the smaller second-floor accommodations, it was joined by an archway to a pleasant octagonal sitting room with windows in each of seven walls, the eighth being taken up by the entryway itself. Colored glass comprised the upper portion of each oblong pane, and though the hour was late, faint streaks of tinted daylight still daubed the hardwood surfaces. Green carpets in each chamber did not totally cover the flooring, and where the rugs ended, oddly angled boards jutted to the wainscoted borders.

In one corner of the sitting room sat an ebony table, a floor-length reading lamp and an overstuffed worn armchair piled with faded throw pillows. Vita's room had an armoire like Creighton's as well as a walk-in closet. The bed she lay on was queen-sized with a dark wood head frame.

On the opposite wall she sees a picture of an elderly woman with an unruly shock of white hair, a spray of violets in one hand, a plain ring on the second finger. In the background, the artist seems to have painted a miniature picture within the picture of a ballerina in tutu balanced *en pointe*, hair sleekly formed to the dancer's head, the cheekbones curiously pronounced, resembling the old woman in the foreground.

The eyes within both pictures fascinate Vita. She would like to rest a little while longer, but she'd promised Merlyn she'd cook and she wanted to have some time to enjoy a cocktail with the men. Vita rose and began to make the bed.

Routine keeps me going, she thought sourly. *No one to please or impress, but here I am, still compelled to be tidy. Why bother?* Nevertheless, she smoothed out the sheets and silken spread with great care, enjoying their cedar-scent. When she was done, she surveyed her finished work. *I still make hospital corners, the way Walter liked. Absurd.* She suddenly grabbed one neat edge and yanked it loose.

Her clothes closet was actually a short corridor between her room and Drew's, shut off from his by a door. *Wonder whether it's locked?* She shifted hangers bearing clothing that she'd hung up earlier, pushed aside the folded slacks she'd worn during the car trip and instantly heard the splattering jingle of forgotten change dropping from a pocket.

"Oh, damn!" She bent down, but it was too dark to see. Remembering that Drew brought along a flashlight, she tapped on the connecting door and waited for him to answer before trying its knob. It turned. She reached for her robe, donned it.

"May I come in, Drew?"

"Certainly," he called.

She pushed the door open and saw Beltane sitting in an easy chair, his chin propped up on his cane, his hands gripping its shaft partway down.

"I'm sorry to bother you," she apologized, standing in the doorway, "but I've got a walk-in closet and I spilled change all over the floor and can't see it. May I borrow your flashlight?"

A simple enough request. Why did he look so startled by it?

Drew took his flash from the nightstand drawer and said he'd hold it while she gathered up her money. She thanked him and walked back into the closet as he approached the door frame.

The closet surprised Drew. His own copy of the Aubrey floor plans was a facsimile of the builder's original blueprints, but there was no indication on them of space between the two bedchambers. His own was the exact shape and dimensions as he recalled them in the second-floor schematic, so the walk-in closet-corridor had to be carved out of Vita's space. *Part of her room must have been modified at some later time.*

Holding the flashlight while she scrambled along the

floor beneath the clothes rod, Drew briefly flicked the beam along the left wall opposite the occupied hangers. Just as he expected, there was a door a few feet farther down that side. His theory, he felt, must be right: additional storage area must have been built for the room's occupant. He supposed the new door merely opened on old garments in mothballs, possibly a few knickknacks. Still, he itched to explore it.

Vita straightened up. "I think I've found all of it."

He called her attention to the newly discovered portal. "Have you looked in there yet?"

"No. I didn't even notice it till now, the closet's so dark. Why? Is it important?"

"Probably just full of old luggage."

"I daresay." It didn't interest her. "Would you like to see my room? I feel like I've always lived here! There's the loveliest sitting alcove."

"I'd be delighted, Vita."

Following her through the connecting space, he brushed against the mysterious door and nearly pitched sideways.

The hammering of a sudden surge of power tightening his chest, clutching at his throat.

My God, I'm right on top of it! In the closet.

The thing hesitates, then swiftly recedes. Drew gasps a needed lungful of air. Heart battering at his rib cage, he totters after Vita, staring at her in disbelief. *Trotted past without sensing a blessed thing.*

"May I sit down a moment?"

"Of course. Drew... you're pale! What's wrong?"

"Nothing. Just need to steady myself."

"Here, try the sitting room. If you don't mind waiting, I'll change for dinner. I won't be long."

Carefully lowering himself into the armchair, pulse still racing, Drew reflected on Vita's alleged psychic ability. *It doesn't exist.* The power, the very unconstant constant roared out of the closet like a ten-ton lorry, no true sensitive could ignore it. But she merely mucked about with her change.

He did not know by what delusions she fancied herself a psychic, but one thing was indisputable: she was a handsome woman. The low-cut dress she'd worn at church was paradoxically daring yet dowdy, but the blouse and slacks she'd donned that morning for the trip delineated an excellent figure.

He glanced toward the room where she was changing. Above the headboard of her bed hung a long mirror. As he gazed into its polished depths, Drew suddenly saw Vita clad only in stockings and panties. Her hips and thighs were full but shapely, her bare breasts large with little drooping. She moved out of view and he forced himself to avert his eyes from the looking glass.

No sense dwelling on impossibilities.

A few moments later, she joined him in the sitting room. She wore a pale blue blouse and matching slacks with a wide white belt. "I know it's early yet for dinner, but might you consider escorting me downstairs just the same?"

"I'm flattered, but perhaps you'd best go on ahead. I'd only slow you down." He wanted to investigate the closet while she was out.

But Vita would not be denied. "I'm in no hurry, Mr. Beltane. I'd be glad to wait for you." She smiled at him. "It's just that it's my first evening here and I feel it'd be appropriate to go downstairs upon a gentleman's arm."

"Well, by all means then, Mrs. Henry." He held out his hand and she helped him rise.

Arm in arm, they walked slowly into the hall.

Aubrey House was one thing in sunlight, another in shadow. Charles Singleton felt its brooding hulk as the sun went down and darkness settled in corners where the light no longer penetrated. He heard the crackle and mutter of old timbers wearily adjusting to the lower temperatures of the night.

Charles helped Vita set the dinner table, gushing happily over Wedgwood, Doulton, Noritake. Merlyn appeared in tailored black with pearls, her makeup subtly done for the precise number of lumens afforded by two candles, and he teased her for it.

"You're right out of *Vogue*, Merlee! Merlyn Aubrey for Chanel. You realize you're the only one who dressed specially for dinner?"

"I'm the hostess, Charlie. If I want to wear nothing but a bedspread, I have the right."

Singleton smiled wickedly. "Your latest scheme for seducing the reticent Dr. C.?"

She blew him a kiss. "Unscrew you, love. By the way, do either of you know where Richard is?"

"In the library with Drew," Charles replied. Merlyn thanked him and left through the main archway. When she was gone, Vita shook her head.

"I almost think she's capable of it, Charles."

"Of what? Flaunting the Aubrey assets in a chenille wraparound?"

"Or something equally outrageous."

"Nonsense, dear woman. By now you ought to recognize her fey moods. She was just playing Little Rich Girl Lost Wants Attention."

"All right, Drew, you don't have to hedge. Come out and say it."

98

"Right. Vita's no sensitive, and I've got grave doubts about Charlie."

Creighton's fingers pause in their passage over the uniform spines of the Harvard Classics. He looks at Beltane seated at the cherrywood desk in the Aubrey study, idly riffling through its stored papers. The unhesitating snap and edge of the Scot's words have their effect. Drew does not strike Creighton as a man given to sweeping putdowns.

"But that sounds a bit imperious, Mr. Beltane. It leaves only you as the Keeper of the Flame."

"Look, Rich, you're a pragmatist. Accept or reject, then, and be done with it."

—There he goes again with the easy labels.

Reductionism necessary to self-image.

"Accept or reject what, Drew?"

"Since we've arrived, I've felt it three times, whatever it is. Too early to put a name to it."

"Three times? Twice on the servants' stair, once down here, once on the second floor. What else?"

"There's a closet in Vita's room that I want to investigate. It—"

He stops speaking, quietly easing the papers he's been examining back into the desk. Merlyn Aubrey enters.

"Dinner in about twenty minutes, gentlemen. Would either of you care for a cocktail?"

Drew declines, Creighton accepts.

"Ah, good—Richard, would you mind fixing the drinks? Scotch for Vita, Jack Daniels for me, never mind Charles, he's saving up for the wine. The liquor's in the kitchen." She tosses the last remark over her shoulder and gives her entire attention to Drew.

Creighton leaves the room, offended by Merlyn's casual rudeness. After their talk in her room, after the long kisses, he thought her hot-cold manner might polarize to consistency.

—But she's back to acting again.

In a play without a title.

Though he wants her in bed, Creighton is detached enough

about it to imagine with amused pity the younger men who must have pursued her to a confused standstill before giving up.

—Charles seems to know her best. She relaxes more around him.

Percipience unclouded by need.

Charles is a strain on his patience, but Creighton does not dislike him. Bouncy, facile, sometimes maliciously witty. Beet-red, too heavy, a battery of pills by his water glass at lunch.

—File him and Vita under D for Dilettantes.

And Drew?

—Too soon to pigeonhole.

And Merlyn?

—C for Cockteaser.

Cocktails are quickly consumed; everyone is hungry. Vita's dinner is simple, prepared with the disinterested ease of a long marriage: broiled steaks; ears of the new corn Merlyn bought at her farmer friend's, roasted before the fresh-picked sweetness could turn to starch; a deceptively simple salad of romaine, leeks, cherry tomatoes and avocado chunks seasoned with a tantalizing mélange of thirsty spices.

They're at dinner now in the Aubrey dining room—tentative, cautious, still feeling their way with one another and the house. Merlyn occupies her rightful place at the head of the formal dining table, Drew and Richard to her right and left, respectively. Now she pays flattering attention to the philosopher, smiling at him with childlike trust as he speaks to her in low tones while judiciously enjoying his food and wine. Next to him, Vita blushes appealingly in the candle glow as Charles, across the table from her, expounds on the excellence of the cuisine. Singleton's flushed cheeks are more than usually florid as he eats rapidly, nervously, downing his pills as he chaffs first one, then the other woman or pontificates with jocular pomposity.

The company is feebly lit by one high, dusty chandelier. The guttering tapers are as functional as they are romantic, but darkness still obscures the further recesses of the room. On the southerly wall, nearly indiscernible in the gloom, hangs a large portrait of Charlotte Aubrey, her eyes gleaming when the dying wicks flare up and flicker.

Merlyn asks Richard about one of the points he made in his lecture at First Universalist. She seems to hang on his every word, yet Charles notices how often her gaze strays to the shadowy painting of her grandmother.

"The hypnagogic state? I made a great deal of it," Creighton tells Merlyn, "because I suspect its phenomenology has long been mistaken for certain allegedly supernatural events."

Singleton picks up on the remark. "Would you care to be more specific?"

"If you really want me to." Creighton sounds doubtful.

"But what are we talking about?" Vita asks.

"Hypnagogia," Charles replies with the air of a pedant lecturing a class of slow learners. "Derived from *hypno,* meaning 'sleep' and *agogos*—'to induce.' Not to be confused with hypnotism. Hypnagogia is a semiconscious state when the body's asleep but the mind's awake, am I correct, Richard?"

"That's a fair approximate definition," Creighton politely states. "The mind *is* more or less awake, but in a condition where the subject is particularly vulnerable to his own thoughts. Adults who drove all day may see landscapes, sometimes even with white-lined highways. Every detail will be so vivid it'll be like being there again . . . except that one is also conscious of lying in bed. Children are said to imagine faces leering down on them in the dark. Auditory hallucinations are also common."

"But what occult events were you referring to?" Singleton prompts.

"Oh, for example . . . dead voices calling. Hags covering their bodies with hallucinogens that convince them they can fly on broomsticks. Handel imagining that the heavens parted for him as he set down the final notes of the 'Hallelujah Chorus.'"

Vita is a bit shocked. "But Richard, how can you be

certain that Handel wasn't actually granted a divine revelation?"

"How can you be sure he was?"

"Well, I suppose I can't, but—"

"But it's a matter of faith." Creighton refills his glass and Merlyn's from the decanter. "I don't want to argue faith versus reason, Vita. I simply find it more probable to attribute a number of reported cases of religious ecstasy to hypnagogic delusion. Have you noticed how many miraculous visions in the Bible take place while the prophets are asleep?"

She does not reply but hears Drew quietly say "refreshingly Velikovskian" with a near-invisible grin. Most of the meal he has remained silent, eating little, drinking only tea or water.

But Singleton is not satisfied. He waves his fork at Creighton. "All right, but what about Swedenborg?"

"What about him?"

"He saw angels."

"You mean, he interpreted his hypnagogic experiences as communications from Paradise."

"Well, doesn't the fact that he chose to do so count for anything? He was a scientist."

"But he gave it up for mysticism."

Charles emphatically bobs his bald head. "Precisely! The man was a biologist, a mathematician, a logician, a philosopher—yet rationalism was not enough for him."

"So he founded a church," Drew murmurs.

Singleton does not hear him. "My point, Richard, is that Swedenborg was well schooled in the discipline of scientific observation. Personally, I should expect that when a man like that says God spoke to him, his testimony would carry a bit more weight with you than, say, that of some unlettered peasant girl."

With a shrug, Creighton tries to appease Singleton. "I suppose that ought to hold some significance, Charlie. Never thought of it that way. But how do you happen to know so much about Swedenborg?" A calculated question, intended to divert the other from the topic at hand.

Charles is enormously pleased by the query. "Well, as a matter of fact, I did a deal of research on him for my most recent book. Surely my publishers sent you a copy?"

"I don't think so," Creighton lies, remembering the book all too well.

"As soon as we get back to New York, I'll see that you get one. It's called *Gods, Ghouls and Ghosts of Western Europe.*" Suddenly, Charles swivels toward Drew on his left. "I devoted several pages to Birnam Cottage in Prestwick. You were involved in that investigation."

Drew comes up out of his own thoughts. "Yes."

"It took me ages and ages to find your address. Didn't you receive my letter?"

"Oh, yes." Drew blots his lips and sets his napkin on the table in two separate and halting movements. "I just couldn't answer it properly."

"Why not?"

"Nothing relevant in it. You lent a great deal of credence to the séances done by Birnam's cousin."

"Mrs. McCallum?" Charles asks with controlled pique. "And why do you disagree with her findings?"

"They have no connection with the truth. The lady's a bit of a romantic. To do a séance or two and then announce that you've made contact with the spirit of a departed cousin is simplistic."

Vita leans across to him. "But surely you've done the same!"

"No. First I read the place, find the residue. At Birnam, there *was* a survival of sorts. Hardly what Mrs. McCallum claimed."

"A survival *of sorts?*" Charles smirks. "I think, as the saying goes, Drew, that you and I are coming from two different places."

"Yes, quite different. You have your ghosts—complete and integrated personalities pursuing their interests after death. But what is personality, actually? Every person has one, of course, but are they 'all, all of a piece throughout'?

I think not. In my opinion, Charlie, personality resembles intricate music. A C major seventh chord, for example— a combination of audible frequencies: C, E, G and B flat, and each note in the combination is a recognizable tone because it vibrates at a certain pitch. Perhaps the human psyche is analogous. But none of us knows all the tones that comprise our inner harmonies, which of them is strongest and likely to continue to resonate after death."

"A fascinating theory," Singleton says with genuine admiration. "And how do you think it applied to old Malcolm Birnam?"

Drew looks away. "Oh, there may have been tones within that he struggled not to hear. He was a retired sar-major, West Highland Rifles. Thirty-five years a soldier, never married, retired alone to the cottage. His papers weren't available beyond some letters very carefully screened by his cousin, but even so, the use of certain words, certain repeated images . . . no, I'd rather not say."

Singleton chews a fatty gobbet of steak trimmed from the bone end. He swallows. "This idea of fragmented survival is extremely intriguing. But how would a medium sort out all those bits and pieces and recognize them as separate from what he or she personally projects? I mean, to extend your own metaphor, Drew, a musical chord also interacts with its harmonics."

"The difficulty has occurred to me," Drew states with unstressed irony, recognizing one of his own published passages closely paraphrased by Charles.

"Well, as far as I'm concerned, I don't want to snoop about my buried life," says Singleton, almost reluctantly laying down his fork. "I'd be quite content simply to discover what's really going on in this house. Has it ever struck you as odd, Drew, that the Aubrey effect was first noticed in 1920, yet the sole death to take place here happened forty-four years later, in 1964, when Charlotte died?"

Drew nods. "It is certainly curious."

Singleton scrutinizes the dimly lit painting at the far end of the room. "Ah, but *was* she the first?"

"Yes, I've often wondered that." Drew turns to Merlyn. "Could you tell me who used to occupy the room directly opposite yours?"

"The one Vita's in? It used to be Emily's."

His brows rise. "Emily Shipperton?"

"Yes. Why, Drew?"

"Because she used to sleep on the third floor. And isn't it strange for a servant to be quartered with the family when the rest of the staff is relegated to the third floor?"

"Not in Emily's case. She was my grandmother's nurse, and long after my father grew up, she continued to care for Charlotte. She was supposed to stay close in the night in case she was needed." Merlyn's tone turns harsh. "That figured. My grandmother never did a damn thing for herself."

"I'm quite interested in Emily Shipperton," Drew says. "How long was she with the family? She just seems to fade out of the record books."

"Oh, she was still with us when I was a little girl," Merlyn replies distantly. "She was an old lady by then, and she slept in the room you asked about. When I was twelve or thirteen, she took ill and my father had to put her in a rest home. She died soon afterwards."

Vita suddenly interrupts. "Was she a dancer?"

"Emily?" Merlyn laughs. "Hell, no! Why?"

"Did she have white hair that stood on end?"

"No. Her hair was dark. She dyed it. She primped almost as much as my grandmother. Why on earth would you ask such things, Vita?"

"No good reason." The other woman tosses it off, but Merlyn stares at her perplexed, as does Drew.

Charles pushes away from the table with a happily replete sigh. "Well, I *was* going to work, but I think I'll postpone it till tomorrow. Too much blood in my stomach, not enough up top where it's needed."

Vita looks from Charles to Drew and back again. "Oh, Charles, I was sure you'd be sitting this evening."

"No, I'm going to let your gorgeous dinner settle, and I

believe I'll retire early." He snaps his fingers. "Though I would like to set up my camera in the back hall by Charlotte's photograph. Would that be all right, Merlee?"

"Sure, why not?"

Singleton smiles at the others. "I hope no one is a sleepwalker?"

"I'm certainly not," Drew answers sardonically. "What kind of camera do you have, Charlie? One of those new Kirlian rigs?"

"No, no, I can hardly afford that. Though maybe I shall once I'm finished writing about Aubrey House. But I hope to snap a few good infrared time exposures of the cold blue light itself."

"Fascinating." Merlyn deposits her napkin by her plate and stands up. "But count me out of your investigations, fellas. I'm going to be plenty busy just getting things ready for the people coming next week, bless their solvent little hearts. Anyone for brandy and coffee in the living room?"

Declining an after-dinner drink, Drew laboriously made his way upstairs, but when he reached the second-floor landing, his body jerked involuntarily and, despite his supporting cane, threatened to pitch him forward on his face. He shot out his hand to protect himself, but just then Creighton—who'd gone to his room to brush his teeth—reemerged into the passage, saw what was about to happen, and dashed to Drew's aid.

"Easy! Are you all right?"

"Yes." Drew collected himself with tight lips. "Damnable nuisance. You may have noticed I haven't touched a drop of alcohol all day. The same goes for my usual lot of pills. That's what's wrong. Without them, there's always a certain level of...of discomfort." He took a tottering step toward his bedroom, Creighton hovering mother-hennishly by his side. "Without medication, Rich, life's like a fingernail on a slate. But I've got to be clear for this house."

"I noticed you were subdued at dinner."

A sardonic chuckle. "Not enough for Charlie."

"Your remarks about Birnam Cottage sort of squashed his toes. I assume your retired 'sar-major' was homosexual?"

"Quite... I say, Rich, you needn't crowd me. I know I wobble a bit, but I generally manage to get where I'm going."

"Sorry." Creighton backed away a step.

Slowly continuing to his room at the front of the hall, Drew said, "You also had your moment as Banquo at the feast. Honestly now, Rich, are you really unacquainted with the latest Singletonian screed?"

"Mea culpa." Creighton smiled crookedly. "I quit after about sixty pages of *Gods and Goats of Western Europe* or whatever it's called. Pretty puerile stuff. But was I that obvious a liar?"

"No. Charles was too preoccupied touting his tome to notice. Also, you threw him a bone."

"A bone?"

"Swedenborg. Whose celestial visions, I suspect, fail to impress you, despite his background as a scientist."

"The only thing it proves is that the need to believe is an almost inescapable trap of the ego."

Something in the way he said it irritated Beltane. Pausing at his bedroom door, hand on knob, the Scot felt a kind of muted sadness mingling with his sense of pique.

"You know, Rich, there are a great many other things I'd rather be than what I am . . . but what I am, I'm good at."

"I'm sure you are, but——"

"You needn't take my word for what's going on here. By all means, observe Aubrey independently. But once you have, will you really recognize what you've seen?"

With that, Drew entered his room, closing the door and the discussion.

—Now what in hell was *that* about?

An open and shut mind.

Postponing the appealing prospect of coffee and a snifter of Hennessy for a few more moments, Creighton goes back to his room and switches on his tape recorder.

click

"Note on Drew Beltane. Has little patience when he thinks you're not on his wavelength. Rude to Singleton at dinner—unnecessarily so in front of Charles' friends. Flared up at me a moment ago, apparently interpreting a casual remark I made as being directed against him personally.

"At this stage, I think Drew lashes out when certain of his basic assumptions seem to him to be questioned. Such as the actual nature of the force he claims to be physically sensitive to. Drew maintains an *a priori* conviction that this unnamed phenomenon, which he allegedly 'reads' on his skin, is that *psi* power which ESP researchers posit. To the best of my knowledge, the issue is still being debated and studied, but Drew has absolutely no doubts that he's in touch with a kind of 'survival residue' or, in lay terms, the stuff of ghosts. Drew has a theory based on the notion that human personality is a complex bundling of disparate, often contradictory traits and factors and that after death, only some of these elements survive—usually without the superego to integrate or control them. It's a new twist on the old theme that all spectres are psychotic. Reminds me of that sci-fi film about monsters of the id.

"Drew's problem is that like many researchers, he forgets that a pet theory may possess the proportions of classic architecture and even fit all the existing facts without being correct. The—"

Creighton stops. The power monitor bulb of his recorder suddenly begins to flicker. While he watches, it grows progressively dimmer and finally goes out.

—Damn! Thought I'd put in new batteries.

click

Drew eased himself into the armchair by the foot of the bed. *Best rest a bit before tackling that closet.*

He mused on his recent conversation with Creighton. Oh, yes, he could have been a great many other things, given a healthy body. But without one, there was pathetically little he could do; even the turning of a page required a separate act of will. Snug in his classroom, he could dissect Pictish or Bronze Age archeology, analyze the finds of the real workers like Burl and Rowley, but he'd never scrape the earth from a new find with his own trowel and sweat. *I'd be useless on the easiest dig going.*

Not a big body, just one that worked, that could allow him to feel the joy of simple health, the pleasure of loving a woman. *That* was certainly out; intelligence taught him that early, but still he had to try—attempts recalled in pain and broken pride. Sublimation was the best remedy for his cruel variety of impotence which left him all the healthy urges and no means of fulfilling them, like certain moths born with mouths but no esophaguses, living just long enough to starve to death, their last hours a frantic search for food that would never nourish them.

With will and careful habit, Drew could more or less ignore the sick joke that was his body, the nerves that received too much but transmitted too little. He could almost forget women. Vita. The way her eyes gleamed at dinner . . .

You will toy with it, won't you? You could end it instead but lack the courage.

But that wasn't it. He still, absurdly, loved life in spite of the diminishing returns his body afforded. *When will I be able to look at a woman without wanting her?* Though Merlyn Aubrey didn't interest him, he read her too well: a vocational virgin, loathing the intimacy her eyes pretended to promise. Vita was another matter entirely. She seemed completely unaware of the nuances of sensuality articulated by her shapely body. Her full thighs and hips, her fine breasts, the graceful curve of her back—all had an instinctive flow, a womanliness that overpowered Drew.

With a normal body, he could communicate the gift to her, let her know in so many ways how her loveliness affected him. Unhurried, letting it become her need as well. He could carry her to the bed, delighting in the tender-cruel pleasure he gave and took—

Christ, pack it in! Like an old maid writhing through a smarmy novel. Dodo Beltane—the instinct for flight without wings. Get to work!

He took his flashlight, tested it, found it wouldn't work. He replaced the batteries, found the new ones dead, too. Putting it down, disgusted, he stealthily moved into the hall. He heard the piano tinkling, a voice wafting up the stairs. Vita playing, Charles burbling more Noel Coward. Not a bad voice, certainly a better pastime for him than mucking about with a séance. Singleton was in the style and sway of antique charlatans like Margaret Fox, Drew was sure . . . turning the whole notion of spirit communication into an occult telephone-answering service.

But genuine sensitives were chary of the risks involved. Birnam Cottage, for instance—its residue could only corrode or altogether destroy an essentially gentle spirit like Charles. *Like wiring together incompatible electronic components—or perhaps too compatible.*

Drew avoided further discussion of Birnam at dinner because of Charles' homosexuality. Malcolm Birnam, as Creighton guessed, also was drawn to men, but he ruthlessly suppressed that facet of his nature, loathing the tendency and himself as the antithesis of manhood and regimental honor. And it was the hatred and disgust that Drew read there in the cottage, that and a leering, tittering tendency lurking round the iron edges of control.

A sensitive is vulnerable and breakable. Unthinkable that Charles could make contact with the vicious aura of Birnam Cottage, that brutal, suppressive, anal-sadistic thing. A *psi* investigator must have a well-integrated psyche, but the irony and danger was that the field attracted so many incomplete personalities.

Quietly opening the door to Vita's room, Drew stepped inside, turned on the lights and went directly to the walk-in closet, stopping at the door. Placing his hand on its tarnished knob, he allowed himself to open just a little, only enough to read the intensity of the power.

Yes, it's there. Much fainter now. Quiescent. Hard to tell if it's moving. But it knows I'm here.

Drew braced his cane, gripped the knob and turned till the latch sprang back with a dull *clung,* but the stubborn door would not open. He ran his hand over the surface till he found the cause. A few feet above the knob was a thick block of plywood fastened with large protruding nails across both the door and its warped frame. He wondered why anyone would go to the trouble and expense of hiring workmen to construct the additional storage space, only to crudely seal it off with a chunk of wood and a few big nails.

Drew returned to his room the short way, through the connecting door, rummaged in his gear till he found matches and a hammer and brought both to Vita's closet. It took a full minute of jerky effort to find his best balance, discarding the cane as he struggled to wedge the claws of the hammer under the edge of the plywood block. He prized it away about an eighth of an inch and then repositioned himself. Again gripping the knob, he bent his knees and hauled, dragging at the warped door with all his wispy ten stone of weight till he heard the groan of the nails gradually leaving their years-old bed.

The door opened the width of a knife blade. Drew yanked at it, breathing hard. Pain in his limbs, but he wouldn't dull himself with pills before bed, even if he rattled apart. Another heave, another inch free. A series of jerks. Another quarter inch. Enough. He had to rest.

The closet disturbed him profoundly. There were plenty of unused storage areas on the second and third floors. There seemed no need for yet another, but one had been built, and now it was a spot of enormous power. The implication was not pleasant, but Drew saw no other way to interpret it yet. Again, he wondered how Falzer could have been so far off when he investigated the house in 1935.

Drew forced himself into place once more. There was enough space now to bend his fingers around the edge of the door itself. He tugged and yanked, and presently the last strength of the nails gave way. The door swung open onto darkness.

Standing in the black opening, he lit a match and moved it from one side to another. Nothing astounding at first glance. *Shallower than I thought.* Two chest-high columns of neatly stacked cardboard boxes, all of a uniform size, surely once white but now grayed with time. The end of each box bore the same gilt-embossed label.

M. L. STRASSER

TOYMAKER

PHILADELPHIA

Lighting another match, he held it higher in an effort to see the top of the pile of cartons. Drew sucked in his breath, startled by the face suddenly leering at him in the flickering illumination.

Seated grotesquely on the top carton, its half-severed head bleeding cotton, the filthy rag doll grinned down at Drew like an idiot surveying the fear-shot work of the Seven Days and calling it good.

A wonderful night! thought Vita. The excitement that seized her on entering Aubrey House hadn't left yet. Part of it was the newness, like the first evening out on a cruise ship when everyone, yourself included, is transfigured with dramatic potentials that vanish in the dawn's revealing light. A sense of infinite beginnings, a radiance of possibilities opened her spirit to meet whatever chose to touch it.

> *I'll see you again*
> *Whenever stars break through again . . .*

While she played Noel Coward and Charles sang, she thought of Michael with that special wistfulness reserved for the ghosts of lost chances. She let 1950 pour back into her its secret vintage, and she lilted with the music and the brandy and the memory of a time when life could have planted summer in her soul.

Oh, Michael, do you ever think of me?

His song ended, Charles begged off from any encores. He sat down, slightly winded, and helped himself to cheese and brandy while Vita played some more. She imagined herself as the hostess of Aubrey House, giving an intimate salon for her cultured friends.

At length, Merlyn rose and said she was tired. Richard accompanied her upstairs. Vita spent a few moments longer at the keyboard, then she sent Charles off to bed, refusing his help with the plates and glasses. Even the task of clearing up was pleasurable, furthering the illusion that it really was *her* home.

On her way to the second floor, she decided there would be no need for her tablets this evening. She felt mellow enough to sleep peacefully all night.

A line of light appeared at the bottom of the door. *Funny,*

I don't remember leaving it on. She stepped into her room and was a little surprised to find Drew sitting on the edge of her bed surrounded by a litter of white boxes. He was holding a shapeless bundle of something, she was too far away to tell what it was.

"Hope you don't mind that I'm here," he said. "That storage space bothered me. I had to open it."

"I don't mind, Drew. Oh! How exquisite!"

Vita exclaimed with delight as she saw the beautiful dolls laid out on her bed. She grabbed them up one after another. Custom-made; even in their own day, they must have been expensive. The Spanish Dancer was almost two feet tall and had joined fingers that moved on springs to control miniature castanets. The costume was filigreed with lace, the mantilla carefully arranged beneath the primly coiffed black hair. Vita fingered the tresses.

"It's real hair, Drew. Feel."

The Southern Belle had seven petticoats of crinoline and silk shaped with intricate hoops beneath the satin gown. The Little Nun wore a full rosary with each tiny bead accurately spaced and held an inch-wide prayer book bound in leather, with printing on every page. The High-Fashion Girl was a page from Godey's Ladies Book, real peacock feather in a velvet hat, a matching basque, bustle and genuine whalebone stays.

Vita felt an urge to arrange them in a scene. She fondled the lace and satin and silks, all uniformly faded by time. None showed any wear.

"They look like they were packed away brand new," Vita said.

"I'd say so," he nodded. "All bought at the same time, too. The sales slip is in one of the boxes."

Vita cuddled the Nun. "They're precious. Merl's so lucky."

"Merlyn? Rather older than she is. The slip says they were purchased in October 1904."

"My heavens, they must have belonged to her mo— no, her *grand*mother. They're heirlooms, Drew. You'd pay hundreds in F. A. O. Schwarz for dolls like these."

He handed her the tattered rag doll without comment. The torn head lolled limply, staring up at Vita with shoe-button eyes and a single painted line of uptilted mouth. She turned it from side to side, studying the stained, half-obliterated features.

"Judging by this one's condition, it must've been a favorite toy," said Vita, taking it with her to the dresser. She rooted through her travel utility case till she found a safety pin. With it, she tenderly closed the rip in the doll's neck.

Drew smiled. "You know, that's just what I've been wanting to do."

It began to rain around ten-thirty. After Drew went to his own room, Vita undressed and showered and put on fresh, filmy nightclothes. Though the long day had tired her, she did not feel like sleeping just yet, so she removed a paperbound novel from her purse and, turning off all but the light in the sitting chamber, ensconced herself in the armchair and opened her book.

But she found it difficult to concentrate. Something heavy in the air weighted her and made it difficult to breathe, and when the drops of water began to tap against the windows that surrounded her in the octagonal chamber, Vita realized the thick air had been the natural harbinger of storm.

Putting aside her book, she gazed absently into her dark bedroom and thought about her wonderful new home and the people she was sharing it with. Especially Drew. *I like how he talks to me*. But it was hard to get used to the way he moved, like one of those old movie flip books she played with when she was a girl, the images starting and stopping and starting, and that was exactly how Drew walked and sat down and got up and ate his dinner and did—*everything?* The thought made her blush. She quickly banished it.

Thunder rumbled. The lids of her eyes began to droop as she slumped farther down in the comfortable armchair. A flicker of lightning briefly lit the two rooms and Vita sees, reflected in the mirror above her bed, the painting of the old woman with the shock of unruly white hair. Like a spirit at a séance, the glowing face vanishes again as the sky goes black. *It's her room, and she likes me.*

The storm dwindles to a whisper as Vita's eyes close.

Angled slants and shafts of rain. Midnight. Flashes of lightning glowing in the puddles of the dark wet ground as the hot drops splash her. The plain is swept with a wall of water plastering down her thin nightgown and can't rise from the damp earth. Her nightgown clinging rainplastered mamabeasts rainfingers down buttocks down skinblood stirring in the waterwall of plain, wet Vita.

Faces. Michael? Mama? Ithe?

Coming it's been before here here it's been before coming I've

Ithe? *coming* It? He?

Cupping her beasts, nipples pointing mutesacrifice to It? Him? Her beasts. The floodwater changing, letting her rise, but the rain no longer water, slicing off her beasts, ripping muscles, arms, stripping bones—

Ring

Yes?

Ring

Yes!

Ring

Deep and distant in the bowels of the house, the clamoring phone rouses Vita from sleep. The dream flickers and dies at the corners of her mind. She sits up, peering at the glowing numbers on her wristwatch. Exactly midnight.

Ring

Vita is amused. The local phone company had all day and more to put the lines back in service, yet they couldn't do it till now, when the household is probably all asleep. *Merlyn will explode.* Convinced it has nothing to do with her, Vita snuggles deep under the covers, waiting for the sound of Merlyn's door and her footsteps on the stairs.

Ring

"Oh, Merlyn, for God's sake, *get it.*"

Ring . . . ring . . . ring . . .

"Somebody answer the damned thing!" Vita mutters into her pillow.

Nobody does. After at least twenty-five peals of the bell, Vita sighs and swings her legs out of bed, poking about till her feet harbor in slippers. She clutches her robe round her shoulders, flips on the wall switch and hurries into the hall, leaving her door open so she can see where she is going.

First dinner, then cleaning up without so much as a "thank you," now this. Vita raps smartly on her friend's door, but Merlyn does not reply. She tries the knob. Latched.

Ring . . . ring . . . ring . . .

"Oh, damn!" No other choice but to get it herself. The only problem is that Vita has no idea where the light switches are. Slidestepping cautiously, she feels where the landing is and slowly descends, carefully placing her feet on the unseen treads.

Ring . . . ring . . . ring . . .

A chilly breeze whispers up the stairs. Outside, the rain patters softly and far-off lightning still flickers. Vita reaches the bottom step. Hands outstretched so she won't bump into any forgotten bit of Aubrey architecture, she creeps across the unlighted hall to the living room's entry arch.

Ri-i-i—

Vita pauses in the archway, disgusted, as the phone stops in midring. *Naturally they hang up now.* The living room is dark except for a few moonbeams straggling through the bay windows. In the dancing points of dim light, she can just barely make out a corner of the piano and the telephone that sits on it.

The receiver is off the hook, its cord stretching upward.

Suddenly, outside on the highway, a truck's bright beams rake the bay windows with a lurid yellow glare. In the harsh wash, Vita sees a hunched figure standing by the piano, back turned on her, one pale hand holding the receiver against a shock of frizzed and matted hair.

What a mess! Merlyn must've gone to bed without drying it.

The truck passes with a noisy grinding of gears and deep night again settles on the room. Then Vita hears the phone being hung up.

"Merlyn, why are you standing there in the dark?"

No answer. Fingers of rain tap the windowpanes. A floorboard creaks.

"Merlyn?"

Silence . . . then there is a subtle rustling, as of cloth. The sound grows louder, closer.

"Merlyn, answer me!"

Vita notices a sickly sweet smell. The air is perceptibly colder.

"Merlyn!"

"Vita, is that you down there?"

The whip edge of Merlyn's voice startles her. Whirling in its direction, Vita put up her hands against the sudden glare as the staircase sprang into brightness. Then she turned back to the living room, but it was empty.

"What're you doing down there in the dark?" Merlyn asked, hurrying down the steps in bare feet and robe.

"Trying to answer your phone. Didn't you hear it, Merl?"

"No."

"Are you sure?"

Merlyn yawned. "The only thing I heard was someone knocking on my door while I was in the bathroom. Who was calling at this hour, Vee?"

"I don't know. It . . . it stopped ringing before I could pick it up."

"Hm." Merlyn turned on the living room lights and padded over to the phone. She picked it up, held it to her ear, jiggled the cradle and listened a moment before slamming down the receiver in disgust. "Christ, the line's still dead."

"Merl, I didn't imagine it."

"Oh, it's those dumb fuckers at the phone company playing around. You can bet they're going to hear from me in the morning!"

* * *

Vita climbed back into bed. The sheets were still warm from her body heat. She stared into darkness and thought over what had happened.

I'm not crazy, and I wasn't asleep. The phone rang repeatedly till someone picked it up. *But who?*

She reconstructed it in her mind, playing it forward and back like on an editing machine. Some small thing hardly noticed at the time niggled at her memory. The phone waking her, rain whispering in the dark. Burying her head in the pillow, vainly waiting for Merlyn to answer—

Suddenly she had it. *I wasn't in bed!* Earlier, Vita had been resting in the armchair in the octagonal antechamber, and the nearby floor lamp was lit. But when the phone broke into her slumber, she was in bed with all the lights out and had no recollection whatever of leaving the sitting room or turning off the lamp.

Peculiar, yet it did not frighten her. She felt more and more certain that this was a special place for her. Suppose Aubrey House chose to speak to her alone, suppose the others were deaf to it. It could well be. Merlyn actively loathed her own home, Richard was indifferent to it, and Charles and Drew were only interested in what it could tell them.

But I love it here. Perhaps that's why it likes me best.

Vita felt her own happiness reflected in the cozy, protective aura of her bedchamber. She knew that only good things could come of such a feeling.

At a quarter past nine, Charles tapped lightly at her door. "Breakfast, Vita?"

"Oh, dear, is everyone waiting for me?"

"Not at all. When will you be down? Is fifteen minutes too soon?"

"No, that's fine, Charlie. You're a dear."

She cleaned her teeth and ran comb and brush through her hair. She liked its sleep-tumbled, healthy gloss. *I won't put it up today. It looks younger down.*

Blowing a kiss to her guardian of the picture, Vita straightened her blouse in the mirror before leaving the room, feeling rested and absolutely marvelous.

She paused at the foot of the stairs. Her breath caught as she looked into the salon and saw a figure hunched over the telephone, her face turned the other way. A stream of obscenities that might have embarrassed a truck driver greeted Vita's ears. Merlyn was on the line, raging like a tethered fury.

"What kind of bullshit are you handing me? I ordered service on this line two fucking *days* ago. It rang yesterday afternoon and again at midnight, and there's still no dial tone. Now you hit me with this *barf?* I told you limited service for one week . . . *what?*" She listened a few seconds, then her voice rose an exasperated octave. "Look, you dumb fart, I *pay* my bills on time. If you'd get your head out of your ass and disconnect it when I tell you to—" She waved one hand in disgust. "Jesus, my grandfather helped some stupid wetback *start* that joke of a phone company!"

Vita didn't need Merlyn when she was angry, certainly not before breakfast. She hurried past the salon, down the hall and through the open pantry door, turning right for the breakfast nook. The room was even brighter and cheerier than the day before. She smiled a greeting at Charles, who

121

was at the sink drying dishes. Richard sat at the table, frowning over coffee. Charles turned and rolled his eyes toward the ceiling.

"Afraid it's one of Merlee's butch days."

Vita took her place and poured hot coffee into her cup. "Well, the phone rang last night at midnight. Did you hear it, Charles?"

"Darling, with Valium I don't hear anything."

"Richard?"

"No. I slept fairly soundly."

"Well, it certainly woke *me* up."

Charles offered the platter to Vita. "Have some eggs while they're hot. Is the pixie stirring?"

"I don't know."

Another burst of obscenity from the salon. "Well, Aubrey certainly has excellent acoustics," Charles observed, stepping into the pantry to close the hall door.

Vita felt compelled to apologize. "Sorry, Richard. She gets this way sometimes."

"So I've noticed."

Charles came back. "The trouble is, you never know what Merlee's going to be next, Little Nell or Fanny Foulmouth."

Creighton sips at his coffee, half wishing he'd brought his own car so he could leave.

Ready to drive again?

—Have to sometime.

Sure about that?

He feels more irritated at Merlyn than either Vita or Charles can possibly know. After their moment of closeness in her room the day before, he thought at least she'd trust him. But when she went to bed, she still chose to lock the connecting door.

—Even after I told her she had nothing to worry about.

Nothing to fear, saith the wolf to the lamb.

—Bullshit. It was an insult.

Then why'd you try the door?

—Merlyn's a sad, mixed-up mess.

And daddy wants to make her all better.

"Morning, all," says Drew, tapping into the room with a dirty rag doll under his left arm and an elaborate figurine in the same hand. "I want to ask Merlyn about these. Thought I'd read the house today. Care to assist, Charlie?"

Stiffening, Singleton shakes his head. "We seem to have vastly differing methods and philosophies, Drew. I plan to do my own investigating."

"I see." Drew takes up his napkin. "I hope you're not still going to conduct a séance."

"As a matter of fact, I intend to sit this evening."

"Well, if you must, I strongly advise you not to probe too quickly."

"Oh, really now, aren't you coming on a bit strong? I'm hardly an amateur. I've held countless séances."

"Never in a place like Aubrey," Drew crisply retorts, spreading marmalade on a piece of toast.

Before Singleton can say anything else, Creighton breaks in, determined to smooth things over. Merlyn is quite enough for one morning.

"Did you set up your camera in the hall last night, Charlie?"

Singleton's frown deepens. "Yes, but it didn't function. The film's still at the beginning of the roll."

"How come?"

"The timer didn't work. I thought I'd put in new batteries, but they were—"

"Shit!"

The door separating hall from pantry bangs open, and Merlyn enters the breakfast nook, fragile and fierce, on the edge of tears or mayhem. "Those bastards I rented to earlier this summer left the place a shambles—dirty dishes in the sink, roaches, cigarette burns on the furniture. Cost me extra cleanup, but if that wasn't bad enough, now I find out the phone wasn't turned off all that time, and they ran up $400 in long distance!" She clutches her arms around her, lumping her blouse over her breasts. Her voice jitters, ready to crack.

"I spend more money than I make keeping this miserable place livable, and—"

Her tirade abruptly stops when she sees the Spanish Dancer on the table. Merlyn's eyes widen, color drains from her face. "Who . . . opened . . . the closet?"

Drew puts down his cup. "I did."

Merlyn walks to the doll and picks it up before addressing Drew. A vein throbs in her forehead. "This is Aubrey family property, Mr. Beltane. Who gave you permission to open a sealed closet and get it?"

"No one, I'm afraid. I beg your pardon."

"You damned well *ought* to be sorry! I never said you could just root through anything you felt like!"

Embarrassment hangs in the air like smog. "Merlyn," Creighton says, "take it easy, I'm sure Drew didn't realize—"

"Who asked you, Dick?" she snaps. "This isn't a fucking flophouse or a public museum. Everybody thinks they can walk on me. The goons I rent to, the phone company and now you people." Staring around at them, ugly with tension, she hugs the Spanish Dancer to her. "You fucking people are all here on my sufferance. Just you remember that."

Her face burning, Vita lowers her eyes to her plate. "I thought we were here on your invitation. And please, Merlyn—"

"Please *what?*"

"Please don't be so free with that word."

Creighton sets down his fork, crumples his napkin, puts it on the table and gets up. "Your sufferance has hardly been abused, Merlyn. Charles prepared lunch yesterday and breakfast this morning, Vita made dinner and did the dishes. As for Drew, you specifically invited him to investigate Aubrey House."

"Please, Rich, it *is* my fault," Drew insists. "I was poking around where I had no right. You have my apology, Miss Aubrey."

—Gracious and complete. Now come off it, Merlyn.

She looks forlornly at her guests, then wilts into her chair, doll still pressed to her breasts.

—Like a child who knows she'll be punished.

"I'm so sorry," Merlyn whispers, eyes bright with unshed tears. She lays a hand on Drew's arm. "No, really, I'm sorry. All of you. I was wrong."

"The doll is your property," Drew admits.

"No. Not mine at all. And I've always meant to pull out those nails and open that closet." She rakes her hand across her cheek. "You're all my friends, and I've been behaving abominably to you. Please, Richard, sit back down. Will you all forgive me—*please?*"

Charles pats her hand avuncularly. "Eat your breakfast, darling."

Creighton sighs.

—Jesus, Miss Wistful again. She's better as a bitch. *Sure about that?*

Breakfast continued, but there was no conversation. Bleakly picking at her food, Merlyn wondered what she might say to ease the tension. *The apology wasn't enough.* After a time, she turned to Drew and spoke. "What I said is true. None of those dolls are mine. When I was a little girl, I had an awful experience with them, it happened twenty years ago, at least. That's why I got so crazy when I saw it." *Lichinsky would call it restimulation.*

"Tell me," Drew coaxed.

"I was eight or nine years old. I was snooping in Emily's room, and I got into that storage space. It wasn't blocked off then. It was near my birthday, so when I found the dolls, I thought my daddy had bought them for me. They were so beautiful, I loved them on sight. Anyway, I brought a couple of them downstairs... this Spanish Dancer was one of them."

Merlyn sipped her coffee, her voice very small. "I didn't know they belonged to my grandmother. When I brought them into the living room, she screeched. It was the most energetic sound I'd ever heard her make. She came at me, clawing and hitting and screaming how I had no right to go into things that weren't mine. She just kept shrieking at me and her eyes were like an old angry owl's. I was terrified.

I backed away, crying, and then my mother said, 'Oh, for God's sake, take the dolls and be *still*, Charlotte!' But my grandmother—I don't know, it was strange, but after all the fuss, she didn't want to take them or even go near them. Finally, mama called Emily and had her put them back where I'd found them. I was—I was very upset. Nobody'd ever hit me before or even raised their voice to me. But daddy made me promise never to touch Charlotte's things again, 'because grandmother is very disturbed about it.' I guess she was, too. She didn't come downstairs again for two whole days. Next time I looked, the closet was nailed shut."

Drew asked, "Do you know when it was built?"

"No idea. As far as I remember, it was always there." She halved a piece of toast, slabbed it with butter. Her elbow jostled the doll, and one of the castanets went *clack*. "You saw her photo in the upstairs hall. Do you know, there are hundreds of pictures of her packed away on the third floor, and they're all like that."

"Yes," Charles put in. "Exquisite."

"No, I mean they're all of Charlotte when she was young. I don't think she ever posed for a picture after she was thirty. 'Old Mrs. Aubrey, what a beauty in her day!' That's what everyone thinks. And the Mona Lisa expression. 'What was in her mind when the picture was taken?'"

"I did wonder that," said Drew.

"Nothing."

"I beg your pardon?"

"Nothing. Blank. Zero. My grandmother had the brains of a lizard. No, even a lizard searches for its own food. Charlotte didn't have to. She was an ornament—bred, corseted, polished and packaged on the Main Line to grace a rich man's house. She was like this doll, nobody ever expected her to be anything but beautiful. I'll bet she and I never said more than two or three hundred words to each other in all the time I knew her. She hardly ever talked to me. I used to think it was because she was so old, but I finally figured out she had nothing worth communicating.

She never read. All I ever saw her with was *Simplicity* or *Vogue,* and that was only so she could cut out pictures of dresses she wanted made. Christ, up until '64, the year she died, she still ordered perfumes and clothes from Paris. Not for pleasure, but because that was what her life was. Nothing else. If she'd had any courage, she would have died long before age turned her face into a road map." She suddenly asked Drew, "Would you like to read her will?"

"Why? Should I?"

"It'll help you see her clearer. She left it all to Blue Boy—my sterling daddy—but that part was written by the lawyers. The only part Charlotte wrote was the rider governing her funeral. What they'd bury her in. A full page of instructions, very precise, from her underwear out. She even ordered a wig. I was twelve. I remember her actually trying out her coffin in the salon and how ghastly she looked. A summery dress and that ridiculous wig and in between them a shriveled old prune of a painted face."

With a shudder, Merlyn passed the Spanish Dancer to Drew. "Please put it back . . . and forgive my bad manners."

"You needn't mention it again. I was prying." Drew took the rag doll from his lap and showed it to Merlyn. "This was in the closet, too. Did it also belong to your grandmother?"

Merlyn looked at it, perplexed. "I don't know. I never saw it before."

"Would you mind if I held onto it for a short while?"

"I suppose not, Drew." Merlyn gave everyone a crumpled smile that suddenly sputtered through a mouthful of coffee. "Well, if anyone needs it, the phone is now in service."

After breakfast, Merlyn drafted Charles to drive her into Doylestown. Both Richard and Drew asked him to bring back batteries of various sizes and gave him money to do so. Once they were gone, Richard went to his room and Vita helped Drew restore the dolls to their closet tomb.

"It seems a shame to hide away such lovely things," she

said, boxing up the High Fashion Girl. She noticed a scrap of paper lying half hidden under the edge of her bed. She handed the brittle scrap to Drew. "We should be thorough. Sales slip."

Drew frowned over it as Vita carried the boxes into the closet. "Did you ever collect dolls?"

"Oh, yes," she replied. "All the foreign costume dolls from Germany and France, Greece, Japan, Mexico. Got them every Christmas and birthday."

"Yes, I should imagine that would be the fun, adding to them one at a time. But these were bought all at once in 1904. Charlotte and Derek were married four years then."

"Well, I guess when you're rich, you can do that. Maybe Charlotte wanted a girl instead of the boy she got." Vita looked at Drew and realized he wasn't listening.

"Eight masterpieces," he fretted, still staring at the old bill, "and a rag thing a dog wouldn't worry at."

"But they're always the favorites, Drew. I mean, I had a stuffed dog named Pal. My costume dolls could stand guard over my bed, but I had to have Pal on my pillow. He stayed there for years, till he just fell apart." She picked up the rag doll. "Do you want to hold onto this some more, or should I put it back too?"

"No, not just yet. I think I'll take her promenading. There's the whole third floor I haven't seen yet."

Vita regarded him shyly. "I know you wanted Charles to help, but . . . well, could I assist?"

Drew hesitated. "Thanks, Vita. I *did* ask Charles, but I think it'd be more profitable if I worked alone."

"Oh." Vita felt rejected. She wondered whether she ought to tell him about what she saw the night before, but decided against it. "You urged Charles not to sit. Would you give me the same advice?"

"Absolutely, Vita."

"Why?"

"I don't think either of you is equipped for it."

"Well." She sat on the edge of the bed. "That's certainly honest enough, but you're wrong—this house speaks to me. I've never been so attuned to a place."

"You're a lovely and very romantic young woman."

Vita flushed with as much pleasure as surprise. "Young?"

"Very young," he said with grave tenderness. "But I don't think Aubrey speaks to anyone."

"People have been holding séances here for years!"

"No, just a few, Vita. There was Olive Masconi, a good hardheaded theosophist who knew what to handle and what to leave alone. Falzer's people all probed a little and drew up neat, dismally wrong conclusions. They called it a 'constant' because they couldn't find any more accurate label, I suppose." Drew stepped to the hall door, paused before opening it. "I didn't mean to be blunt. It's just that I'm concerned for you and Charles."

"You needn't be, Drew, but thank you for the honesty. And the compliment."

"It's sincere. You're very lovely."

"But an amateur."

She could see him searching for the right words. "Let me ask you this, Vita—you're a Christian, aren't you?"

"Of course."

"And Charles?"

"The same. Why? What's that have to do with Aubrey House?"

"Everything. Both of you share a working mind set based on God, redeeming Christ and the whole-cloth survival of an integrated personality after death."

"Very much," Vita asserted. "The world makes no sense without it."

Drew smiled bleakly. "I'm afraid it doesn't make much sense with it, either."

"I made my choice long ago, Drew."

"Of course you did. And I respect it. There's very little else but faith to keep out the cold. But this house has nothing to do with what you believe, Vita. Psychically speaking, it's a whole new equation. Good, Evil, God, Heaven or Hell—I doubt that any of those words have much relevance in Aubrey House."

Vita shook her head. What he postulated ran counter to everything she lived by. "That just can't be."

"That's what the Burtons thought, I suppose."

"Who?"

"Wait till Charles returns. I'd better tell you both." He raised the rag doll in salute. "Well, have a good day, Vita."

Something silent in the house. A thing without a name.

As Drew moved from floor to floor from the basement up, he made notations on the strength of the psychic current. The wine cellar showed nothing. Traces were barely detectable on the first floor, were stronger on the second, but reached their peak at the rear of the third-floor hall that opened on the long-disused servants' rooms. The penthouse attic had no discernible energy at all.

Drew worked to find a pattern to the current rather than its centers of power. *Powers can mislead.* He'd already found several spots whose readings surged significantly higher than their surroundings: near Charlotte's photo; the storage area where he'd found the doll, the doll itself—and now, a tiny room at the rear of the third floor.

The small chamber retained its original gas jets. No electric lights. Near a half-circular window, a heavy antique jug and wash basin stood by the slant wall that formed the inner line of the roof. The window was broader than high and set low in the wall.

Here. The room swelters.

Emily Shipperton may have moved into the second-floor bedroom across from Charlotte later on, but when she first came to Aubrey, this tiny chamber was where she slept. The Burton book confirmed that fact.

Socialites and flamboyantly mystical, Harold and Phyllis Burton were permitted by their friend Charlotte Aubrey to use the house in the summer of 1927, while the family (Charlotte and her son, Jason) were at Saratoga. Left alone in the house, they interpreted their guest rights very broadly, rooting through bushels of old pictures and papers. They used them freely in their book without Charlotte's knowledge or consent. The carelessness of amateurs ignorant of libel; it *was* an invasion of privacy, but without it, valuable

Aubrey data would not have existed for the researcher.

Drew could hardly condemn their methods; his own were no more scrupulous. While negotiating with Merlyn's agents for a week in the house, he was supplied with a list of the local people employed for the maintenance of Aubrey. He selected the lowest-paid scrubwoman and offered her $200 besides postage and insurance for any letters and accounts between the years 1900 and 1920. These, he assured her, would be duplicated and returned to her personally to be tucked back into Aubrey House, all transactions most confidential.

God bless venality. He received several ledgers, photographs and a thick bundle of papers, Xeroxed them quickly and expressed them back to the sender in less than a week. The material provided a wealth of information as well as a lot of new questions to anyone who cared to read between the lines.

The land on which Aubrey House was built was originally granted to one Colonel Ezekiel Lambert, Continental Army, who built his house on the tract in 1789. Drew understood that the foundations of Lambert's farmhouse could still be seen a few hundred yards north of the present mansion. Lambert married, had a son and daughter, died circa 1820. The daughter married away from Bucks County, and Lambert's widow and son went west in 1849, leasing the property to cousins, though the deed remained in Ezekiel Jr.'s hands. In 1870, his son, Ezekiel III, needed capital to finance a business venture. He sold the property to Addison Aubrey.

The one surviving daguerreotype of Addison showed a barrel-chested, sharp-eyed man glaring at the photographer's birdie as if it were stealing his valuable time. A speculator in land and finance, Aubrey moved that same year, 1870, into rails and beef. The land in Pennsylvania became a tool in his portfolio, used for collateral when needed, never improved beyond a "No Trespassing" sign. In ten years, Addison Aubrey was a magnate more or less centered in Chicago, herding Aubrey beef into Aubrey railheads while his son Derek—Merlyn's grandfather—marched stylishly through prep schools and Princeton, groomed and courted by the cream of Philadelphia society where he found—

> "—a goddess, Father. To see her is to love her, and so I have asked Charlotte Danefield to be my wife. Everyone says we are the match of the season—"

Busy in Chicago, the tycoon wired his preoccupied blessing, a draft for $10,000, the controlling stock in a small but expanding Philadelphia insurance firm, and as an afterthought, the deed to an almost forgotten property.

> "A nice place, Son. Full of rabbits. Build your goddess a temple."

Derek and Charlotte moved into their new home in September 1900. Their married life commenced and continued on a lush scale. They entertained, they subscribed, they gave regular monthly fêtes on the rolling green lawn when the weather permitted. Photographers' flash powder competed with sunlight to capture the abundance and glory of gracious living, of Derek's affable smile, but mostly of Charlotte in white satin and organdy; Charlotte waving by the Carrerra marble fountain; Charlotte pensive in the study. Always Charlotte. Derek was obviously enchanted with her image.

And yet—very odd to Drew—in an age of large families even among the privileged class, Charlotte bore Derek only one child, their son Jason, father of Merlyn Aubrey.

For all her place in the sun, Charlotte was a shadowy figure in the family journals. A few of her letters survived in a back-slanted hand, mostly instructions to servants from abroad or various watering places, never expressions of personality. The rare passages of personal feelings were turgid and stiff, sentiments proper to a young matron in her position, always precisely and rigidly centered between the

faded ruled lines, never crossing them. Her phrases might
have been lifted whole from a manual of etiquette, and
perhaps they were.

Derek's letters were not much more interesting. Usually
addressed to his parents, they were newsy, respectful, filled
with Charlotte, *see her latest picture enclsd* . . . Charlotte
yet again in specially made stereoscope slides.

Their gilded lives, if their letters were a measure, had
all the drama of a poodle's. Against the bloated background
of New American Wealth, they stood flat and unmoving,
paper cutouts on a cardboard stage. Though Derek had found
a goddess, his letters were remarkably mundane. Only once
did the velvet curtain part to expose a flicker of the man.

> "—afraid I have been imbibing too much these last months,
> which is reckless and bad for my health, though I confess
> I am not as happy as before. But it is just foolishness. We
> have everything."

He wrote it in 1905, one year after Emily Shipperton
came from Garfield Hospital in Washington, D.C. She was
identified in the Burton book *(Aubrey House, Home of the
Spirits)* as "a hired nurse for Charlotte's illness." Evidently,
Derek went to some pains to secure a competent person.
Drew Beltane's purloined cache of documents contained a
letter from the administrator of the Washington hospital
dated November 1904:

> "—her desire to accept your employment, we are pleased
> to recommend Miss Emily Shipperton. In her capacity as a
> practical nurse, she has shown a sobriety and competence
> well beyond her years."

Dated the same month was a short note from Shipperton
herself acknowledging receipt of train fare from Derek.
*"Will arrive in Philadelphia at 8:17 on Thursday of the
coming week."*

There was a photograph of the woman in the Burton
book, a poorly focused silhouette of her against the half

circle of the third-floor room Drew was now in. In the profusion of half-forgotten pictures his accomplice shipped to him, Drew found the original. On its back, Shipperton's neat hand had written: *me in my new home, Christmas 1904*.

That was the last record of Charlotte's new nurse for a long time. Having arrived at Aubrey House and the tiny bedroom, she proceeded to become nameless. From her letter, Drew recognized the travel fare entry in Derek's ledger, but it was listed as "miscellaneous." Then—seven years of silence. Notations in Derek's careful hand of everything from food to furniture, servants' names and salaries, bonuses, Christmas gratuities, even 9¢ for birdseed allotted once a year to the groundskeeper. Nowhere did Shipperton's name appear, though there was a nonspecific weekly outlay of $15 commencing in December 1904, rising to $17.50 in 1908. Derek just labeled it "overhead." Then, abruptly, in 1911, the ledger began to list "E. S., nurse to Charlotte," and her salary shot up to a princely $70 a week.

Why?

Drew wondered whether that was when she changed her living quarters to the second floor.

Another thing that bothered Drew was why Charlotte needed a nurse when she was twice in Paris, three times in Saratoga. Shipperton presumably stayed at Aubrey House while her patient was far away. *For reasons of marital privacy?* Not likely. According to one of the Burtons' more gossipy chapters, Charlotte always had a suite to herself, a bedroom, bath and dressing room that she could not think of sharing with anyone, not even her husband. The idea was "so foreign as to upset her," the Burtons reported. "Derek's room was indeed adjacent to Charlotte's, and there was a connecting door, but it was generally kept locked."

The Burtons had a theory about Emily Shipperton: "We knew Charlotte for years and years, she was one of our oldest friends, yet she always showed a modest reluctance to speak of her companion and nurse. She may well have come to Aubrey House under a cloud, a working-class girl inconveniently pregnant. In those unforgiving days, such women disappeared when possible and took whatever shelter and employment their situations permitted."

The implication was clear enough, Drew mused. *They think old Derek put Shipperton in a family way. Could be true, of course. Charlotte must have been rather a disappointment. "Admire the display, but don't touch."*

Shipperton's third-floor room was a dynamo of residual energy. Drew's head ached with it. He moved down the hall to read the other servant bedrooms. Every chamber had a stale smell of disuse. Thick dust covered a collection of household trivia that would now fetch ridiculous prices: Amazon-breasted dress dummies, old razor strops, chamber pots, a hand-painted porcelain hand cooler (a must for young ladies at a ball in Charlotte's dancing days), calfbound books with small print that no one read even when they were new and considered uplifting.

"Hello. Haven't seen one of you outside of a museum."

He picked up an old stereoscope with a box of assorted views: the Matterhorn, a mock wedding, an overfed Tosca. And Charlotte in Paris and Versailles and at home. Drew recognized another pose from the Burton book, much clearer in the original: Derek and Charlotte on the lawn, Derek natty in white linen, Charlotte in an Empire gown standing partly behind him, her usual smile gone. The back of the view was inscribed in her stilted hand: *D. and my disgosting Self. Sept. 1904.* The absence of her smile surprised Drew; it was there in every other picture he'd seen of her. *What did Merlyn call it? A Mona Lisa smile.* Could that be what he'd seen in the large photo hanging at the rear of the second floor? According to Gerald Kersh, *La Gioconda* bemused centuries of critics with a mysterious close-lipped expression that hid no more than bad teeth. Perhaps Charlotte's mask was just a veil drawn over a thoroughly banal mind. A void.

Bad spelling aside, Charlotte's written comment was incongruous for someone never shy of a camera until she started to age. Drew fitted the picture into the stereoscope and held it to his eyes. Early 3-D, popular as the telly in those days. Two photos on cardboard, each taken at a slightly different angle from the other, affording the illusion of depth when they merged in the lenses of the viewer. Drew moved the holder back and forth to focus it and achieve the three-dimensional effect. *Yes . . . much sharper than the flat book reproduction.*

A faint tingling of the skin.

When he entered the storage room, the place registered no more than a residual energy trace, but now Drew feels the power slowly build, approaching the intensity he felt at Vita's closet.

In the hall. Coming.

Alert but wary, Drew puts down the stereoscope and walks out to meet it. The corridor feels cold. At its opposite end, a blue glimmer disturbs the air like summer heat waves. *Too faint to judge shape or magnitude.* The energy pushes against him and he winces at its force. Then it slowly begins to retreat.

Standing motionless, the rag doll in his hand, Drew reads the thing, still close by, probing at his mind like a treacherous undercurrent. Oddly, he detects in it a degree of bewilderment.

He takes a step forward. The presence gives way an equal distance. He moves toward it again. It lurches backward.

Peculiar. Almost as if it were afraid. But if that were so, if it could perceive him in so sophisticated a manner, then—his own smug theories notwithstanding—Charles must be right, after all: it had to be a complete personality or close to it. Its precise level of awareness, of course, could not be determined without probing deeper, but Drew didn't think it saw him in the usual visual sense. *It probably moves about Aubrey like a blind man in a familiar room. Except my presence must disorient it.*

But even if it was confused by him, he had to remember it was potentially dangerous, all the more so because it could not yet be defined. Charles and Vita, with their unquestioning belief in an essentially caring savior, could well go the way of the Burtons. *And so could I.*

Drew cautiously follows the presence toward the rear of the hall. It does not enter Shipperton's old room but drifts past in the direction of the servants' stairs. *Probably means to escape from me down there.* He waits till the thing passes through the door, then quietly follows. Standing at the top of the dark, steep flight, he feels the energy surge up at him from below. *Even stronger here than in Shipperton's room.* Of all the power centers his skin detected, Drew decides the rear staircase dominates the rest.

Moving forward, Drew's foot brushes the worn top step and glides too far, overshooting its lip. Drew flails his cane, suddenly wobbling alarmingly as the fear of falling seizes him. He grabs the dim outline of a gas jet with his free hand and holds tight, praying it will support his weight. It does. Steadied, Drew slumps onto the landing.

God, I almost bought it that time.

He waits for his heart to subside, for his meager control to reassert itself over palsied muscles. The thing hovers in the darkness below, throbbing like the unmedicated ache in his limbs. He craves his pills. *Prescriptions to keep me from rattling apart.* Sometimes he wondered why he bothered continuing, but he hadn't the courage to call a halt just yet. If things were only as neat and reassuring as Vita believed: a nice dualistic cosmos with reward and punishment built into the system; a tidy balance of marshmallow Goodness opposing bitter-chocolate Evil; medieval stock characters, God and Satan *ex machina*. But somewhere on the staircase there was a person or a large fragment of one who'd already died and yet was still as lost as Drew himself. *So it doesn't end, it drags on like a sick joke without a punch line. No comforting Beings of Light to show the way, no endings—*

Not far below, the silent thing begins to climb toward him. Drew notes its coldness, yet as it approaches, pain ebbs from his raw nerves. He relaxes a little, ever so cautiously opening to the presence. The relief he feels is more satisfying than morphine.

Quite near now.

The air shimmers with the vague hint of visible motion.

It's going to materialize. Rising excitedly to his feet, eager to be the first to solve Aubrey's sixty-year-old mystery, Drew Beltane welcomes the soothing energy laving him in plangent waves; he exults in its healing tide and opens more to receive the full flood of well-being—

No! Pull back!

His peril suddenly flickers in his mind like tongues of flame. *Too late!* Before he can set up defensive barriers against the tardily perceived danger, agony lances into the base of his skull. Psychic currents seize him like a scarecrow buffeted by a hurricane. He twists aside, but the effort jerks his body out of control. He crashes against a wall with jarring force. His cane drops from senseless fingers, his head lolls limply on his neck.

With hideous clarity, Drew realizes the thing never meant to show itself at all. Instead, it wants to draw him down to its own level, sucking his spirit like quicksand. Marshaling the tempered strength of a mind used to fighting desperate battles against Death, Drew wills numb limbs to waken, sluggish senses to rally.

The struggle is won with surprising ease. As soon as he begins to resist, the thing releases its stranglehold and flees down the steps to the darkness below.

Drew shudders with the deluge of returning sensation. His knees buckle. He tries to steady himself with a cane he cannot find. His foot skitters off into space. With a cry of terror, he lunges for the gas fixture, but this time he misses. One leg twists beneath the other. A sickening moment while he sways uncertainly—then Drew jackknifes down the stairs, cracking his jaw smartly against a hardwood tread.

Spread-eagled halfway down the flight, bruised limbs throbbing, he opened his mouth to call for help and blood gushed over his lips and chin and beard.

"Vita...Rich...help..." But he knew no one could hear a voice as weak as the mew of a sick kitten.

Bloody hell, what if it comes back?

Sitting on her bed under the watchful eyes of the old woman and her miniature companion, the ballerina, Vita considers what to do. Perhaps she should have accompanied her friends into town, but she'd really had enough of Merlyn for one morning.

Her young friend confused Vita, zigzagging between winsome little girl and dirty-mouthed vixen. Even when New York put her through its worst trials, Vita never lapsed into the habit of casual obscenity. That word Merlyn used so much concerned a part of love that Vita never really experienced. Incomplete and frightened with Michael, unsatisfied with poor Walter, who never knew the difference, who was always too embarrassed to discuss it. No, she could not bring herself to utter that word ever. She could not think of it in any context except its primary meaning, and that disgusted her. Love was a poetic thing, should be poetic, though Vita was intelligent enough to realize that her poverty of fulfilled experience probably made it loom all the more romantic.

And yet.

Something in her *could* use that word, was not afraid of it. The séance where she had her breakdown—the voice came from her. And the recurring dreams, the sensual flood of warm water washing her, the presence in the darkness coming toward her, everything exaggerated: the immensity of Him? It? The helplessness as she lay open to It? Him?

Ugly. Like cats on a back fence.

Her cat was kenneled. Spayed and kenneled, just like her. And the men she met on those rare fumbling occasions weren't much better. Clumsy, all of them wanting it done with, so they could zip up their pants and go away and talk about it with other men, exaggerating how good it was. *Everyone wants sex but not love. And here I am, forty-seven*

*and still unused. God, I'm a joke. A pointless joke with no
end. Let it end.*

But later on, walking in the middle of the field, Vita felt
better. She looked back once to see the house awash in the
early sun, then strode on over the rain-moist ground toward
the woods, filling her lungs with fresh, sweet morning-after-
the-storm air.

The morning smiled on the trees, burnishing their amber
and gold against the bright unclouded blue of the sky. A
breeze carried the faint smell of woodsmoke that she always
linked in her memory with autumn. Vita broke into a jog
that lengthened to a lope and then a run, bounding over
rocks and hummocks, faster and faster until she reached the
edge of a copse, plunged through and dropped down by a
fallen maple branch, panting, pushing her tumbled hair from
her face.

*Haven't felt this good in years. Almost fifty, and I'm
scampering like a kid. Thank you, God.*

God the Father. She always thought of Him as a man.
Growing up with her own father in his pulpit at St. Thomas
Episcopal on a Sunday morning, dressed in full canonicals
and invested with authority, it was easy to accept God as
masculine.

And yet.

All through the years with Walter, whenever Vita considered the nature of God within *her,* she did not conceive
a maleness but something so primordially female it frightened her. Like the woman-spirit that once possessed her.
Though anything but a god, *she* was quite as powerful in
her own way: a harsh-voiced, steamy bitch in heat. It scared
Vita when she came unannounced. Drew Beltane could say
what he liked about her having no calling as a medium, but
Vita knew otherwise. She had a talent so huge, it drove her
to Bayview. *And what about last night?*

What about it? The phone rang, and it was answered.
By whom? The ghost of Charlotte Aubrey? Of Emily Shipperton? Or someone else? Who? And why hadn't she told

Merlyn or any of the others about it? Charles, after all, was her friend, she'd sat with him on several occasions and planned to do so again tonight. Yet Vita was reluctant to share the experience with anyone. It was hers, the house's special gift to her alone.

She got up and walked ruminatively through the thicket. A chipmunk sped around a tree trunk in front of her. Vita caught her breath and laughed. "Oh, Michael—look!"

It was her secret game, imagining Michael with her, sharing all the little joys. She got into the habit when he was away in Korea, both of them counting the months and weeks and days till he came home. 1953. She was twenty that year, dating Walter mainly for something to do but writing every day to Michael. She would walk alone and talk to her invisible love beside her, planning the life they'd have together, redeciding all the important things they'd already agreed upon before he left, not to change their decisions but only to live the precious moments again. There'd be two children, no more, and of course they'd be baptized and raised in the church.

But Michael always argued about that. "Why? How'll they know they want to be Episcopals?"

"They've got to be *something*. What's wrong with Episcopal? It's daddy's church."

"Oh hell, yes. Daddy."

"Well, you aren't anything. What's wrong with Episcopal?"

"It's just Catholic without the juice. Is it such a big thing where they go to church?"

"Well, of course it is!"

"Why, Vita?"

"Because, it just—because. I can't explain, you have to know."

She couldn't answer satisfactorily then. Hindsight told her why. *It makes no difference.* There was God the Father, there was Death and Hell and Redemption, and those things mattered, but the sect didn't.

1953. Michael was coming home. Suddenly all the dream-plans might come true—and Vita was afraid. Steubenville was too small now for Michael. He'd made a good friend of an Australian in one of the NATO brigades, and he wanted Michael to join him in a sheep-ranching venture.

"I want to go, Vita. It's a new life, a good one. I've got my GI loan approved. All we have to do is get married and go."

She thrilled at the idea of a new continent far away from dreary Ohio, but then her fat mother began to erode the excitement, deriding the absurdity of it all. "That boy's unsettled, unpredictable, you can't get a straight answer out of him, Vita. He's...peculiar. Walter, now, there's a different story. Going to divinity school. And he adores you. For God's sake, girl, be sensible!"

Vita thought she had more sense than her mother credited her with. She could just go, couldn't she? Simply pick up the phone when Michael called and say, "Yes, I'll marry you. Come for me." So easy.

So impossible.

Somewhere back along the years and the Sundays and the dusty afternoons in the rectory, in the smothering folds of her father's constricted lectures and her mama's flabby hands and tiny, mewing, disapproving mouth, she'd lost the courage to tell him yes and go away.

Michael called, and she said no. Three times he tried her that evening, but her answer was always the same. That was a bad night, with her mother and father hovering over her like birds of prey, all her aunts and uncles called in, encircling her in the living room as if she were a castle under siege. If only she could have raised her head and defied them—but she didn't have the nerve. And so Michael went away, and Vita did the only thing she could: marry Walter.

Leaving the curve of the trees, Vita climbed a rise and saw the lake before her. Her breath caught at the beauty of it, a large glimmering sheet of bright blue-green with an undulating shoreline densely overgrown with bushes and weeds. On the side nearest the house, an area of perhaps thirty feet had been cleared away. There was white sand, a few beach chairs, and the rowboat Merlyn mentioned. Vita crossed the lawn, removed her footwear and padded barefoot in the cool sand. She let the water lap her feet and ankles.

For the first time since Walter died, she felt refreshed, renewed. Even Drew noticed it, calling her lovely and young when she was nearly old enough to be his mother, but he was right; it was Aubrey's gift, bringing her an abundance of possibilities and beginnings . . .

Oh Goddess, let life come to me. I'm so ready now. Give me one more chance and I'll take it. Use me up.

The placid lake rippled softly in the late summer breeze. Vita walked over to the rowboat and examined it. The interior was dry and clean; the outside brightly painted. On an impulse, she got in, pushed away from shore with one of the oars, then worked the paddles till the boat drifted into the middle of the water. A shame she couldn't share it with Drew or Richard, but it didn't matter this morning. Her breast felt too full of hope to contain it all; in the next second she might laugh or cry or burst with the sorrow and intermingled ecstasy of just being alive.

The boat rocked gently. The sun felt warm on her cheeks. Vita closed her eyes and thought about the new things that soon would fill her life, things only possible now because of the wonderful old home that silently welcomed and protected her. Drowsing toward sleep, she thought: *I ought to be a witch.* A creature of leaves and shadows and sorcery worshiping a warmer female goddess than the great cold Daddy-God that watched the world's agonies and nodded over them without saying a word. A big, laughing healthy goddess with large breasts that loved the feel of men's hands and lips on them, a goddess who would roar contempt at Fat Mama and tell her—

"Mama, I want to marry Michael."

"And what do you plan to live on? Ask him and he'll never give you a straight answer. Take Walter now, there's a boy with his feet on the ground. Going to divinity school. And he adores you."

"I don't want Walter, I want Michael!"

Mother stands up, so fat the rectory kitchen can scarcely contain her. Her double chins shake like aspic. "Take your hands down, girl! That's *filthy*." She slaps Vita's fingers away from her bosom. "Leave those beasts alone! Don't you know you're not supposed to touch them? It's a sin!"

"Mama..."

"Be glad Walter thinks so well of you, girl, he's a whole different story from that irresponsible boy you want to run after. There's only one thing Michael wants from you, and if you let him have it, he'll soon toss you away like—never mind what!"

"Mama, I want to tell you something!"

"What? And take your hands away from your beasts."

"They're breasts, Mama, *breasts*. Tits. Boobs. You've forgotten you have them, Mama. That's because you're castrated. You didn't know it then and you're dead now, but that's what feminists would have called you. Somebody took the woman out of you and left you no sex at all, just an eating machine, Mama!"

Impossible tears well up in her mother's eyes, spill down blubbery trembling cheeks. Vita's father fixes her with his sternest unrepentant-sinner scowl. "Look How You've Upset Your Mother, girl. All Because of a Worthless Boy."

"Daddy, shut your mealy mouth."

Shocked. "Vita!"

"I hate you both."

"*Vita!*"

"You know what you and Mama can do? Go fuck yourselves! You hear me, Daddy? Fuck you! Fuck you, Mama! Fuck you both, fuck you, *fuck you*, FUCK YOU!"

"*Vi-i-i-i-ita!*"

The distant shout carried clear across the water. She opened her eyes, momentarily confused, her brain logy from her nap.

"*Vi-i-i-i-ta!*"

Shielding her eyes against the midday sun, she peered toward the house. Richard was gesturing to her from a second-story window. She waved back at him, grabbed the oars and rowed to shore, pausing only long enough to retrieve her shoes and stockings but not bothering to slip them on. She ran across the wide lawn, slipped through the back door and arrived breathless at the foot of the main staircase.

"That you, Vita?" Creighton asked, his footsteps clattering on the stairs.

"Y-yes. What's the matter?"

He stopped halfway down, looking at her over the slant of the bannister. "Drew hurt himself. Come quick."

Vita woke at 4:15. *Lord, what a sleep. I'll be awake all night.*

Voices came to her through the partially open hall door. *Must be having cocktails downstairs.* She got out of bed, shut the door and walked through her closet to the portal separating her room from Drew's. She tapped on it gently.

"Drew? Are you up?"

No answer. She went back to the hall door, listened for a moment, thought she caught Beltane's muted Scottish drone beneath Charles' higher tones. *He's all right then.* It had given her quite a turn to see him stretched out on his bed; his face and whiskers dabbed with blood. He was really quite lucky, though: nothing appeared to be broken and the bleeding was the result of numerous minor lacerations of his lips and gums. The greatest injury he'd sustained was to his pride.

Shutting the door again, Vita slipped quickly out of her slacks and sweater, took clean underwear from the dresser and carried it to the bathroom. She showered, brushed her teeth and freshened her makeup, adding a little more eye shadow than usual. She could get away with more than Merlyn and didn't feel like being shown up at dinner again.

Returning to the bedroom, Vita selected a sleeveless, after-fivish dress that displayed her smooth neck and shoulders to best advantage. She added a touch of perfume, hoping Drew might notice.

Richard's accounted for, anyway. And I like Drew better.

Most of her life, Vita was vaguely uncomfortable in clothes too old and sober, but today she felt beautiful. She imagined her two friends of the picture crinkling their eyes approvingly.

She blotted her lipstick with a tissue, tossed it away, emerged into the hall. As she reached the stairs, the voices below rose in sharp conflict. Drew and Charles, and not very cordial.

They were all in the salon. Richard and Merlyn, still in casual clothes, sat side by side on the sofa. Her friend waved the brush she was doing her nails with by way of greeting. Charles sat alone, his customary good humor nowhere in evidence as Drew—white-faced, tense, his chin and jaw bruised and discolored—wobbled up and down the carpet, besieging the rotund little man.

"Really, Drew," Charles said with lips pursed tight, "to advise me is one thing, but to come on like Einstein instructing an idiot is quite another."

"Charlie, I'm sorry if I give that impression," the Scot replied, his speech slurred, the Ayrshire glottals more pronounced, "it's just that I'm worried."

To Vita, Drew seemed more awkward and disoriented than ever. He was obviously feeling the whiskey he gulped rapidly from a jigger. He paused long enough to acknowledge her presence with a smile that ended in a twinge of pain.

"Drew," Vita asked, "how can you drink with all those mouth cuts you got? Doesn't it burn?"

"It did at first. Not now." He turned back to Charles.

Vita slipped onto the sofa next to Merlyn, who seemed more concerned with her nails than her guests. "What's wrong, Merl? Why are they arguing?"

"Oh, Charlie wants to sit tonight and Drew called him a very naughty name."

Richard leaned over to Vita. "We're the referees. Do you want a drink, Vita?"

"Just sherry, thanks."

He brought it. "I like your perfume."

Vita smiled at him, relishing the compliment. Merlyn, she noticed, was wearing a sweetish, musky scent as inappropriate as the color she was daubing on her nails.

Charles rumbled, "And what, precisely, makes you think I'm not equal to conducting a séance at Aubrey? And why do you suppose you're the only one who can solve the mystery? Especially now when you're half drunk."

"It's not the whiskey, it's my pills," Drew replied thickly. "You're no' up to it because I'm not, and I'm better than you."

Vita thought Charles would burst a blood vessel. His already florid face flushed deep crimson, but he bit his lip and said nothing other than, "Vanity, vanity."

"It's not at all vanity," Drew replied fuzzily but with great earnestness. "Something new happened to me this morning, and it was quite horrible. I made contact but there was absolutely no control. It was like stepping into a quagmire."

"But you're all right now," Richard said drily. "Happily smashed."

"Ri' enough, Rich. I'm on a bloody pink cloud with pills. First I've taken since coming here. And I just may stay that way."

Charles set down his wineglass. "Then you'll be in no condition to sit or probe or anything else. I keep reiterating, Mr. Beltane, that I am an experienced psychic. I've been at this game longer than you have, and my results, if I may say so, are much better known."

"More popular, at any rate," Drew sniped.

"Yes, since you bring it up, there's that side of it, too. My publishers are very interested in a book on Aubrey House. There's a good deal of money involved."

"I've no doubt," Drew mumbled. "Another Perry . . . business as usual in the Great Beyond."

"Now that's plain arrogance!"

"*Is* it? And have you reread Perry, as you promised your sheep you would?"

"I've been just a bit busy."

"And what about good old Harry Price, whom you lauded the other night in church as one of the great psychic researchers of all time?"

"Well, he was."

"Then I imagine you never troubled yourself to read Dingwall's debunking of Price's precious 'most haunted house in England'?"

"Hold it, Drew," Richard rose to quiet them both. "This

is becoming an emotional knockdown-dragout without any point. You've done some investigating today. Charles hasn't. Correct?"

Drew nodded. Charles grumpily agreed.

"Okay, then Drew seems to feel there's reason to be cautious. Do you have any objection to hearing him out, Charlie?"

"Not so long as he keeps it reasonably civil."

Richard looked questioningly at the other. Drew took a thick folded paper from the lamp table near him. "Right, then. I'll show you."

They gathered about a low coffee table, where Drew spread out an enlarged composite photostat showing the floor plans for the different levels of Aubrey House. Vita watched his laborious, segmented movements as he flattened the paper. Shaking visibly, his hand pointed to the features of the diagram.

"To begin with, I do owe you an apology on one important point, Charlie. The thing is more than a fragment of a personality. It has to be to react to my presence with such a complexity of discernible emotions. Fear, confusion. It may be nearly whole. It might even be a complete entity."

"In other words," said Vita, "a ghost."

"Yes. As traditionally defined . . . for lack of any other."

"Thank you for the admission," Charles said, slightly mollified.

"Wait, Charlie, hear me out, I only said *may* and *might*. I'm far from positive at this point, it's—it's too different."

"Well, go on."

Drew proceeded to trace the results of his day with one unsteady finger. Each level on the plan was peppered with red marks that he said corresponded to pressure of the psychic force on his skin. The photostat revealed how the power grew as he ascended in the house, peaking at the entrance to the servants' stair on the third floor. Other pools of activity could be found at Charlotte's photograph, in the sealed-off closet and within Emily Shipperton's old bedroom on the top floor.

"This is all based on what you felt on your skin?" Charles remarked suspiciously. "That doesn't seem very accurate."

"I know. But until someone comes up with a black box to do the same work, the human body's still the best receiver. Even mine."

Vita glanced at Richard and wondered what he was thinking. Usually he looked faintly skeptical, but there was something else now she couldn't quite pinpoint. *Certainly not partisanship. I don't think he's on anyone's side at this stage. Not even his own.*

Continuing, Drew said, "I took readings at least twice at each point, more when there was rapid power fluctuation. On the second floor, no reading stayed constant for more than ten minutes. On the third, shifts were as frequent as every three minutes."

"And the back stairs?" Charles asked, interested in spite of himself.

"Moment to moment changes." Drew traced a long pencil loop through each of the active areas. "See what these fluctuations suggest, Charlie?"

"Indeed, yes. Our spirit is moving in a definite pattern."

"Correct. And a very restricted pattern, considering the great size of the house. Any idea why?"

Charles shook his head. "But we're only dealing with a single day's reading, Drew. Shouldn't we reserve judgment till we can examine a spread of, say, two or three days?"

"Absolutely. I'll be glad to provide more readings for you." Drew began to fold the blueprint. "But that's all I'll do. I'm not up to that thing—whatever it is. I found that out today."

Vita stared at him in surprise. Drew did not seem the sort who'd give up so easily. His tone, too, had softened uncharacteristically, restoring Charles' usual benign temperament.

Feathering his fingers over his bald head, Charles regarded Drew curiously. *Almost sadly,* Vita thought. "You don't mean you're actually quitting?"

"At this point, Charlie, I suspect I am. At the very least,

I'm calling a retreat. I hope you do too." Drew's brows drew down as he made an effort to rise. His muscles did not seem to want to work, but when Vita stretched out a hand, he only glared at her. "No, I'll manage—" But he couldn't. Risking his disapproval, she grasped his arm.

"Do let me, Drew. I think I know what you've been through."

He argued feebly, but she helped him to a chair and, at his request, refilled the jigger he'd been using. Meanwhile, Charles went into the library and returned with a heavy ledger. He put it on the coffee table and began thumbing through.

"Grant for the moment that you're right," he told Drew. "The restriction of movement chiefly to the second and third floors and especially the servants' stairs would suggest our departed spirit to be that of a household servant whose normal sphere of activity was the second and especially the third floors. Very interesting. With Merlee's permission, I've been reviewing this book of household records. I'm sure you never saw this, Drew. I know your methods are unusual, but there's still a certain amount of spadework to be done, you know."

Vita sighed. *Charles is being smug again.* She detected a flicker of emotion in Drew, but all he said was "Hear, hear."

"Of course," said Charles, smoothing out a spread of two ledger pages, "your work is very thorough as far as it goes, but there is history to consider. Now we know the only person of record to die here was Charlotte Aubrey in 1964. But let's note this nurse, Emily Shipperton. She came here from Garfield Hospital in Washington, D.C., that is. According to my research, she was the illegitimate daughter of a Liverpool cobbler and an Irish farm girl from Mayo. Liverpool was a collecting place for poor Irish. Emily seems to have jumped at the chance to emigrate."

"Didn't they all?" Drew gulped his fresh drink, dribbling some.

"You ought to be careful with that," Charles admonished.

"An investigator shouldn't get drunk."

"I already told you, Charlie boy, I'm not going to probe that buggering thing at all."

"You mean, that spirit," Vita corrected gently.

"You've got the floor, Charlie," Drew said. "Tell us more about Shipperton."

"For many years," the florid investigator went on, "Emily was carried in Derek's accounts merely as 'overhead.'"

Drew toasted him. "I commend your thoroughness." He sounded sincere to Vita.

Charles ducked his head like an actor acknowledging proper adulation. "I confess that up to yesterday, I was of the opinion that Emily died in the house and for some reason it was hushed up, but Merlee said she lived here as Charlotte's nurse and companion till the 1960s.

"This afternoon, Drew, while you were resting from your fall, I prevailed on Merlyn to let me examine Aubrey records. I traced Emily till December 1911, when she is suddenly inscribed in the ledger as a real person, and at a considerable advance in salary. The force of moral disapproval being what it was back then, I suggest she was brought to Aubrey House under a cloud—'with child' or close to her time. She raised her infant on the upper floors. In 1911, the child must have died. Out of pity, Charlotte and Derek decided to console Emily by giving her a handsome raise in salary and station. They installed her across the hall from Charlotte—in Vita's present room. Merlyn's father was born in 1910. What better way to occupy a sorrowing mother than to put her in charge of the family offspring?"

Vita said to Drew, "That might explain why they built that small room. Maybe it was a nursery, and later they converted it to a closet. What do you think?"

Drew shrugged. "Possible, I suppose."

Merlyn's head came up from her nails. "It's also possible you're all full of shit." She bent her attention again on to the tips of her fingers and did not enlarge on her remark.

Charles favored her with his best Noel Coward smirk.

"Just for that, princess, I shall send you a poisoned apple."

Merlyn finished a brush stroke with extreme care before replying. "Just for that, duchess, I shall send you a poisoned actor."

Charles laughed, a fluttering epicene sound. "Well, despite our earthy friend's salty doubts, may I also mention the crude rag doll that Drew found? How out of place it is with the others. Surely the plaything of a domestic's bairn intermingled with patrician toys." He waggled a finger. "There is also Drew's own evidence of the peculiarly restricted movement patterns centering about the third floor room where the putative mother took care of it... and also the closet where the rag doll, presumably a favorite plaything, was kept locked for so many years."

"But Charles," Vita interjected, "what about the rear stairs and Charlotte's picture?"

He shrugged. "Let's hear what Drew thinks about it."

The Scot's voice was husky with fatigue. "It's a tempting theory, Charlie. And yet, I don't know..."

Charles pushed his advantage. "You've admitted it may be a whole personality. Would you venture a guess as to sex?"

"No."

"It's female," Vita suddenly said, very positive. Charles and Drew turned startled glances on her. She blushed. "I... at least I think so..."

"Hm. Allow you're right," Drew persisted. "Sex doesn't matter much here, the important thing is how to determine its identity. Not easy when there are no birth records. And considering what happened to me today, how can we approach it?"

If Charles heard the "we" he showed no sign of it, but Vita didn't miss the word.

"Well," said Singleton, "I plan to sit before dinner. Right now, in fact."

Drew banged his empty glass on the lamp table. "Don't do it."

"*That* again? Drew, I have tried to extend you every courtesy—"

Creighton interrupted. "Charlie, hold it. You too, Drew. We've heard out both of you. Now let's get some other opinions. It's your house, Merlyn, so you go first."

"I couldn't care less." She went on with her nails.

"All right. Vita?"

"I don't know, Richard. Perhaps we're all feeling and reading different things."

Creighton spread his hands and clasped them over his knee. "Tell you what *I* think, gentlemen. You've both done interesting work. Whether or not I agree with any of it is irrelevant at this point. But I feel compelled to mention one thing, Drew, even at the risk of offending you."

"You shan't," the Scot said impassively. "Go ahead."

"It's your physical condition. I don't mean the way you got hurt falling down the steps...I'm talking about your bodily status quo. What happened today might have been a natural byproduct of your affliction."

"You're remembering the way I stumbled in the hall yesterday, aren't you? Rich, I tell you I've never lost control like I did today. Never."

"But you also haven't done without your medication in quite a while. I'm not ruling out the possibility that you had a genuine paranormal experience on the back staircase, but I have to consider other alternatives too. It comes down to this—I don't feel the fall you took is a reason to deny Charles his séance. After all, you're along for a free ride, but he's got a book involved."

"Which reminds me—" Drew said, hefting the empty jigger and staring into it as if its dregs revealed all their futures, "Charlie, have you ever read a book called *Aubrey House, Home of the Spirits*?"

"Just excerpts. It's quoted, as I recall, in the Falzer report. I never could lay my hands on a copy. Why?"

"You remember who the authors were?"

"Not really."

"It was written by Phyllis and Harold Burton." Drew took Vita into his glance. She leaned forward, remembering the last name Drew mentioned to her that morning. Lowering his voice, Drew spoke with a crisp intensity that brooked no interruption. "Now everyone kindly pay close attention. The first Aubrey investigator was Olive Masconi. Charlotte hired her the same year Derek died in his Philadelphia office. 1920. Masconi had the sense to withdraw after two sittings. Her findings are couched in guarded terms. I suspect she honestly didn't know what she'd found here but was smart enough to leave it alone. Now Falzer's team came fifteen years later to conduct a very dry, astringent group of experiments. Controlled and safe and quite wrong. The Burtons came in between.

"They were tall, genteel, elegant Main Line Philadelphia psychic dilettantes. Old money, without any wit to put it to good use. Acquainted with Charlotte through Derek. In 1927, while Charlotte and Jason, then seventeen, went on summer vacation, the Burtons were invited to use the house and lake for a weekend. They leaped at the opportunity and proceeded to rummage through all the family papers and albums, borrowing some for their projected book. They only sat once that weekend, and the results were insignificant. The book was published the following spring. As a record of a serious psychic probe, it's worthless, but it's got rather considerable historical value for the researcher."

"I remember the Burtons slightly," said Merlyn, looking up with her first glimmer of interest. "A very old couple, always half in the bag. Damned if I ever heard about any book they'd done."

"I shouldn't think Charlotte would have said a word about it," Drew replied. "She all but obliterated the thing. Not only did the Burtons print family photos without permission, they also included unauthorized remarks made by your grandmother and even Emily Shipperton. Had Charlotte taken them to court, she would have had a good case, but she settled for buying up practically every copy of the book and destroying them all. Yet the Burtons managed to restore themselves to her good graces, surprisingly enough. Falzer met them in 1935 at the house, though they weren't permitted to participate in his team's investigation."

"Interesting," said Singleton, "but how is all this germane?"

"A bit more patience, and you'll understand. Now we must move ahead to 1964—the year Charlotte died. Could you tell us what happened after she was buried, Merlyn?"

"No." She sounded suddenly strange. "I don't know."

"But didn't your parents close up the house?"

"Oh. Yes, we went to Europe." Vita thought she understood why her friend's voice had a hollow ring. The family's trip to Paris ended with Ariella Aubrey abandoning husband and daughter for a French musician with whom she still lived in Cannes.

"Part of the preparations for your overseas jaunt," said Drew, "must have been deciding to rent the house. The Burtons managed to secure it for several months. Did you ever hear your father mention it?"

Merlyn shook her head. "If it was business, you can be sure my mother handled it. I was—how old then?—twelve. They didn't discuss family business in front of me." She recapped the polish bottle and set it aside. "Not much else, either. Daddy never had a lot to say. Nothing worth listening to."

An uncomfortable pause which Drew finally broke. "To continue with the Burtons, they seem to have picked up a smattering of psychic technique over the years, but by 1964 they were well into their seventies and heavy drinkers, too. Poor risks. Phyllis kept a daily journal. For two weeks, she and her husband held séances here, but they were fruitless. The only entry worth noting is the last... '*We were so wrong. It's lower. Deeper.*'"

"What?" Creighton asked.

"No idea, Rich. Presumably whatever nearly got me today." Drew hobbled back to the scotch. "Now for a few facts. The day Phyllis Burton wrote that line, the domestic couple they'd hired for the summer had the evening off. They left a light supper for their employers and went to a movie in Doylestown. As they walked out the front door, they noticed a table and two chairs in the middle of the salon. Obviously, the Burtons planned another séance.

"Next fact: the domestics drove back after the film and came in by the rear door so they wouldn't disturb the Burtons, since the living room lights were still on. It was about 10:30 when they returned. They heard nothing, noticed the food hadn't been touched, but that wasn't unusual. The Burtons often forgot to have dinner once they'd been drinking for a while. The couple took the back stairs and went to bed, so it wasn't till the following morning that they found the Burtons down here. Phyllis was slumped over the table, Harold was sprawled on the floor, his chair overturned."

"Both dead?" Vita asked.

"No. Charlotte was the only one, remember?" Drew took his time refilling his glass. Had it been Charles, she would have suspected the pause as a theatrical device. *But not Drew. He doesn't like what he's about to say.*

"The Burtons lived another week. They were taken to a Philadelphia hospital. Considering their condition, they might have been allowed to die."

"Oh, come now," Singleton scoffed. "Euthanasia's a bit extreme, wouldn't you say?"

"I'm not suggesting it was mercy killing, Charlie. What I mean is this . . . it's never been a publicized facet of hospital medicine, but in hopeless cases, while no regular care is stinted, perhaps no extraordinary measures are taken to prolong a life of which the patient is no longer aware. Whatever the Burtons encountered that night in this room, it totally devastated the cortex and limbic systems of their brains."

"Then they went mad?" Vita faltered.

"No. You need a mind for that. They had none left. Every trace of memory, personality, cognition had been burned away. When the ambulance came for them, the Burtons were nothing but vegetables."

A long silence. Drew wended his difficult way back to his chair. He had less control than ever. His cane wobbled. As he sat, he apologized for drinking so much. "But it helps the pills."

Creighton was the first to speak. "All right, it's up to Charles now."

The rotund medium clasped his fingers over his ample middle and meditated for a moment before making up his mind. At last he raised his head and addressed Merlyn. "I'll use the dining room table if that's all right?"

Drew exhaled noisily. "So you're still going through with it?"

"Of course. You've said nothing to negate my own experience. However badly the Burtons suffered, this poor confused spirit is surely in even greater torment. My conscience would never rest unless I do what I can to help it find peace."

"Charlie, Charlie," Drew mourned, "why is it so hard to think *new?* We've been out in space for twenty years, revised our concept of the universe, mass, matter, density, even time, all without a murmur. And yet we cling to a notion of survival after death that hasn't essentially changed in four thousand years."

Vita could no longer keep silent. "Isn't there any place in your theories, Drew, for God? Where does He fit into all this?"

"Who said he has to fit? Or that he even exists?"

"My heart tells me so. If I couldn't believe that we *continue,* that we go onto a better place after here, if I thought there was no God watching over us all, I couldn't get out of bed in the morning!"

Creighton laughed without mirth. "Oh, yes, you would. Believe me."

Charles was too concerned with Beltane to answer Richard. "I find your philosophy and approach impossibly bleak, Drew. Agnostic, elitist, sterile. If believing in God is subjective, I'm guilty. I want Meaning. A reason somewhere, even if I don't know what it is. Peace, as the Indians say, beyond understanding. Believing in things, finding their true shape requires courage."

"Christ, Charlie, this isn't Dunkirk, they don't give the bloody VC for tilting at things that go bump in the night. You're taking a dreadful risk because something inside you won't let you beg off graciously."

Charlie hauled his bulk out of the deep chair. "Have you quite done?"

Vita felt a twinge at the haggard expression on Drew's face. "All right, get it out of your system, but won't you please take one bit of advice from me? *Please?*"

The earnestness of his appeal touched Singleton. "Yes, I'll consider it. What?"

"If you feel any pain in the base of your skull—the least ache, or even unusual euphoria, come out of it as fast as you can."

"Noted." Charles bobbed his head decisively. "The dining room in ten minutes. I hope you'll all join me."

When Merlyn switched off the chandelier, shadows deeper than the outside dusk enveloped the long dining room. Charles sat at the head of the table facing the portrait of Charlotte Aubrey at the far end of the chamber. Merlyn took the first seat on the medium's right. Creighton, next to her, held pen poised over a small memo pad.

Vita entered the room, rounded the table and sat nearest Charles on his left. Drew had the seat next to her. As soon as she was settled comfortably, Charles spoke to them in a soft voice.

"Please relax, everyone. Vita has sat with me before. For the rest of you, my method is very simple. I'm a mental. I use no spirit guide. I merely empty myself to become a receptacle for whoever wishes to communicate from the other side. It will help me if you all remain silent, no matter what you may hear."

Whenever Charles prepared and conducted a séance, there was an unction in his voice that reminded Vita uncomfortably of her own father delivering a sermon. *The same buttery condescension, as if he'd just breakfasted with God.* She dearly loved her pompous little friend, and she knew he'd brought comfort to many, yet something perverse within her wondered, even after all the successful séances she'd sat through with him, whether Charles was really a gifted medium or merely a lucky actor.

Singleton bowed his head. "My dear Lord, who hath helped me so much throughout life's trials, help me now bring to living voice the spirit that wanders lost in these halls."

He paused. In the corridor, Vita could hear the faint tock-tock of the great grandfather clock, even the lesser metallic creakings of its inner works.

Charles spoke again. "Emily Shipperton's child. Emily

Shipperton's child, if you are near and can hear me, I am open to you. Speak to me." A deep breath swelled his chest, then his chin sank onto his breast. Vita knew he had slipped into a light meditative trance.

Richard glanced at his watch and noted the time on his pad.

The minute scratching of his pen reached Vita's ears. All her senses were heightened now. Without even opening her eyes, she could catalog the separate presence of each person at the table, each distinctive attitude registering almost subliminally: Merlyn's indifference, Richard's clear-eyed reserve, Drew's ragged concern. She smelled her hostess' musky perfume, so much heavier than her own; Richard's aftershave; Charles' cologne, the sharp tang of whiskey and scrubbed skin emanating from Drew.

Time and silence stretched out. Minute protestations of a house settling in the surrounding twilight. The clock struck the half hour. Beyond the curtained window, the sky still glowed with sunset. Muted breathing from all around the table as she focused on the dim, unmoving figure of Charles Singleton.

And then—a movement seen in the corner of her eye. *Why doesn't Merlyn stay put?* A quick turn of her head to cast a sharp glance across the table at her friend rising from her chair.

But it isn't Merlyn.

The disturbing movement is that of a pale blue smudge hovering in the air above Merlyn's blonde tresses. Against the deeper gloom, the smokelike twisting thing folds in and out of darkness, flickering and filling with tiny points of light.

Vita's lips part, but no sound emerges. She checks the impulse to touch Drew.

The dribble of faint illumination grows thicker, resolving to a pale grayish blue. A new scent heavies the air. A pungent chill grips Vita's limbs.

"Child of Emily Shipperton, are you in this house? Is

there anyone who wants to speak to us?"

My God, Charles, can't you sense what's actually here?

Apparently not. His eyes remain closed while the light continues to cascade like mist behind and above Merlyn's chair, widening as it descends with a growing hint of definite shape. Vita glances left for an instant, but Drew also seems oblivious.

Two tubular clouds float away from the pale column. They lengthen and articulate into joints and clearly identifiable arms. The central pillar of ectoplasm undulates, each billowing movement shaping it clearer. The suggestion of a head, only a lump at first, then a hoodlike thing that becomes a tumble of wild, unruly hair. The hint of an oval face with curiously pronounced cheekbones. The lower part of the mass separates with the unbroken flow of an amoeba to become two legs.

Still not entirely distinct. One blurred hand lifts to stroke the hair above large, eloquent, familiar eyes. The woman sways in the enveloping glow like seaweed waving on the ocean floor. And now with liquid grace it drifts toward the hall door, fills it, then fades into nothingness.

Bong . . . bong . . . bong . . . bong . . .

The grandfather clock struck six. Vita was amazed. *Just a moment ago, it was five-thirty.*

Charles stirred. "Turn on the lights, please." He sounded ill.

Drew's chair creaked, but it was Creighton who snapped on the chandelier. Though its light was feeble, they all blinked at its relative brightness.

Vita had to smother a giggle. The famous Drew Beltane on her left, the popular Charles Singleton laboring away on her right hand, yet neither saw a thing. *My God, this house is beyond them both!*

Rising, Merlyn regarded Charles ironically. "Well?"

"Nothing," he said glumly, massaging his eyes. "My concentration was good, none of you were blocking me, but . . . nothing."

Richard asked Drew whether he'd noticed anything. Beltane glanced oddly at Vita before shaking his head. "No. Nothing."

"I should have read *some*thing," Charles pouted. He looked ashamed, disappointed, bewildered. "The auras here are so strong, so close. I've never failed like this before."

"*I* fail more than I succeed, Charlie." Drew was uncharacteristically sympathetic. "Failure is the beginning of experiment."

"This was *not* an experiment," Charles countered, unconsoled. "I know what's out there, I just don't know who. Or why I cannot get through."

"Face the truth, asshole."

They all turned around, stunned. Merlyn stood rigidly by the sideboard, her face chiseled into an expression both familiar and disquietingly alien.

Creighton was equally chilly. "What truth?"

"This is Charlotte's home. She's still here. You're the ones who don't belong. Why in hell would she want to talk to a hopeless old fruit like Charlie?"

No one spoke or stirred. In the silence, the hall clock tocked monotonously. Merlyn glared at them, her features as immobile as if molded from plaster. And then, suddenly, all the tension drained from her body. She smiled at her guests as if nothing out of the ordinary had occurred.

"I'm starved. Anyone want supper?"

She left the room. Drew exchanged an embarrassed glance with Richard. They both shuffled out, careful not to look over at Singleton. After a moment, Charles sighed profoundly and levered himself from his chair. He followed the others.

Only Vita remained at the long table, forgotten.

How like men. Her own impressions had been completely overlooked during the Great Opposition between Drew and Charles. Well, let those two egomaniacs rattle off statistics and historical minutiae to impress one another . . . the phantom showed itself only to *her*. She wondered whether it might be the same one who answered the telephone at midnight.

Men. Vita brooded indignantly over the way the three tacitly ignored her mediumistic gifts. An old memory surfaced: back in Steubenville, she had one divorced friend, Rena Burke. Sometime between her third and fourteenth vodka collins, Rena would slur her views of the masculine sex.

"Sure, Vita, men'll love you and work for you and even be faithful to you—maybe. But there's one thing they just can't manage."

"What's that?"

"They'll never let you be *you*. If you're a woman, Vita, you're a nigger."

click

"Friday evening. Quarter to ten. A strange day. Small wars and crises. Merlyn has been less than glamorous. Mistress of the manor warning the peasants to shape up. I had a few things to say about that, but maybe I should've kept my mouth shut. I shamed her into making dinner this evening. As a cook, Miss Aubrey would be lost without a can opener.

"After supper, she suggested I take a walk with her around the grounds, but I declined. At this stage, my feelings about Merlyn are rather mixed up. True, I still want her, but I don't think I like her much. She's capable of some thoroughly unattractive behavior. Still . . ."

Still you'd like to screw her.

—I'd like to help her. Something's wrong, but I don't know what.

Galahad to the rescue.

"Drew went investigating today and had an accident. Up on the third floor. There's a laundry room off the kitchen. Half of it's filled with preserved food, a lot of it moldy. Don't know why Merlyn doesn't throw the slop out, it's disgusting to look at. Anyway, while I was in there I heard a faint moan. Naturally, it was rather eerie, especially after my foolish little episode yesterday in the wine cellar. But the sound turned out to be Drew calling for help. He was two flights up, but the staircase acted as a kind of wind tunnel and carried the sound down to me. He was more shaken up than actually hurt. We had a long talk about what happened. Drew told me a few additional details of Aubrey history. Later, while we were having cocktails in the living room, he gave us some disquieting facts concerning the unfortunate Burton couple. I asked Drew more about it afterwards . . . especially his sources. Turns out they're solid enough. He used whatever method there was at hand to prize out nuggets of Aubrey information. Had to promise him I wouldn't say a word to Merlyn.

"He and Charlie had another wrangle over methodology. I negotiated us into wasting half an hour in the dining room listening to Charlie attempt to invoke the spirit of Emily Shipperton's hypothetical child. Another prime example of researchers' blindness. Charlie's mind leaped from a mere educated guess to thinking he'd uncovered Holy Writ. He failed miserably. Maybe it'll teach him some needed humility. Like the statesman said, he's got a lot to be humble about.

"Out of all this welter of theorizing and fact gathering about Aubrey House, no significant psychic facts have as yet evolved. Not to my mind, anyway. *If* there is a constant, and *if* Drew ran into it today, all it would seem to suggest is that there is a kind of stored energy that we have not definitively charted as yet. No reason to assume it's in any way connected to the survival of the human spirit . . . other than the possibility that it's emitted by the body during moments of great emotional stress, turning the walls of certain houses into sponges of electric power of a type unlike other familiar forms. A sensitive person might well resonate with certain frequencies of this *psi* force, and his brain could perhaps interpret the experience as supernatural. Thus the whole complex mythic structure of four thousand years— ghosts, demons, heavenly visitants—might be reducible to this one bleak physiopsychological fact.

"It's interesting to note Drew's terminology for his traumatic experience—the 'presence' attempting to 'drink' his essence. Freudian-Strangelovian overtones aside, could it be that Drew's on or close to the house's frequency (assuming there *is* such a thing) and it's just a case of a greater magnet drawing the lesser one? In this regard, every battery brought into this house yesterday was drained dry by this morning."

—Drained?

"Correction: was found dry. Would need a meter while it was happening to prove whether the power in them was being siphoned off unnaturally."

So easy to slip.

"Let me extrapolate further the physiological corollaries to this line of speculation. Vita said something rather—"

A tap at the door. Creighton reaches for the Stop button.

click

"Come in."

She studies herself in Charlotte's mirror. Her hair? Quite acceptable. Good color. Lustrous. Fine skin. Hardly a furrow on her forehead, and those are the hardest lines to control. Her temples? Absolutely perfect, not a single wrinkle. A long time ago, an actress friend showed her how to isolate those muscles and hold them immobile while only her lips smiled. The trick kept her from developing crow's-feet, one of the first signs of aging.

Now . . . a touch of powder, a soupçon of blusher to accentuate her creamy cheeks. The merest whisper of highlight brings up those excellent facial bones. Lipstick should be blotted gently, and there must never be too much applied when one has a delicate complexion. A quick whisk of her old pearl-handled hairbrush, and all is in readiness.

Time to knock at his door.

"Come in."

Richard—

She opens the door slowly and puts her head into a room lit only by the fuel lamp. She sees him sitting in the armchair.

Richard, please—

"Are you busy, Richard?"

"No. You can come in."

Stepping through, pulling the door closed behind, she sees the minute widening of his eyes that indicate he is impressed by the beauty of her appearance, and well he should be!

Richard, please help.

Shyly framed in the lamp's dim glow, Merlyn looks exquisite to Creighton. Clad in sheer silk pajamas and a loose, diaphanous robe, she stands motionless, her shadow darting this way and that in the dancing flame that tints her hair silver-yellow and paints her pale skin now amber, now pink, now colorless as whey.

Creighton does not rise. "What do you want, Merlyn?"

"I came to say I'm sorry."

"Oh?"

"I know I got off on a bad foot with the phone company business this morning. I was rude to everyone today."

"Especially Charlie."

"Charlie?" She repeats it in a puzzled tone.

"He's the one you most owe an apology to. He feels rotten enough because his séance fizzled."

"I'll speak to him first thing in the morning," she promises with a vague shrug of her shoulders. "May I sit down?"

"I suppose so."

She walks to the edge of the bed and sits facing him. She reaches out and touches his cheek. He neither draws away nor responds.

"You're very angry with me, aren't you?"

"Just disappointed. I find you extremely difficult to fathom."

"I hope you'd still like to try."

—Christ, what movie does she think she's in?

"I told you where I am emotionally, Merlyn. I don't have much to give right now—least of all patience for your frequent lapses in manners."

"Yes, I know. I'm really a wreck." Hands clenched, head down, her small feet angled in toward each other, Merlyn looks as if her whole body might buckle from the stress of facing her faults. "My shrink says it's just that I'm suffering growing pains."

"At twenty-eight?"

"Then what was I like as a little girl, right?" There is a hint of a bitter smile on her lips.

Creighton shrugs. "From what I've gathered, that was not a very good time for you."

"It was a nightmare, Richard," she says, her voice deepening. "There was no love in this house. Practically the only time my grandmother displayed emotion was during the doll incident I told you about this morning. She and her crony Emily always had their heads together. They reminded me of a couple of old birds twittering in the wind. Charlotte hardly ever spoke to me, Emily not much more, though by then she was pretty old and none too sharp. Neither of them paid much attention, either, to my parents, except to order daddy around. Mother was the only one who'd talk back to Charlotte." Merlyn's large hands claw at her cheek. "And then there was daddy—care to hear about him?"

"Yes."

"I'm joking, Richard. There's nothing to tell. He was a goose egg, a porcelain Blue Boy. A genteel wino without an original thought. It was always Mama Thinks This or Mama Doesn't Care for That. *His* mother, not mine." Abruptly, Merlyn bounces off the bed and paces, her shadow bloating and dwindling in the lamplight. "Tell you something terrible . . . I prayed for my grandma to die. I thought once she was gone, daddy'd take over here and it'd be so much finer, and I could walk around without being afraid to make a noise. Only Charlotte did pass away and it just made things worse."

"How?"

She stops suddenly. "I don't want to talk about it anymore." Her voice climbs a thin hysterical octave. "Could you just hold me for a while? Please?"

With slightly rusty compassion, he gets up and takes her in his arms. After the first cool touch of silk, her warm flesh burns him like sudden fever.

The wary, wry observer in his brain catalogs her scents: shampoo and soap and mint-tinged breath and subtly cloying lavender perfume. She tilts her head up and he gazes into her eyes, seeing in them total trust as well as something more—an alluring yet enigmatic light. Their lips meet. Creighton's inner voices are, for one sweet moment, stilled. He feels her pulse quickening in sympathy to his; his fingertips delicately trace the soft descendent curves of her spine.

Stiffening in his arms, she suddenly pulls away from him.

"Merlyn . . . what's wrong?"

Without a word of explanation, she goes to the door between their rooms and opens it. Standing framed on its threshold, she regards him with an expression as cold, calm and remote as a death mask: all the planes and contours of her face perfectly replicated, only the lambent spirit missing.

"Good night, Dr. Creighton."

He watches numbly as she enters her room and shuts the door behind her, turning the key with a terminal *click*.

A picture.

Michael with overgrown hair, a deep tan. A beard. A plump, plain-faced woman embracing two children.

A letter.

Received by a friend of a friend: How Michael loves Australia and his life in the outback.

. . . isn't she fat, though, Vita? Well, those Aussie girls get big. And she had the two children bang bang, one after the other, and maybe she didn't have time to get the weight off. But doesn't Michael look wonderful, Vita?

Father-God on your bench in your all-male court with only men for a jury, I am all mouth and you have no ears.

My face? Down all?

Coming

Faces. Michael. Mama. Angled It? He?

Slants and shafts, rainfingers down buttocks down beastsstirringblood

Flashes of lightning, glowing in the dark wet puddles that pock the plain. Plain, plain Vita.

Beautiful, Michael?

Swept with a wall of warm water, her hot drops splashing down her thin nightgown clinging in the waterwall that presses her to the damp, dark earth.

I've coming been here before it's been here coming before

It? He?

Cupping her beasts. Her nipples pointing, a mute sacrifice to the myth of Him? It? Floodwarmwater changing into steel needles, slicing off her nipples, no pain, only the warm blood flowing with the ripped muscles, bones stripped and nerves torn raw, and the curse rivering ripplefast strippleasurepai

Ring

172

Yes
Ring
Yes!
Ring

Vita turns over and wakes. The red digital dial of her bedside travel clock revolves as she blinks the sleep from her eyes. Exactly midnight. Her bladder urges a trip to the bathroom.

Ring

Well, at least now with the phone in service, there's no need to wonder. Probably one of Merl's SoHo friends. They ring her up late all the time in New York.

Ring

In the bathroom, Vita takes her time, brushing her hair for no apparent reason or need. But when she returns to her bedroom, she still hears the shrill summons clamoring downstairs.

Dear God, is everyone else deaf?

Exasperated, she snatches up her robe and goes into the hall. Turning on the now-located staircase lights, she goes down to the first floor. The phone jangles monotonously. She pauses at the bottom of the steps before slowly crossing the gloomy hall.

No moonlight, but the spill from the stairwell feebly illuminates the living room arch. The rest of the salon is deep in shadow. She fumbles her hand inside the entryway till she finds the switch, flicks it.

The bulb flares briefly, then goes out with a muffled pop.

Absolute silence. Standing just outside the salon, Vita feels a growing tingle down her spine. Coldness engulfs her as suddenly as a tidal wave.

Ring

Vita's throat constricts as she sees the reflection on the polished panels of the library's sliding doors: a wan blue glimmer swiftly spreading in the salon's farthest corner. This time the column forms more rapidly as the figure slowly advances on her. A heavy scent clogs her lungs. Still halfway across the salon, the spirit grows steadily clearer. A frizzed mat of white hair so unruly it reminds Vita of Harpo's fright wig. Grotesquely protrusive eyes, like Mama's hypothyroidism. Closer and ever closer, unsubstantial arms eagerly outstretched to fold her in their clasp. The face—

Ring

Down all?

Reluctantly, the wraith veers away from Vita. Glides to the telephone, picks it up.

Now it is in the same attitude she'd seen it on the night before—hunched over the receiver with a kind of mute desperation while a mysterious caller speaks on the other end. The woman's shriveled lips twitch in response. A single syllable: No.

It's not fair. She's answering my *call.*

As the apparition hangs up the telephone and looks again on Vita, Drew's voice suddenly sounded from the top of the stairs.

"What's going on down there? Who is it?"

Vita involuntarily glanced over her shoulder at the staircase. When she turned back, the electric light was on after all, but the woman was gone.

Back in the octagonal sitting room, Vita perched on her vanity seat, brought in from the bathroom.

Clad in yellow cotton pajamas, Drew rested in the comfortable reading chair by the floor lamp. In the background, her FM portable played soft mood music from an all-night Philadelphia station. He could have dispensed with it, but it was Vita's radio and room.

Before coming back upstairs, Vita had helped herself to a pair of tumblers and the open Hennessy. Now she sipped brandy with Drew as she described to him in detail her visions of the past few days.

"I must say," he nodded when she was done, "I felt something—uh, odd—from you during Charlie's sitting tonight."

"And no one else did."

"Which seems to fill you with pleasure." The Scot sounded worried. "Why? Because the renowned Drew Beltane failed after having the brass to scoff at your mediumistic powers?"

Her face flushed. She did not reply.

"I see by your unwillingness to offend that I'm correct, Vita."

"Well, it's only that, you know . . . well, I'd heard such impressive things about you . . ."

"I can imagine the rumors. Suckled by toads, raised by druids, compacted with Satan in the Dark Ages, a man of many lifetimes—eh?" He shook his head. "A few raggy periodicals have perpetrated ridiculous legends about me, chiefly based on the coincidence of several ancestors named Drew Beltane. The one in the 1840s was also a psychic investigator."

"But that could have been you in a past life."

Woman, woman, how can you reconcile pagan reincarnation beliefs with your professed Christianity? "Very well, Vita—there was another Drew Beltane in the 1300s, a priest, according to my mother. Another born circa 1520 was an alchemist. A poor clan, but colorful. Of course, the line ends with me."

"Oh, no! Oh, Drew, that would be tragic."

"Hardly that." He smiles at her with sardonic affection. "Can you honestly imagine me dandling an infant on my knee?"

"Yes, with help."

"You are a sweet and indeed romantic young lady." He savored his cognac. "But before the dandling one must first be able to cope with the getting."

Vita looked stricken. A brief, painful silence, then she attempted to stammer an apology, but Drew waved it away.

"No offense taken, Vita. You couldn't know. I'm not particularly sensitive about it any more. It's just a fact I have to live with."

"Impotence?"

"Technically, no, not according to my doctor. But he doesn't take into account the futility of my pitiful past attempts to master the mechanics involved. But what about you, Vita? I'd think you'd be a fine mother. Didn't you and your husband want children?"

"Oh, yes. I certainly did, and I suppose Walter did, too. Only . . ."

"Yes?"

"He . . . had a problem."

"Of a sexual nature?"

She nodded.

"If it embarrasses you, we don't need to speak of it."

"No, I think—I think I want to. I'm just not used to opening up like Merl. She does it all the time, but I was brought up not to discuss or even think about certain topics."

"Yes, I understand. Merlyn's generation overdoes it a bit, but the idea's right, I suspect. What was your husband like?"

"Oh, you probably would have liked him. Most men did. They found it easy to come to him with their problems, even though he was a minister. A 'man's man,' they used to call him. Their wives would look at me, obviously wondering how I was so lucky to have a steady rock like Walter. And all the time, we didn't have so much of a marriage as an arrangement."

"Tch. What was the trouble?"

"He . . . there was something wrong with him, Drew. He just couldn't seem to be able to maintain an erection very well. I think he had problems reconciling the act of love with his calling."

"They say it's not uncommon in the ministry." Drew finished his brandy. "Tell me, was he the only man in your life?"

"No, there was someone else once, but that's a very old story."

"I like old stories."

"Well, his name was Michael—"

Drew sat back in his chair and let Vita tell him about her past. Though he closed his eyes, he listened more attentively than ever.

As if by common consent, Saturday breakfast was casual and late. Drew came down first at ten-thirty, his inspiration limited to brewing tea and coffee and setting out orange juice. As he took the kettle off the stove, Richard Creighton arrived looking like he could have used a few more hours sleep. They nodded to one another, then sat quietly until they'd jolted their metabolisms with infusions of caffeine.

They observed the leaden sky over the fields and woods and lake. A chilly morning, the first day of real Pennsylvania autumn. Drew said he'd heard a weather forecast the night before on FM: high winds off the Atlantic bringing a bad storm, possibly by nightfall.

"Perfect weather for Catherine and Heathcliff," Creighton murmured lugubriously. "Drew, will you be running your second day of readings?"

"Promised I would. Care to come along?"

"As an observer? Yes. But I wanted to suggest that you offer to work in tandem today with Charlie."

Drew nodded. "That would be considerate."

"Yes. He's pretty low after last night. You'll try to get along with him?"

"I'll be gentle, Rich."

The rapid clatter of footsteps pounded on the front stairs.

"Well, sounds like Merlyn's up," Drew said.

"Uh huh. Hope she's in the mood to cook."

Vita Henry bounded into the room in jeans, sweater and a short jacket.

"My God," Creighton laughed, "we thought you were Merlyn galloping down the stairs."

"Vita, you look ravishing," Drew said over his teacup. "Going hiking?"

"Yes. I love the woods out here. They help me get my head together." Her smile absolutely glowed. "Now aren't you going to eat a proper breakfast?" When the men merely shrugged, she turned automatically toward the direction of the kitchen, but stopped herself. "On second thought," she said, leaning against the jamb with hands in pockets, "if you little boys are too lazy to fix it for yourself, the hell with you." She strode to the stove, poured herself half a cup of coffee and drank it without bothering to sit down.

The two men stared at her in surprise. In her jeans and jacket, glossy hair tumbling loosely over her shoulders, Vita exuded an unguessed-at hoydenish desirability. The casual, self-confident attitude of both body and manner was so completely out of character for her, they were both struck dumb.

Looking ten years younger, Vita took a few sips from the mug, then set it down, leaned over and kissed Drew full on the mouth. "Have a good day, love, and don't work too hard."

The mud room door flapped in her wake and she was gone. Creighton blinked. "Is it my imagination, or is that woman growing sexier by the minute?"

Drew did not reply. He watched Vita through the window jogging toward the woods, jumping playfully high, buoyant as a girl at hopscotch.

Creighton observed the retreating figure. "How on earth did I miss the way that woman is built?"

"She was always beautiful," said Drew, "but she actually didn't know it. That's how." He swallowed some tea and looked moody. "I'm worried about her, Rich."

"Why? What's the matter?"

"That's the hell of it. I don't honestly know. And that disturbs me even more."

Or perhaps, Mr. Beltane, you're really upset at her un- anticipated kiss, he told himself. In that unexpected instant when Vita's lips met his full on, Drew experienced a star- tling flash of virility. Even at the séance the night before, if he read anything, it was Vita—her perfume, the musk of her skin, the sudden vibrancy of her persona charging the dark dining room with electric potentials. Trying to concentrate on Charles, Drew could consider only Vita and the pang of excitement she brought where before there had been nothing but numbness. *Shades of Boccaccio: "The Resurrection of the Flesh." Well, my atrophied libido, it's been a long time, no semen.* Best have a sense of humor about it; might prevent him from reverting to long-buried foolishness.

Charles pottered morosely about in his room till shortly after eleven, then dragged himself down to the breakfast nook. He was dismayed to see both Drew and Creighton still sitting there.

"Good morning, Charlie," Drew said while Richard rose and poured coffee into Charles' cup. "I'm going to start taking readings again soon. Care to work with me?"

"Kind of you, Drew." *Victor's largesse.* "Since I'm back to square one, I might as well. Whenever you're ready, I am." He got up and rooted in the pantry for muffins and jam, found them and brought them back to the table.

Richard brewed more coffee. The next several minutes were devoted to mapping out the procedures for systematically recording the house's residues.

"May I make a suggestion?" Charles asked Drew.

"Of course."

"Invite Merlyn along. She probably won't be interested, but if she decides to be civil, it might prevent a recurrence of another episode like yesterday morning with the dolls."

"A damn good idea," Creighton declared. "Tell me, Charlie, has she always been like this?"

"Seesaw, Margery Daw?" Singleton spread wild blackberry jam on his muffin. "Ever since I've known her, Dick. Back and forth. Totally in control or Alice cutting her wrists en route down the rabbit hole. I will admit the house seems to exacerbate Miss Aubrey's moods, but she never hurts anyone half so much as herself. You simply have to ride her out."

She came down just before noon, polite and demure, a coiffed production number in powder blue sweater and

matching slacks, pearls carefully selected, her blonde hair
not merely combed but elaborately done, her careful daytime
makeup applied with deft perfection. She was as far from
the rumpled virago of the day before as a woman could be.

"As soon as you've had breakfast," Charles said to her,
"would you like to come along with me and Drew and
Richard?"

"To do what?"

"Drew's going to read the house again."

"All right," Merlyn decided with easy grace. "Why not?
With this weather, there's not much else to do. I'll give
you the official guided tour, and maybe for dinner I'll have
Liza prepare—" She broke off, wincing comically. "Good
Lord!"

"What is it, Merlee?"

"Liza was our old cook. She hasn't been alive since I
went away to college. Now what made me think of *her?*"

A few minutes after one, they began their tour. Vita
didn't come in for lunch, and no one else wanted any food,
so they started in a group for the basement. The work pro-
gressed slowly. Charles was put off by the pragmatism of
Drew's approach, but cooperated without comment.

Drew's readings occurred at the same points he'd sensed
the day before. He waited the identical intervals before
taking secondary soundings. They too matched his initial
findings.

By the time they were halfway through the second floor,
Charles could see that Drew was growing tired. The Scot
read a power pool in Vita's room by the closet, but he said
it was a bit fainter. He got the same strong reading he did
Friday at Charlotte's photograph in the back of the hall. He
politely invited Singleton to verify his observation. The
older man tried, miserably embarrassed but game.

"Sorry, Drew. I don't seem to work this way."

"Nothing at all?"

"Traces, yes. Feelings. Nothing localized."

"I see. All right, let's move on then. Merlyn?"

She was so rapt in her grandmother's picture, Drew had

to call her a second time. Charles looked at Merlyn thought-
fully, then forgot her again in his absorption with Drew's
readings which, he certainly agreed, were anything but constant. But then Charles had always preferred the term "Aubrey Effect," he didn't know why. Perhaps he'd always
been suspicious of a spirit that never moved.

They spent a few moments on the second-floor landing
of the servants' stair, then—at Drew's insistence—returned
to the main staircase before mounting to the third floor.

Here there were more and longer readings. Creighton
frequently suggested additional verifications from Drew,
and Charles could see it was beginning to annoy Beltane,
whose fatigue was now quite perceptible to all of them.

They came to Shipperton's room. Drew read it in silence,
then passed a hand over his eyes. "Another high pool. No
change."

Creighton watched Charles write it down. "Sure about
that, Drew?"

"Sure, *sure,* bloody SURE! Please stop asking me that!"

"Sorry."

Charles shut his notebook. "Well, I'd say we've got
enough to confirm yesterday's readings. Only the closet
varied slightly. You ought to rest now, Drew."

"I don't need to. There's still the rest of this floor and
the attic."

Merlyn put a comforting hand on his frail shoulder. "Don't
be stubborn. You're worn out."

"I can push on," he argued. "But see how it gets to you?
Reading the power is actually the first step in going under.
That's the danger—like the 'rapture of the deep' that drowns
so many divers. Euphoria, and after that—"

"A child once lived here!"

Standing stiffly in the middle of Shipperton's old room,
his back to his three companions, Charles Singleton is suddenly sure of himself. Ever since coming to Aubrey House,
he'd detected a familiar aura. *This is why the séance didn't
work.*

Turning to face Drew and Richard and Merlyn, Charles

confronts them with a bewildered, laboring honesty, all his epicene urbanity gone.

"What is it, Charlie?" Creighton asks. "A child?"

"Yes. I'm not a machine, Dick, I can't read the currents like Drew can, but I know this feeling. A child spent time here alone, and it was unhappy." *Like me. Wondering when Papa would return from touring and step on Mama. Wanting him to, hating him for it.*

"You still hold to the theory, then, that Shipperton arrived here pregnant?"

"Yes, Drew. Don't you see, it explains why the child was reluctant to come to me last night? I should have held my sitting in here. A child whose mother worked on the lower floors, a child considered a disgrace to begin with. It wasn't permitted to go downstairs."

Creighton looks grim. "You're suggesting they practically imprisoned Shipperton's child here?"

"Or at least the extent of the third floor. This room cries with it . . . or, no, nothing quite so strong or articulate as that . . . but wanting *some*thing." Singleton's hands spread in an appeal almost like pleading.

Drew felt an unfamiliar humility. The force of Charles' earnest conviction stirred greater depths than he himself had. *Charlie might indeed have cut his own throat in Birnam Cottage.* Singleton was far better acquainted with the color of unhappiness than Drew, with his loved, secure childhood, could ever know.

"Shall we continue?" Charles asked, subdued once more. And they did. Their survey brought them eventually to an eastern room cluttered with photo albums and other Aubrey memorabilia. Drew Beltane glanced at his watch: four-thirty. The fading afternoon light came and went as black clouds blotted the sky. The air felt thick with lowering purpose.

But Charles' customary playfulness was returning. "What a garage sale one could hold from this room alone! A veritable trove of Belle Époque!" He lavished fond attention on each antique, every item of accumulated nostalgia, costumery and paraphernalia. Presently he found a stereoscope already fitted with a picture. He pulled the exposure from the holder and examined its penned inscription.

"What's this? '*D. and my disgosting—*' sic '*—my disgosting Self.*' Dated September 1904."

"Oh, yes," Drew recalled, "I was looking at that one yesterday, Charlie, when the power began building out in the hall. Derek on the front lawn with Charlotte, she looking uncharacteristically camera-shy."

Peering at it through the viewing lenses, Charles said, "I remember this picture from the Burton book."

"Mm-hmm," Drew nodded. "Much clearer in three dimensions, isn't it?"

"Indeed it is." Charles lowered the stereoscope. "You know, Drew, this photo bothered me when I first saw it, and it still does."

"Why?"

"Because 1904 was a year for hourglass figures, but Charlotte's wearing an Empire gown. You can see it's a style with no waist at all, it just gathers at the bust and falls."

Merlyn took the stereoscope away from him. "Well, if there was anything Charlotte was conscious of, it was style. Let me see." She studied the sliver of frozen time. "It's nothing. They still wore Empires then, I'm sure. They were probably just planning a fancy ball or—" Merlyn's breath caught; she squinted carefully into the viewer lenses, then put down the device and chuckled. "Hell, you *men*—so smart in so many ways, and yet you miss the obvious. Of *course* grandma tried to hide from the camera."

"Why, Merlee?"

The blonde planted a wet kiss on Singleton's bald head. "Because, my fey little friend, Madame Aubrey was knocked up, can't you see that? Charlotte had perfect posture right up to her deathbed. That's how they trained young ladies in those days. But here—just look—she's so pregnant, she's swaybacked. Feet wide apart. Comes from the shift in weight. That's the reason for the Empire gown and the hide-and-seek attitude. She thought she looked 'disgosting.' Here, Richard, what's your opinion?"

He studied the pose, then replied in a flat tone, "I think you're right. My wife stood like that just before my daughter was born."

A sudden gust rattled the windowpane, a few raindrops spattered against the glass. Merlyn placed her hand on his. "I think I know how you feel, Richard. Sort of. It's strange for me to see Charlotte with my daddy hidden under a yard of crinoline. I mean, knowing he's been dead eight years, and here he wasn't even born."

Drew spoke with great reluctance. "Merlyn, when your father Jason died in 1972, how old was he?"

"He was sixty—" The color drained from her face as the arithmetic snapped into place. "Sixty-two."

"Aye," Drew nodded. "Which means he was born in 1910. But this slide was taken in September 1904 according to Charlotte . . . two months before Emily Shipperton arrived at Aubrey House."

The implication hung in the troubled air. Outside, more dark clouds massed in the late afternoon sky. Looking half puzzled, half annoyed, Merlyn frowned as she turned her back on the three men, walking away from them to wrestle with the strange new thing. Time passed. The rain beat steadily on the roof and walls. The men huddled in a tight knot by the window to discuss it in hushed voices.

"My God," Charles muttered, "and I thought it was Emily's child. A brother or sister that Merlyn's father apparently knew nothing of."

"I think we can assume it was a girl," said Drew, glancing worriedly at Merlyn's rigid back. "Remember the dolls? Roles were rigid in those days. All were bought at the same time, too, in October 1904, just before Emily was hired."

"And the rag doll?" Creighton asked.

"Something safe and soft I suppose," Charles ventured. "The kind of toy one gives a child who perhaps couldn't be trusted not to break those fancy figurines."

They looked at one another, sharing the same ugly thought. Creighton voiced it. "The child was possibly deficient somehow. Deformed or retarded . . . who can tell?"

"I'd guess so." Drew nodded. "Derek sent all the way to Washington for Shipperton. Why? Perhaps because she was experienced in dealing with birth-defective infants?"

Charles shuddered. "And Emily kept her up here, away from her parents?"

The Scot shrugged. "I'd guess it was Charlotte's doing. Hundreds of family photos but not one of the child. No wonder Charlotte wanted the Burton book destroyed."

Merlyn again faced them. "You needn't whisper on my account, the acoustics in here are excellent. Christ, I'll bet Charlotte never even gave the poor baby a name."

Creighton tried to say something consolatory, but Merlyn impatiently silenced him.

"So now I know," she bitterly proclaimed. "That's why the dolls were packed away brand new—so that cold bitch wouldn't have to be reminded of the little monster—oh, God, she was my aunt—that little girl at the top of the house. Even afterwards . . . that's why she attacked me when I brought the dolls downstairs. That's why she didn't want to take them from me. Drew, you seem to be the unofficial Aubrey historian, wouldn't you say I'm right?"

"Yes, Merlyn." But another jagged fact raced through his mind, a thought he couldn't bring himself to express in front of Charlotte's granddaughter.

"Christ almighty," Creighton uttered with profound disgust, "how can a so-called woman do that? Put her own child away in a room with a nurse and just forget about her? How could her husband allow it?"

The sound Merlyn made was part laughter, part pain. "Richard, love, when you're rich, you can do anything. A Roman senator once bought the entire world. My grandfather would have spared no expense to please precious Charlotte. He owned the whole damned county and all its little kissass mayors and sheriffs and clerks. I mean, fuck morals, fuck human feelings, fuck motherly love . . . Charlotte didn't have them, didn't want them, didn't need them. She had money."

She sounds almost proud of it, Beltane thought.

Creighton's reply was full of crisp loathing. "I didn't think anyone could be that poor."

A tense silence. Distant thunder crackles in the darkling sky. The air is suddenly charged with pent fury. Unexpectedly, the woman whirls on Creighton, her voice jittering near the top of its range. "How dare you criticize Charlotte Aubrey in this house? What gives you the right, Doctor? Because you're a man? God's sceptre of power between your legs?" She trembles with loathing. "You men are so proud of it, aren't you? A filthy fold of flesh you pass water with. But it makes love so easy for you, doesn't it? *Mes petits poissons, allons, allons, vite, vite!* You don't have to watch and feel your body bloat you out of your clothes while the greedy parasite inside drains your vitality and trots you to the bathroom every ten minutes—and then they spread you naked on a hard table while the little animal rips its way out, and all you feel is pain and smell the blood."

"Merlee, for heaven's sake, calm yourself!" Singleton tries to put his hands on her shoulders, but she slaps him away.

"Don't touch me!" she shrieks. "You're still one of *them.*" She sweeps across the room, her face white with rage, but abruptly stops by the entrance. "Would you like to know, Doctor, why I lock my door at night? Because you *revolt* me. You want to climb on me and push your dirty thing into my body, just like you did to the wife you used to have. Before you *killed* her . . ."

She smiles triumphantly at the sudden agony on Creighton's face. She leaves, her footsteps sharply clacking down the hall. A door opens, closes. Silence.

"Rich, go after her!"

Creighton glared disbelievingly at Drew.

"Rich, do you hear? Follow Merlyn!"

"Like hell I will. If you think it's necessary, send Charlie."

"Me? I can't even deal with her when she's butch; right now she's thirty times worse than I've ever seen her. I think

I'd better call her doctor in New York."

"Later, Charlie," Drew said urgently. "Don't you understand? She just took the servants'—"

A sudden piercing scream.

They all stood frozen for an instant. Then Creighton lunged for the door, Singleton immediately behind him. Drew followed as fast as he could, but he was exhausted and by the time he emerged into the third-floor hall, the others were already pounding down the back steps. Drew had no wish to try that route again, so he hobbled to the front staircase and took it all the way to the first floor.

Passing the salon, he saw Charles standing with the phone to his ear. His flushed clown features were screwed into an anxious mask; his stubby fingers impatiently drummed the gleaming piano top. When he noticed Drew, he put his hand over the mouthpiece and said, "They're in the laundry. There's a flashlight on the kitchen counter."

Drew tottered down the main hall, energy nearly spent. He found the flash where Charles said it would be, took it and entered the dark laundry room. He immediately heard Merlyn whimpering.

"Rich, where are you?"

"The last aisle over."

Drew cautiously made his way to the easterly wall where the servants' stairs began. He darted the beam along the shelves of rotting foodstuffs. The air reeked with a pungent sour-sweet odor, and shards of something brittle splintered beneath his feet.

Merlyn lay at the bend of the last row before the wall. Creighton squatted on his haunches and held her head in his lap, soothing her as she pleaded over and over for him to help.

"I think Charlie's phoning for an ambulance," Drew said. "What in hell happened?"

Creighton answered for her. "Merlyn says that just as she came off the stairs, she heard a sort of muffled explosion and next thing she knew, she stepped into a slippery mess and fell. On the way down, she twisted her ankle and cut her face on something sharp on the floor."

In the feeble lightspill of his flashlight, Drew saw the welling cut at Merlyn's temple and the beginning of a purplish discoloration above her left eye, which was swollen shut. Her cheek was spangled with blood that streamed from several lacerations and punctures, a few of them large, with ragged flaps of skin hanging loosely.

Drew ran the weak flashbeam over shelves and flooring till he located what he was afraid he'd find: the broken fragments of a large jug, the same one he'd seen slowly oozing bubbles two days earlier. He'd figured that whatever it contained had begun to ferment and was building up gaseous pressure. *But I forgot to warn Merlyn about it.*

Singleton poked his head into the laundry. "I just got through, Dick. We have to drive her over to Bucks County emergency. There've already been a couple of serious highway accidents because of the storm, and none of the ambulances are available."

He and Richard gently carried Merlyn to the living room while Drew prepared a few cold compresses. After they'd all helped her into a coat, Drew looked at her ankle with Creighton.

"Probably only a sprain, Rich, but be sure they X-ray it."

"I will. I've got a hunch we'll be there quite a while. Better not wait dinner for us. I'll call from the hospital and let you know how late I think we might be."

"All right," Drew replied.

Singleton opened an umbrella and dashed out to the car. He wheeled it closer to the front steps. Cradling the suffering girl in his arms, Richard brushed his lips against her forehead and quickly carried her through the pelting rain to the rear seat of the Rolls.

Drew watched the huge car back up, turn around and then vanish into storm-swept twilight.

"...receive thee into Paradise...may the martyrs receive thee and bring thee to the Holy City of Jerusalem..."

Go away, daddy.

"...and with Lazarus, once a beggar, mayst thou have eternal rest."

Fuck you, Walter.

A soundless snarl. Baring her teeth. All mouth, and down all the way licking the sugarstick death.

There.

So low, where cobwebs shimmer before her closed eyes, and she knows the warm rain is only her familiar dream. A wall of water sweeping the plain, plastering her nightgown to her body, bearing her down to the damp earth.

Faces float in darkness. Michael's. Her mother's. The rain is like Michael's fingers fumbling at her BREASTS, MAMA, brushing over her buttocks, the touch on her skin stirring her blood, arousing her as she senses Michael coming, Mama trying to stop her from going to, being with, meeting him.

No. Not Michael?

Who?

I've been here before, I don't like it here, Mama, Mama, take me back, it's coming for me.

It? He?

Something coming.

Warm rain indistinguishable from blood

> It's raining, it's pouring,
> The Old Man is snoring.
> Jumped in bed and bumped His head
> And didn't wake up till morning.

And she opens her eyes, and underneath the green leaves it is really, really raining. Vita laughs at the goodness of

189

the world and all its unpredictable joys. Though autumn is etched in dying amber tints, she feels her soul budding in the sudden crystal flood of Heaven's tears.

Goddess, thank you for these good new things you bring me!

Laughing in the rain, she runs eagerly toward Aubrey House.

After the Rolls slogged off down the muddy driveway, Drew felt the accumulated toll of his fatigue and tension. His nerves too jangled for sleep to come, he poured two jiggers of scotch into a glass and took it to the salon. Sinking into a beige armchair, he swallowed a large mouthful of liquor before taking out a pad of paper and pencil from his breast pocket. He jotted down the salient features of the day's investigation, putting in the things he'd reserved from Merlyn.

While he wrote, the strain slowly retreated from his body under the benediction of the whiskey. His pencil scratched and labored till its point was dull. At last, he put it away and scanned his notes.

A productive but painful day. Certainly he felt somewhat humbled in the light of what new information had emerged; he certainly had no monopoly on Aubrey. Charlie might symbolize for him all the sentimental tripe he'd long ago abandoned, but he'd been right enough when it counted. Right enough to change the picture.

The picture...*D. and my disgosting Self*. No iron-clad proof, of course, that there ever was a child. Just Charlie's painful intuition, a photograph bearing a damning date and a curiously undeclared household expense: seven years of paid anonymity for Emily Shipperton.

How could Derek Aubrey permit the thing to happen? *Why?* Because it was deformed or retarded, severely deficient in some way; there could be no other explanation for Shipperton hiding in that high, distant room—for the secrecy that shrouded the whole affair. And yet...*he was her father. How could he do it?*

But as he poured more scotch and drank it, Drew graduated from his first shocked reaction to Merlyn's coldly practical acceptance. It could very well have happened and probably did. There was that bothersome scrap of letter from Derek to his father—

"—afraid I have been imbibing too much these last months, which is reckless and bad for my health, though I confess I am not as happy as before . . ."

A boy is born to wealthy, busy parents whom he rarely sees, is set into the pattern of a certain standard of life: private schools, exclusive spas, Princeton. A nice boy, never rocking the velvet-lined boat, never biting at the silver spoon—dutiful, naive, unused to adversity or difficult decisions. At the right age and time, he meets a beautiful girl groomed to be an ornament. No question of the alliance, their backgrounds are compatible. A handsome match in their families' eyes—both young, attractive, well-bred and rich. Perhaps she is the first girl the shy, respectful lad has ever touched. Can he be expected to listen to her impartially or look cannily into her properly limpid eyes? Why should he question, this boy born into a world forever gilded and secure? What is there to challenge in Eden?

And so they marry and their life is chronicled in orderly days, pictures, letters. He enters the world of business. His mind begins to grow, expand—perhaps he tries to reach out and touch his wife's thoughts, her inner Self resting at the center of their servant-tended home. He draws back, baffled. There is an emptiness.

Not that they quarrel. Charlotte probably never says a cross word to him. The days pass by, the years stretch out before him, and still his perfect marriage somehow lacks, vaguely disappoints. He hungers at the feast.

After four years of marriage—in an age when pregnancy was the universal condition for young wives—a child finally comes. Born very likely when Derek was away in Philadelphia, a longer trip in those days. He learns by telephone of the birth of his little girl. Perhaps, in the haste of happiness, he doesn't wait to hear more. Or maybe the caller is afraid to tell him. The proud father rushes out to buy an armload of expensive dolls for the new daughter who he knows is just as lovely as her mother.

Only she isn't.

Charlotte can't cope with the sight or even the thought of the nasty thing that made her ugly for so long. Pleas on both sides: Derek, agonized, torn by love and instinct; Charlotte, disgusted and bewildered, craving only escape from responsibility.

In the end, Derek does what she asks. The nurse takes the unwanted child to its third-floor confinement. The beautiful dolls are packed away and replaced by a simple rag thing that will not endanger the incapable little girl. Years later, it finds its place among its more elegant cousins. As if someone—Derek?—could not quite bear to throw out the pitiful reminder of a child that never was.

It could be. It could have happened like that. An unrecorded doctor or midwife. Servants well paid, threatened with dismissal with no hope of another position if they indulged in careless talk. A note to Derek's father in Chicago: an infant dead at birth. And only one telltale drop of blood shed by a man who would die at fifty, weighed down by flesh and sorrow: *I am not as happy as before.*

Was Charlotte a cruel woman? Drew did not think so. *Cruelty requires a mind, a capacity for strong emotion.* All the time he'd been seeking some elusive quality in her picture on the second floor, it was, instead, an absence of higher feeling that he'd detected in her eyes: the kind of vacuous self-absorption one sees in lower animals. Vapidity reflected in Charlotte's empty penmanship, elegant without sufficient character to shape a single tall "h" or one deepened, venturing loop.

And while that sculpted imitation of a woman strolled about the sunlit Aubrey grounds, high above her a little girl knew the world only as a picture to look at through the panes of a low window—a fairyland sometimes green and blue, sometimes brown and dying gold, sometimes white. Did she ever reach out tiny hands to the two beautiful people walking arm in arm far below, never ever looking up to see her watching them?

Painful, inhuman, he didn't even want to imagine it. And all these years he thought life put *him* in a cage?

The storm slashed the shut bay windows. The chair felt good, but bath and bed would be even better. One final fortification from the whiskey bottle, then he'd begin the tedious stair-climbing marathon. The hall clock struck the half hour. Drew swallowed his pills with a gulp of scotch and glanced at the final note he'd made on the pad of paper. Just then, he heard the slam of the rear door.

Good Lord—Vita! The long, tiring day and Merlyn's accident had wiped her completely from his mind, ever since she'd unexpectedly kissed him goodbye that morning in the breakfast nook.

"Hello?" she called from the pantry. "Anyone downstairs?"

"I'm in the living room, Vita." Now that she was back, his concern for her reawakened. In the developing equation that was Aubrey House, where did her phone-answering apparition fit? *It doesn't.* A midnight summons that no one heard but her, a spirit only seen by one out of five people at a séance—none of it had anything to do with the dark history reconstructed by Drew and Charles and Merlyn. He was afraid—

"Hi!" Vita trotted into the room in bare feet, looking flushed and happy . . . no, more than that: *high*. Bits of damp leaves clung to her jacket and a few wisps of dewy grass dangled from one lock of unbound hair. Her soaked sweater and slacks molded her body's graceful curves. She ruffled her hair with a kitchen towel.

"You'd better change into something dry before you catch a cold, Vita."

"I won't, I won't," she laughed, spinning giddily about.

"I love the rain, it's glorious. But I'm famished—I forgot to eat all day. Where is everybody?"

"Oh-uh—I'm afraid Merlyn had an accident. They drove her to a hospital in Doylestown."

Vita smiled with distant amusement. "So Little Nell finally has a real problem to deal with."

At the hospital, Charles paced worriedly in the crowded waiting room next to the emergency entrance. Merlyn, looking a bit pale, sat in a corner staring at but not reading a three-month-old issue of *Woman's Day*. Her face had been temporarily treated, but it would need one of the more experienced physicians to assess the actual extent of the damage. *Pray God there's no scars. Merlee couldn't handle it.* It would take hours before her cheek could be examined properly, and then there was also her ankle, which might be fractured. The auto crash victims had priority on all facilities, X-ray and labs included. It was quite possible they'd have to wait till 10 or 11 p.m. or even later before it was Merlyn's turn.

At least she's calmer now. When they'd arrived at the hospital, her childish fright had been more than a little embarrassing to Charles, especially with Richard's automatic acceptance of the role of protector and guardian. *If she'd only act her age. And stay there.*

Richard was out getting them all some food. Glancing through the waiting room window, Charles saw him returning. Dashing across the glistening street, then working his way along the side of the hospital building, he made his way back to the emergency entrance and carried the sopping bag of sandwiches and coffee to the table next to where Merlyn sat. He was dripping wet himself.

Charles came over and helped him separate the food from the clinging brown paper container. Charles found his roast beef on rye, bit into it—ghastly stale—and followed up with a mouthful of coffee before asking Creighton, "Did you phone the house to say we'd be here a while?"

Creighton shook his head. "The storm knocked down

some power lines. The phone at Aubrey's out again." He lightly touched Merlyn's uninjured cheek. "How are you feeling now?"

She pressed his fingers to her lips. "Better. A little hungry, Rich." He handed her an egg salad sandwich. She held it in her hand but did not hurry to eat it.

"So Drew and Vita are cut off by the storm," Charles remarked with a lugubrious attempt at humor. "Appropriately gothic, wouldn't you say? Alone in a haunted house at night, no telephone. If there's a bridge handy, it's surely washed out."

Creighton lit a cigarette. "They're warm and dry, they've got good food and plenty to drink. They're a hell of a lot better off than we are tonight."

"I suppose so," Charles said, rejecting the rest of his sandwich.

Vita cooked beef ragout and limas and served Drew on a platter in his room. After they ate, she brought coffee and brandy and sat beside him on the bed, clinking her glass to his. He smelled the sweet fragrance of her washed and tubbed body, wrapped now in a warm bathrobe. Her hair hung in loose strands about her shoulders.

"Cheers," he said, "but what are we drinking to?"

"To freedom, Drew."

"If you say so." He lofted his snifter in a saluting gesture and took a small sip of brandy, savoring it in his mouth for several seconds before releasing it over the back of his tongue. It made him feel slightly giddy on top of all the scotch he'd consumed earlier, not to mention the medicine he'd swallowed. Her aura, too, was overpowering. She flaunted it now, her warm leg pressed next to his. Deep within, a drum began to beat a quicker tempo for his pulse to mark.

"To freedom." Vita drank again. "Freedom to be beautiful. You said I am."

"I did."

"And meant it?"

"Yes."

"Well, then, you've helped to make me real. Finally."

He was sure she wasn't drunk or on pot, yet he still sensed something not quite natural in her suddenly heightened glamour. At the moment, though, he was too fascinated to question it. He wanted to kiss her so much, he was even considering whether he could manage it without dropping his drink.

Vita finished her brandy and stretched luxuriously across Drew's bed, her stomach flattening. The motion made her robe slip open a few inches, revealing the inner contour of her right breast. Drew felt himself hardening in response to her implied invitation. *Exactly on schedule.* He'd always been normal enough to have an erection, but if he tried to pursue his natural inclination, he was sure his body would betray him when they got down to it, leaving Vita unsatisfied and scornful. He didn't want to face that acid humiliation again.

"I feel so safe and good with you," she said.

"Thank you, Vita...but...well, I...I told you..."

"Told me what? I've forgotten." Her smile enticed him to forget too.

"We shouldn't begin something that I can't finish."

"Don't you want me, then?"

"Of course I do. But my body's been accurately described as a factory reject. I have very little control—"

She put her fingers on his lips, hushing him. "I want you, Drew. Very much." Her hand moved up and down his arm.

"But I've failed repeatedly," he argued, his will weakening. "And by now, I'm afraid I smell like a brewery." He set down his glass.

Vita leaned close, breathing deeply. "You smell marvelous, Drew. Perspiration, just a whiff. A touch of what you've been drinking. A trace of after-shave. Lovely. Kiss me."

By God, he told himself, *I can do that much, anyway.* He pressed his lips to hers. Vita's mouth opened under his, searching his tongue with her own, a long exploratory kiss that did not stop when they lay down side by side. Her skin's perfume mingled with the gentle thrust of her hips, dizzying him. Yet his fear of failure mounted with his heart's quickening tattoo. If it was now, this very instant, he might actually be able to perform the feat, but the prolonged sweet torment of foreplay would take its toll on his erratic system and soon he'd go limp. *It always happens.*

But Vita's flesh urged its own rhythm on him, pressing, releasing, pressing again while her mouth held his fast and she guided his hand to her bare breast. Impossibly, he felt himself hardening even more, and now he feared the old flaccid failure any moment now, all the more convinced it was coming because it had not yet occurred. And though he'd warned her, he knew Vita would be disgusted with him when it happened. Or rather, didn't happen. *Going to be worse than ever before—*

"Don't go away."

"But I'd—I'll disappoint you."

"No." She pulled him close again. "Not if you really want me."

"I do. So much that it's agony. Practically since the first time we met."

A gentle laugh. "Oh, no, that was someone else, not me. *I'm* beautiful . . . and so are you. Feel how beautiful you are." Her pelvis moved urgently against him. "It's not just the entering, Drew, it's . . . it's more. I'll show you." Rising quickly, she removed her robe and revealed to Drew the incomparable silhouette of a woman's body—familiar yet new and as mysterious as the first time he'd ever beheld the wonder.

He fumbled with his shirt buttons, fear finally drowned in the flood tide of passion. *All right, then. One last try. She wants me so much, maybe I won't fail. If there's no God, at least there's statistical accident.*

The musk that aroused him during the séance again stirred him as Vita kneeled on the bed and helped him take off his clothes. She brushed her breasts over his chest, along his cheek and mouth.

"You can," she whispered. "We can."

I think so, Vita. I actually believe it's possible.

Her breath was hot against his skin as she drew her lips and tongue along his limbs and hips in narrowing circles until her mouth finally engulfed the head of his penis.

But even in ecstasy, Drew could not completely abandon his lifelong habit of observation. This passionate, vibrant lover was the same tentative, tremulous Mrs. Vita Henry that he'd met four days earlier at the church. She was right in saying that woman was someone else entirely; the two Vitas were completely irreconcilable. A mouse of warning instinct skittered over the floor of his mind, a gnawing sense of something ineffably *wrong*. Still, there was no passion for him without fear, and maybe that was all it was.

Her mouth again sought his. His hand, moving as smoothly as if he'd never been afflicted, caressed the moist warmth of her vagina, found the font of her passion, and now there were no longer any doubts. No need to hurry; for once, his body would not behave traitorously. His thoughts blurred to instinct in the starved urgency of their mutual need.

Later, much later, lying beside Vita, legs entwined with hers, Drew noted the various twitchings of his astonished muscles with amused contempt. *Surprise!* At last he'd driven his inadequate body as it should be driven, thanks to her transfiguring belief that he could. If once, he could do it again. A vista of new possibilities. Why, with a woman who was as fine and full and open as Vita, he could even get used to it. He leaned over and kissed the dim outline of her upturned face.

"What time is it?" she asked.

"Does it matter?"

"Yes."

Drew covered a yawn. "Nearly midnight. Surprised they aren't back yet." Not that he was worried. In such wild weather, the hospital was probably bedlam. He'd tried to phone earlier and knew the line was dead. Richard was probably needlessly concerned that he couldn't get through to them.

Drowsily, Drew tried to pay attention to what Vita was saying, but it was difficult. Her voice was deep and husky and hard to understand, especially while she nuzzled his throat with her lips.

"...me that haunts this house, Drew. Why should it only be the dead? I've haunted the edges of her life for..."

Her?

"...and now I'm real..."

There were more things whispered against his skin, but the pills and brandy coupled with the delicious lassitude following sex lulled him gently toward sleep. Yet just at the brink, the bed moved and his eyelids fluttered open.

Vita was sitting up, alert and listening in the dark. *But when did she turn off the lights?*

His sluggish mind protested being expected to work again. Moving his lips to shape words was a major effort.

"Vi'...wha'?"

"Shh. It's just the telephone."

"Rich?"

"No. It's for me."

"Hm?"

"Nothing. Good night."

She kissed his forehead and left the room, leaving her robe behind. He tried to tell her she'd catch cold without it, but she was already gone before he could focus on the thought. It was the last effort his overtaxed physique could tolerate. Sleep came as suddenly as if a switch in his brain had been flicked off.

Later, when he fought to remember, Drew was sure he'd never heard the phone.

Hu-rrr-y...hu-rrr-y.

The telephone calls to her like the Sirens that sing to sea-weary sailors. Her bare feet pad on the stairs. The air feels refreshingly cool upon her love-flushed skin. The storm wind blows kisses for the glory long denied but now forever hers. Her supplication fills the house, echoes in the magic forest beyond, resounds upon the rain-swept Pennsylvania plain *coming down all* and goddess hears her prayer and grants her the lost moment at last.

Hu-rrr-y . . . hu-rrr-y.

Three times Peter denied Sweet Jesus, three times Michael called and was denied, once for each night she'd spent in Aubrey House, and this the third.

Hu-rrr-y . . . hu-rrr-y.

Not for Merlyn or Richard or even brilliant Drew did the house break its silence. For Charles? Never. Good and well meaning and devout though he was, how could he probe the essence of a life he'd never joined? Blaming his failures on mistakes of upbringing some fifty years dead. Praying to a Father-God who never marred one line of what was past. Only goddess granted hope to those who learned at last to love.

("Promise me you'll try to finish it, Vita . . .")

Hu-rrr-y . . . hu-rrr-y.

In the parlor, the cold blue woman holds out her arms to clasp Vita to her ample bosom, but she is powerless to stop Vita from lifting the receiver or shaping the long-feared answer.

"Yes."

Silence, but Vita knows He is on the line and listens to her every word.

"Come for me. I'm ready."

She hears the receiver at the other end click down. *Coming.*

Garish lightning. The sharp thunder is like steel slivers lancing her eardrums. The hag's abnormally protrusive eyes are filled with anguish as her shriveled lips try to shape some desperate message.

. . . protect . . .

Strange that Vita never noticed before how fat the spirit woman is. Wasn't it she who, on the first night at Aubrey, turned off the sitting room lamp and tucked Vita into bed with motherly care? And intercepted her midnight calls from *Him? It?*

Gusts of rain drive against the walls in rhythmic warning . . . *wanted* . . . *protect* . . . and for one brief atavistic moment, primal terror seizes Vita.

My God, my God, Who have I invited to come?

A scrabbling noise on the front porch. The doorknob begins to turn. The hag fades to nothingness. Vita's fear slips from her like falling leaves.

Hu-rrr-y . . . hu-rrr-y.

Taking the stairs two at a time, she bounds into her room, lights one small lamp at the dressing table and quickly washes, careful not to make noise and wake Drew next door. She dries and powders herself, then sits at her vanity and draws a brush through the dark thickness of her hair with languorous strokes. Her body feels nearly weightless.

A trick of light. I can't be that beautiful . . . can I?

Yes.

Footsteps slowly mount the stairs.

Hu-rrr-y . . . hu-rrr-y.

Michael, I know a place where they'll never find us, even if they cheat 'n' don't count to a hundred, and we can play post office, fifty special delivery letters for me, and wait for your return postage, oh Michael, Michael, don't touch me there Mama says

The footsteps reach the second floor landing.

Hu-rrr-y . . . hu-rrr-y.

She sets down her hairbrush. Blood pounding, feverish, the rhythm quickens between her legs, even as the old woman *so fat!* flows down from her portrait and ghostfingers reach for Vita, the woman's disapproving flabby cheeks quivering Mama, come to me and I'll pry open your weak flabby mouth and stuff your bottomless box of chocolates down your throat and up your ass and you can choke and

His footsteps coming down the hall to her.

Hu-rrr-y . . . hu-rrr-y.

Smiling at herself in the mirror, Vita laughs at the hag woman whose silent lips shape the answer *No, Vita, let me protect you from* but Vita ignores her, spraying perfume on her wrists *faster* her throat *oh faster* thighs *oh faster oh* white heat of passion consuming her as He? It? puts his hand on her knob and turns it *yes oh yes faster ohhhurrr-y* . . .

Cupping her beasts, Vita feels the peaking thrill that the hag still tries to prevent by hugging her in a cold protective clasp, but now the door opens and the midnight caller that Vita told Yes come for me is in the Aubrey bedroom with Vita and He? It? beckons her to bed *coming* spreading her legs *downall?* but far beneath the ecstasy, it's lower deeper needlestrippleasure*painsinbaseof*

michaelmam

Shortly before one a.m., Charles parked the Rolls in the driveway. He got out and slogged through sheets of water to the house, Richard and Merlyn right behind. Inside, the couple wanted drinks, but the only things that sounded good to Singleton were dry pajamas and sleep.

He went upstairs. On his way past Vita's bedroom, Charles noticed her light was on and the door slightly ajar. *She'll want to know we're back safely.* He tapped and waited for her response, but there was none.

"Vita?"

Silence.

Charles hesitated briefly, then decided she wouldn't mind him pushing her door open.

Singleton's screams woke Drew.

Every nerve and muscle protesting, he staggered out of bed, searched for but couldn't find his cane. By the time he stumbled through the open door to Vita's room, Rich and Merlyn were already there, faces white with shock. Clutching a dresser beneath a large portrait of a ballerina *en pointe,* Charles wept bitterly.

Vita lay naked on her bed, hands clutching her maimed breasts, legs drawn up and parted like a woman about to receive her lover. Livid cuts and scratches covered her thighs, some of them so deep they bled upon a bedspread already stained with urine that basic muscles were no longer able to control.

Drew stared in stark horror at her tangled shock of frizzed and matted hair, now completely white. Her grotesquely bulging eyes seemed symptomatic of advanced hypothyroidism. Spittle ran from lips spread wide in a congealed mindless joy.

Her imbecilic grin reminded Drew of that empty leer sewn long ago in thread upon the rag doll's ravaged face.

SOMETHING
SILENT

■

Sunday morning, the sun shone high and cold. Though the rain had stopped, bitter winds still whipped small swirls of leaves and bits of bark along the muddy ground. A brackish stench clogged the nipping air.

Charles was grateful for any reason, no matter how minor, to get out of the house for a few moments. Large as it was, Aubrey was beginning to feel confining, oppressive. Inside, he found himself laboring to catch his breath.

He'd wisely decided to pack rain things with his gear—though Merlyn's accident had hustled him out of the house the preceding afternoon without a thought for slicker, vinyl hat or overshoes. He had them on now. His galoshes squelched deep into the runny earth as he headed toward the woods on the far side of the great rolling lawn. His eyes were red from recent weeping and his forehead felt flushed. He sneezed repeatedly. *Coming down with something, I shouldn't be surprised.* He hardly cared if he did.

When Charles got back, Richard was sitting in the breakfast nook munching on dry toast and drinking his usual cup of black coffee. He looked disinterestedly at the stout, gnarled branch Charles set by the sink.

"For Drew?"

"Indeed," Singleton averred. "Till he finds where he put his cane." He ran fresh water into a kettle. "Do you think he'll want tea?"

"I don't imagine he'll want much of anything. Me either, really." He dropped a bit of crust on his plate. "Just eating out of habit."

Charles buttered a slice of bread but forgot to taste it. "I started to pack for Vita. I don't suppose she'll be coming back here."

"No."

207

"It's so personal," Charles murmured, "going through someone's things, even an old friend."

"Especially an old friend."

"Suddenly, they're all laid out for your inspection, and it feels like a kind of voyeurism. Mended sweaters, underwear with holes. A Bible, a sexy novel, a few pictures. Prom night, young boy in white jacket and tie, Vita in fancy gown, a spray of violets in her hand, looking no more than sixteen, seventeen. Another one of a good-looking fellow in beard and Aussie hat. None of her husband or parents. D'you know Vita saved uncanceled stamps? I . . . I had to stop."

Creighton stared down at his plate. "I know. Sometimes it's just a shoe . . ."

"You think you knew your friend, and then you realize she was a stranger."

"Yes."

"Vita and I were very close, Richard. We told each other most of our troubles. She didn't have much luck with men on the singles market."

"How long was she married to what's his name?"

"Walter? Too long. Years."

"You think she would've married again."

Charles gave Richard a sad, knowing smile. "People who want to be married, are. Period. She never talked about her husband at all after he passed away, that in itself is indicative. And the losers she'd meet at the church meetings—suggest a week's acquaintance to them before going to bed, and it's an affront to their masculinity." He absently began to crumble his piece of bread into bits. "Sometimes when . . . my life wasn't going too well—you know how it is—she'd listen, try to help. We prayed together occasionally. Or bitched mutually. Each of us trusted the other enough to be able to be weak sometimes, or petty, or—or wrong. That's how well I knew her."

Creighton's eyes met his. "In that case, Charlie, what in holy hell happened to her last night?"

"All I can think of is what Drew said about the Burtons.

But why Vita? I mean, he warned me, and I risked a séance, anyway, and drew a total blank. But she went down without even looking for it, and oh God, I'm talking about her in the past tense when she's still alive."

"If you want to call it that."

Charles went to the stove and adjusted the flame beneath the kettle. "Strange how silently Drew took it. Just standing there by her bed without a word."

"Not so strange . . ."

"Do you think they were lovers?"

"What? Who?"

"Drew and Vita."

"Come *on*, Charlie! He can barely get up the stairs."

Ever since they'd lifted Vita from the bed and carried her away, Drew hadn't closed his eyes. All the rest of the night and long past sunrise, he lay and stared at the ceiling. *Only a few hours.* His body still remembered the feel of her, the smoothness of her flesh against his, being inside her, her fading scent on his skin.

So mutable. A few days' acquaintance and she's gone. One hour's worth of love and part of me will keen over her the rest of my useless life. If it were just one of those casual trysts some people had, he might well accuse himself of mawkishness. But Vita gave him the gift, showed him he was still a whole man, able to experience the simplest and most complex joy that men and women could share. Despite their spiritual age difference, there'd been no gap in their emotions. They might have had a go at it and turned up whole new years of maybes.

Charlie was fortunate, he could weep. *A blessing to be able to translate emotion into the balm of tears.* For himself, there was only the thing to be done and the white rage chilling into black determination. His body was crying out for its accustomed sedation, but it would just have to go on crying. He wouldn't allow it. Not yet.

When I'm done with you, Beastie.

Beastie, constant, presence, it took her, that thing that swirled in a predictable tide between the second and third floors of the house, that almost dragged him under once. *I should have been alive to what was happening to her.* She had a distinct aura for the past two days, the same euphoria he'd experienced, an overtone that warned his senses even as it excited them. Vita it took more slowly, her sudden loveliness a lightning before death. And death it was, too, no matter how long her untenanted body might endure.

Like the Burtons, Aubrey destroyed her without actually

210

killing her on the premises. But now Drew had grave doubts that Charlotte was the only one to die in the house. It might well be the child. But whatever, whoever it was, conscious or unconscious of malice, the presence was as real a danger as a sunken wreck in a shallow channel.

All night long, while he silently grieved for Vita, Drew felt it prowling on its endless round. After a while, the idea surfaced, a thought so basic it had never before occurred to him: that a psychic entity moving in an unvarying path from point to point must be restricted in a physical sense to real time and place. It couldn't be in two places at once.

Which meant it could be tracked.

Richard Creighton glares out over the same fields and lake he called Vita in from two days earlier.

—When she was just beginning to change.

Hindsight. You were too busy tabulating Beltane's intellectual incapacities to notice her.

He leaves the window, sits at the small table, roots through his attaché case and finds an unused cassette.

click

"Early Sunday afternoon. Ghastly thing happened to Vita. Not quite sure what, waiting for call from Merlyn at the hospital to assess the damage. Some kind of traumatic shock. Merlyn prays she'll be able to recover from it, Drew's positive she won't. I wouldn't bet against him at this point, though it's possible the condition we found her in has colored our thinking. When you watch a shy woman blossom into a ravishing beauty virtually overnight and then the next time you see her, she's a horrible old hag, the effect is devastating. Still, symptomatic observation is only worth so much. Have to wait till Merlyn calls.

"She held up surprisingly well, considering. Helpless at first, of course, but when the ambulance arrived she put her foot down and said Vita was her best friend and she wouldn't leave her side. Rode back with them, and she's been there ever since. I would've gone, but there really wasn't room and I didn't trust Charlie to drive the Rolls. He was in no shape, especially with the roads the way they were."

And Dr. Creighton doesn't drive.

—Oh, shut up.

The tape revolves for several seconds before he speaks again.

"The big question is why it happened. Several possibilities immediately suggest themselves to me:

"*A* Massive cerebral stroke or an aneurism that blew out her mind like a fuse. True, she seemed as healthy as an Amazon, especially during the past few days, though that needn't contraindicate this theory. But neither stroke nor aneurism would produce the anomalous condition we found her in, at least I don't think so. Admittedly a lay opinion, but based on some familiarity with physiological morbidity.

"*B* Emotional collapse following sexual attack. Idiotic, of course . . . she was alone in the house with Drew, and the state of his paralysis strongly suggests he is incapable of consenting sex, let alone using force on a healthy woman. Vita could have beat the hell out of him if he'd tried. Still, it's a theory I'm afraid is going to occur all too readily to the local police. I don't think it'll be long before they pay us all a visit.

"*C* Vita took some sort of drug. I suppose the hospital staff will pursue the possibility, but again, I only catalog it for completeness. She didn't even smoke. Drank a little but never excessively so far as I could observe. And alcohol, even mixed with pills, had nothing to do with . . . with what she became.

"*D* Drew Beltane is correct. Aubrey House contains a psychic pool of energy that found Vita a vulnerable target. He would characterize it as a presence, Vita would have termed it a spirit and Charles would write it down as a ghost, his readers would prefer it that way, I imagine, or at least he'd think they would. Anyhow, this possibility has no built-in objections other than the lack of verifiable evidence. But even if one could prove this hypothesis, it would not automatically validate Drew's claim that *psi* energy derives from whole or fragmentary survival of—"

Charles raps on Creighton's door.
"Dick, it's Merlyn on the phone for you."
"Be right down."
click

No trace now of the frightened little girl. Merlyn's voice is deep and steady and sad.

"My ankle's all right, Rich, don't worry. They gave me one of those silly aluminum canes, but I can walk without it."

"And your face?"

"He thinks I may need surgery."

"Oh, Christ—"

"Minor surgery. Comparatively. Don't worry about it. I'm not."

Creighton hesitates. "And . . . Vita?"

A long pause before she answers.

"No change."

"Any tests yet?"

"Yes. What's that thing that measures brain waves?"

"EEG. Look, Merlyn, did Vita have any history of cerebral hemorrhage? Or aneurism? Anything, even high blood pressure?"

"I don't know. I don't think so. I never saw her sick. What's the difference now?"

"Just a need to know why. What were the results of the EEG?"

"Nothing. I mean, the lines on the paper barely moved. The doctors say there's nothing left."

Longhand was a taxing business for Drew Beltane, but he was assiduously enduring its tedium and minor aches when Charles rapped at his bedroom door.

"Come in."

The knob turned and Charles stepped inside carrying a long, thick branch.

Drew raised his eyebrows. "Is that knobkerry for me?"

"Well, I asked Merlee to bring you a cane from the hospital, but she probably won't remember, so I thought you'd better have a workable substitute in the meantime."

"Thank you, Charlie. I may have to hunch a bit to control it, but I suppose it's better than grabbing the backs of furniture."

Singleton rested the stick against the foot of Drew's bed. "It's rather late, but I'll be glad to fix breakfast just the same."

"No, no, I have no appetite. I'm going to finish this, then I want to try to get some rest. I couldn't sleep at all. Please apologize to Rich for me for keeping to my room all day."

"Certainly. We're all drifting around like shadows, anyway. What are you working on so diligently?"

"Oh . . . just some notes. You can read them later if you like."

"Mm." Charles grunted disinterestedly. "Merlyn called from the hospital. No change in Vita."

"There won't be, Charlie. It's the Burtons all over again." He passed his hand over his eyes. "Wish I knew what she meant."

"Meant by what? Who? Vita?"

"Phyllis Burton. The last note in her journal. 'We were so wrong. It's lower. Deeper.'"

Charles walked slowly toward the door. "Frankly, I don't care if I never find out."

* * *

Assured now against intrusion, Drew eases himself down onto the bed and opens his senses to the presence.

Got it: past energy-peak and ebbing.

But still close. The power arcs slightly on his skin as the thing approaches and hovers in the hall near his door, aware of him as always.

Moving away now. A predictable cycle. In ten minutes it would drop to its lowest point, its period of "rest." Plenty of time. Straightening his legs, abandoning by degrees the awareness of tendons, nerves and atrophied muscles, Drew regulates his breathing to the rhythm of his pulse: *in-two-three-four-hold-hold-out-two-three-four* and over again and again. His body's messages fade as a drowsiness like the onset of a shallow doze begins to lull his mind. Behind closed eyelids, a retinal afterglow focuses high above his brows, like a tiny penlight beam centering on his forehead.

Gradually his thoughts flow again. The psychic counterparts of limbs grow loose within the prisoning shell of flesh. Exhilarant expectation; he feels like an ocean diver about to ascend to a level of lesser pressure.

Suddenly, the glorious double moment arrives: his spirit rushes ceilingward, his body remains on the bed, and Drew is simultaneously aware of being in both places. Then he concentrates on his liberated self and capers above the inert wreck of his body below, revels in supple power and utter release from pain. Against the grayish light and elongated lines of the room, he sees his astral umbilica etched as sharp as a midnight star.

And now he floats toward the dim angles of the door and with a slight effort of will, flows through the closed portal into the hall. Gray turns black. Points of light reflect from picture glass, doorknobs, bronze sculpture lancing in all directions across the corridor, shooting out to infinity. On another plane, he could see it as it normally appears to the conscious eye, but Drew knows he must scry beyond physicality to detect the cold blue light.

Tangled ropes of pale light thread along the hall. *Human*

*energy residue. Identifiable as fingerprints. The strongest
are surely Rich and Merlyn, the paler ones Charlie and me.*
Following Vita's to her room, he notes how her older tracks
are normal and robust, the newer ones adulterated with that
color characteristic of the "constant." The last strong pool
is at her dressing table, but the crude outline of her body
still glows over the square of the bed, its residue completely
corrupted with the hue of the presence. *If it were organic,
I'd call it cancerous.*

In the hallway again, Drew hesitates only long enough
to differentiate the tracks, then moves on to the slightly
distorted square of Charlotte's picture. Beneath it hovers
the wide centrum of residue he detected in his first readings.
Years of it. On his present level of perception, Drew can
still make out Charlotte's features, though the angles of
brow, cheekbones and chin seem oddly highlighted.

A milky puddle of faintly glowing slag directly beneath
the photograph leads back to Vita's closet, snakes through
recent traces he'd left himself and goes out and up the back
stairs, following the unvarying route he first mapped in
varying pressures on his skin.

The door to the dark stairway stands out luminously.
Tiny points of light still dance from the last passage of the
presence a few minutes past. Drew flows through the portal
and up the steps to the third floor.

In front of Shipperton's room: the strands fresh enough
to flicker with isolated charges of static energy. The imperfect rectangle of the door shimmers with it. Drew moves
closer and the trail momentarily brightens.

Know I'm here, don't you?

Increasing agitation; the thing reads a difference where
change has never before come. Drew penetrates into the
room, not expecting to see the presence clearly yet, not on
such an unexalted astral plane, that is his deliberate safety
valve. *Deep enough to see the trail, close enough to snap
back to my body.*

The nurse's old room is as misty as a steam chamber,
thick with residue drifting over every inch of space. Drew's

other vision probes the fog, separating fresh from old till it fixes on a point in front of the distorted half circle of the low window.

Within the opalescent cloud, something moves.

There you are. Ready or not.

The swirl churns furiously. His thoughts grope for it. *Charlotte?*

It eddies away from the window on an angle meant to elude him.

Can you hear me?

Drew inches forward, projecting silent questions, but quick as a silverfish it wriggles in a lateral dash to the opposite wall.

Is that you, Charlotte? Answer me. You can't hide anymore.

With surprising speed, it flows around him and out into the corridor, but for an instant at the core of it, Drew glimpses the merest nuance of shape. Against the dark wall of the hallway it is clearer, a glowing daub against black velvet, bleeding a fresh trail of energy as it flees from him, following its unvarying route, back and forth from one room to the next as if searching for something.

Allowing it no chance to rest, Drew flushes it from each chamber as soon as it enters, driving it faster along the hall toward the back stairs. On the second floor, it stops by Charlotte's picture. Drew takes advantage of the pause to slip around and wait in front of Vita's room, blocking it off from the presence, pushing it to retreat.

Into and up the scrawled shape of the narrow stairway again, in and out of Shipperton's old room through another full circuit, door by door, floor by floor, up and down. It begins to falter noticeably; there is an odd, jerky quality to its movements, leaving a trail no longer thick and whole but rather blunt-ended worms of energy ash as its power reservoirs dwindle. Not trying to overtake it, Drew permits it no rest as it flees yet again into the dark well of the servants' stairs.

Never goes to the first floor. Never backtracks. Pure

energy, and I'm burning it up. Measurable. Must be a way to symbolize it as a property, graph it across time and space, even predict—

Midway up the rear stairs, the presence halts, pulsing feebly.

Tired, Beastie? That's too bad, because we're going to do it again and again, you buggering little remnant. You destroyed Vita, and now you're going to run until there's nothing left of you. He has no mouth to shape the snarl of his vengeance, but Drew lunges up the stairs to frighten the presence into yet another circuit. His mind echoes with the unheard reverberation of its muffled wail—

—and then the presence on the steps above flares impossibly brighter.

OH, JESUS, YOU BLOODY FOOL, PULL BACK!

Drew silently curses himself for being so carelessly overconfident, his passion for revenge blinding him to the way the presence stealthily drank of his own resources all the time they ran the endless circuit of pursuit. Now the undertow that almost pulled him to death once before tugs at him again. He fights wildly to resist. The contours of the stairwell warp above his head as Drew feels himself whirl into the vortex. The presence waits for him and now he can see more clearly as a face ripples into definition, distorted but unmistakable: the graceful arch of the brows, the set of the eyes, wide and bleak, no more than a glimpse while he bends his entire concentration to struggle against the lethal suction.

No doubt of it, it's her. And weak. Couldn't steal much strength from me. Her fatigue saves him; with a supreme effort, Drew breaks away, ascends, stabilizes. Her shape blurs as he moves up, becoming merely a pulsating glow again. The hard reality of the servants' staircase once more solidifies around him.

Got to let them know.

In one dizzying instant, he whips back to his bedroom and sinks with relief into the pitiful twisted shape of his own real body still stretched out on the bed, asleep.

* * *

His raw, unmedicated nerves always felt worse after out-of-body flight. As Drew opened his eyes to blinding sunlight, a deluge of sensation crashed down on him like a wall of water. He waited a moment till his laboring heart eased, then raised his left wrist to read the watch face. Elapsed time, twenty-five minutes. He'd driven her through two cycles in half the normal time, and still she almost dragged him under.

Then maybe if I approach on her own level to begin with, her only weapon will be useless.

Feeling wretched, Drew levered himself up to sit on the edge of the bed, groping for the pad and pencil on his nightstand. His hand shook too much for legible script, so he began to print laboriously.

RICH: Out-of-body travel is the only way to get near the thing, so I've gone OB to track it down. It is definitely Charlotte. Got a flash of her before I realized how she kills. God knows why she's in Shipperton's third-floor room, surely she didn't go there while she was alive.

The Burtons were careless amateurs, but they tripped over the truth. Remember Phyllis' diary: "We were so wrong. It's lower. Deeper." Deeper in the mind, Rich. That's why Masconi's results were inconclusive; she was afraid to probe in depth. The Falzer people found a constant because they tend to dismiss out-of-body travel as unreliable. But at Aubrey, it's the only way to make real contact. One must descend to a primitive level of mind. The Burtons could not have figured this out without going under themselves, but they stopped in time and even had enough wit to analyze what had occurred. Since they must have done just that, Rich, I suppose they deserve a bit more credit as psychics, after all. The question is, once they knew the risk, why the hell did they try it again? Perhaps liquor—they were heavy drinkers, remember? Might've thought booze would sufficiently alter state to bring them into contact without actually resorting to OB travel. Idiotic. They must've been blind drunk when it got them. The danger—

Drew tore off the sheet and began another, smirking grimly at the last word. The danger was immense. Sucked down rapidly into one's own id, unprepared and totally traumatized, the effect on the neocortical areas of the brain would amount to a lethal electrochemical concussion for which "shock" was an impoverished identification, like trying to equate the word "boom" with a nuclear explosion.

Suicidal. The most rigidly controlled id-regression experiments demanded subjects as stable as Gibraltar, and even then most of them came out of it screaming lumps who had to be tended for hours. A vital byproduct of these experiments at Edinburgh was birth regression. Drew went through it under control, his private descent into the pit, reexperiencing the natal trauma, the pressures on his soft infant skull as his mother's body squeezed him into the world. He remembered and dealt with it and was one of the few volunteers who suffered relatively light side effects, but it was a gradual, stage-by-stage process. Sudden immersion, especially during an OBE, would kill him just as surely as it had crushed the Burtons and Vita.

The pain in one's skull—remember I mentioned it to Charlie—that's the first symptom of birth memory. I've been through it, Rich, and believe me, there can't be much of anything harmful rattling round my little Ayrshire id. Except for the animal wish, sometimes, to be free of pain for good and all, but that's one of those irrelevant urges that I've had to ignore through the years. The greatest danger I face at present is Charlotte. I'm going OB again to finish her. In case anything should happen to me, you may want to review my OB work in the Falzer journals. As with my skin, I believe trained out-of-body travelers can eventually assign arbitrary values to energy units, perhaps

Drew ripped the print-covered sheet away from the pad and went to a new one.

even come up with a viable equation as to the longevity of these things generally called ghosts.

You'll also find some observations on Vita on another sheaf of papers beneath this pile. Things she told me the night before she succumbed to Aubrey may explain why her experience was so very different from all the others recorded here.

Now I'm on my way down to meet Charlotte on her own ground, the id level. I have the advantage this time. I've run her energy very low and she won't be able to siphon mine because we'll be on the same plane. By now, she must be scared out of her vacant little mind, probably thinks it's Judgment Day, and she has good reason to fear that event, I'm afraid.

The pencil twitched in Drew's fingers. He gripped it tighter, glancing at his watch. No more time for elaborate rationales, he didn't want to give her an opportunity to build up power.

Please thank Merlyn for the chance of a lifetime. Never thought it would become this personal, but it has. So, whatever happens . . .
                              Love,
                              DREW

Since Richard had no more interest in lunch than Drew, Charles skipped the meal, too. While Creighton paced the living room with eyes downcast as if the rug was some cosmic hieroglyph that needed decoding, Charles sat on the piano bench steadily imbibing sherry. As he tipped more into his glass, his hand trembled a few drops on the keys. He quickly blotted them with an already-purpled handkerchief.

"Aren't you overdoing it a little, Charlie? Thought you were under doctor's orders."

Singleton sighed muzzily. "The exception proves the rule, Richard. My body can handle a few ounces of alcohol better than it can manage cold-sober stress."

"Hope you know what you're doing."

"Look, you choose to pace, Drew is sleeping and I elect to drink."

"Okay." Stopping by the fireplace, Creighton stared with somber interest at the portrait hanging above it of Derek Aubrey. "You're right, of course. We've all got our own ways of trying to deal with mortality. Some systems just work better than others."

"What's yours, Richard? I hope you didn't come here thinking Merlyn was an out." It was the first time Charles had even obliquely alluded to Creighton's personal tragedy. *Blame it on the wine.*

It didn't upset the other. He shrugged offhandedly. "If I had any such illusions, Charlie, all it took to kill them was experiencing Merlyn at close range. Actually I've had my own emotional deadener down pat for at least fifteen years. Ever since my mother died."

Singleton peered at him over the rim of his glass. "Well?"

"The details? Obliteration of the past."

"Hm?"

223

"I mean, not dragging around chains. Cutting away childhood, old graves, last week. Excision of everything unreachable except by memory." He resumed pacing.

Charles gaped in blunt disbelief. "You *can't* be serious, Dick! Our past is what defines us . . . it's what the world grows on."

"Bullshit. It's what we're dying from. Traditions, superstitions, religions. Adults warp children who grow up and cripple adults."

Charles found that hard to argue with, but the idea was simply too appalling to confront. "Richard, how can you possibly live without roots? It's inconceivable."

An acknowledging nod. "It's tough at first. I don't suppose that over the years I've really achieved better than, say, eighty-five percent efficiency, but it's like any habit. The more you do it, the more it begins to take command. Isn't that the basic principle behind organized religion?"

"Now you sound like Drew," Charles said through pursed, disapproving lips.

"Maybe. But he and I are actually miles apart spiritually."

"It hasn't seemed so, here at Aubrey."

"Because we both respect scientific method. At least Drew does up to a point. There's only one way to investigate a phenomenon, Charlie, I don't care if it's ghosts or the undiscovered properties of a new element: you gather, collate, synthesize, form hypotheses — and always remain open for new interpretations. Unfortunately, Drew accepts personality survival *de facto*—"

"So do I."

"Assuming there is something there, Charlie, whatever Drew reads through his brilliant pores doesn't have to be Charlotte or anyone else, no more than the trunk that the blind man felt had to be the whole elephant."

Charles sloshed the last wine dregs into his glass. "My thoughts are slightly muddled at the moment, but even if I were sober now, I'm not sure I'd follow where you're coming from, Richard. However, I *do* sense things, no matter what you may think after that abortive séance. Would you like to know what I detect in you?"

"Be my guest."

"For all your elaborate intellectualization on the folly of attempting to objectify—or shall we say rely?—on paranormal experience, I have the distinct impression that, given a choice, you would dearly like to believe."

Creighton's lips crooked. "How can I argue with that, Charlie? Don't we all, deep down, want a spiritual nightlight?"

The phone rang. *Thank God for a diversion,* Charles thought, answering it.

"Aubrey residence. Charles Singleton here."

"Mr. Singleton, I'm Mariella Willet from Bucks County General. I'm in charge of the ICU where Mrs. Henry was brought."

"Yes?" Charles' throat suddenly went husky.

"I'm afraid I have some bad news."

"About Mrs. Henry?"

"Yes . . . partly. There . . . there really was nothing we could do for her."

"I don't suppose there was," he said numbly. "When was it?"

"Less than ten minutes ago. She experienced no pain."
No, that part happened here.

"What else is wrong? Is it Miss Aubrey?"

Richard came to a halt. "Merlyn? What?"

The nurse told Singleton, "She reacted quite violently to Mrs. Henry's death. We had to sedate her."

"I see. Where is she now? May I speak with her?"

"No. She'll be unconscious for several hours. We had to put her in a private room. There were no other available beds."

The irrelevance of the detail, coupled with her apologetic tone, struck Singleton funny. "It's all right," he tittered, "Miss Aubrey can afford it. Though when she sees the bill, you may have to sedate her again."

"What's the matter with Merlyn?" Charles gestured for Creighton to wait.

The nurse had more to say. "Before Miss Aubrey fell asleep, she mumbled something about a Dr. Creighton. Do you know where we might get in touch with him?"

"He's right here. But he's not her physician, just a friend. I'll put him on, though."

Creighton listened on the line for a short time, then hung up. "She was in the room when Vita died. Merlyn leaped on the resident and almost knocked his brains out beating his head on the floor."

"My God!"

"Who, Charlie?"

Two minutes later. Richard upstairs. Charles rose wobbily to his feet, fumbled for his wallet.

Dick's mad at me. Too bad. I'm in no shape to drive. Creighton wanted to be with Merlyn when she woke, but was loath to get behind the wheel of the Rolls. *Probably because of that accident. No matter what he says, that's one piece of his past I don't suppose he'll ever bury.*

Carefully placing the contents of his wallet on the lid of the piano, Charles began to turn over cards and scraps of paper, holding them close to unfocused eyes.

Creighton came downstairs carrying an old flight bag packed with a few necessaries for Merlyn, in case she had to stay overnight at the hospital.

"I think Drew's asleep, Charlie. His room's quiet. We'd better leave a note."

"No, no. I'll stay here with him. He ought not to be alone when he finds out about Vita."

Charles knew Richard wanted company on the drive, but he just couldn't face the prospect of the bumpy secondary roads he'd have to endure. His stomach wasn't up to it.

Richard said a curt goodbye and slammed the front door behind him. Charles returned to the business of rummaging among the accumulated paraphernalia of his billfold. At last, he found what he was looking for: a 2 by 3½ once-white business card.

Time to call Sam Lichinsky.

A firm step in the hall: Richard Creighton moving past his door. *Funny how people make more noise trying to be quiet than they would if they just clumped away.* The footsteps recede, a door slams. Silence.

Ebb to peak to ebb again, Charlotte's cycle takes twenty to thirty minutes in real time. *Her ebb's longer now.* He'd caught her at her weakest point and chased her without rest. Her basic drive was a vast but not inexhaustible reservoir of id-energy from the deepest seat of human emotional need. *Easier for me to replenish energy than she can. Eventually, I'll literally run her to extinction. It may take a while, but I've no engagements elsewhere. Charlotte saw to that.*

Her last cycle barely registered on his skin. *She's very weak.* He waits through one more circuit to rest himself, then prepares to start down.

Drew gathers his concentration. Physical awareness drops away by degrees. His limbs cease their twitching, become pleasantly numb, then no longer exist for him. Slowly, conserving his energy, he rises from his body and begins the steady descent through the surface layers of his existence. Hovering near his shape on the bed, he regards it with distant pity: poor, pathetic lump of imperfect flesh, why would anyone go back to it at all? Only one obstacle stands in the way, the absurdly stubborn will to survive.

Easy on, Beltane. It's going to be loud and messy down there. Don't confuse the issue.

Contours and dimensions abstract further, darkening and warping as Drew completes his second level of descent. Distance reverse-telescopes, sounds die. The world turns achromatic, gray-white and black, but he knows the senses of color and sound will come rioting back at the id level where the deepest animal instincts are unbridled, where hue and noise are warnings needed for survival. Day, night, enemy, friend, food—need: stimuli triggering the deep limbic layers of the mind to its oldest aggressive functions.

Ready now. Not too fast.

The trick is to maintain an override by the higher cortical centers, a control to keep him stabilized. Doing his best to maintain a dual awareness of inner events, Drew begins his final descent, passing through a layer of infant fear and anger, a momentary, phantom pain like the last vestige of birth trauma, something Vita and the Burtons must have felt just before Charlotte pulled them under. *A quicksand effect. They killed themselves, really. Charlotte was just a catalyst, destroying them without even knowing it. But then, she was always a vacuous bitch.* Drew's reason grips him tighter. *Steady on. The anger's part of it. Don't get carried away.*

Sinking, he notes as long as he can the gradual disconnection of the cortex. *Mustn't leave me entirely. That's my lifeline back to the world.* One strong thread of superego controlling those primal instincts already tugging at the bottom of his will.

Color seeps back, silence thrums like audio hum thrust through powerful speakers at maximum gain. The most minute sounds—Singleton stumbling up the stairs, the creak of a board—now reach Drew as sharp and clear as digital music over stereo headphones. The room's dimensions warp and twist, the door a hazy approximation of a rectangle crayon-scrawled by a two-year-old. Inundated by glaring color and jagged sound, Drew crouches on guard against the unknown, his ghost-fingers curling in prehensile memory, vision darting back and forth in response to each potentially threatening stimulus.

Almost there, his will whispers. *Here we go, last stage.*

Vibrations batter his hearing. Waves of light beyond the visible spectrum stab sharp, lewdly flicker. A phrase he read once trumpets its own weird hue: *the red of blood and sin and fire.* Angles split apart, join again in impossible couplings, shooting up and over and around him as he plummets into the dark cellarage of his mind, where nightmares always lurk. Though once before he'd descended so far and scoured away the worst terrors, primal fear still remains, incapable of being expunged. *Necessary survival tool.*

Whole and functional again, Drew merges through the skewed shape of the door into the tunnel of the hall. He winces at the brilliance of the energy trails threading the long corridor, the newest, writhing like a snake, leading to Charles' room. Drew's vision, exponentially more acute than before, clearly discerns the adulteration of Vita's final residue and its unmistakable similarity to his own wake. Naked id: and she collided with it unprepared. *Literally knew herself to death.*

As he crouches over the traces, Drew does not notice one of the distorted door panels behind him suddenly gaping with a tidal wave of lurid light. But the shrill whine makes him turn in time to see a mottled horror charging toward him, its vague chromatic shape etched in veinal-crimson flame. Drew screams as the fireball roars straight at him. He crouches in a fetal ball of fear, but the apparition passes through him and surges down the chasm of the front stairs.

Trembling with fear, then reactive anger, Drew forces his reason to take hold again. With weak amusement, he suddenly realizes what he actually saw.

Jesus God, that was Charlie's aura.

Then all the live inhabitants of Aubrey House must look like monstrosities of energy and thunder to Charlotte. *No wonder she fled from me!*

Returning his attention to the trails of light, Drew finds Charlotte's latest, no longer a continuous thread but ragged pools of energy that bleed all the way from her photograph to Vita's room and out again to the back stairs.

Weaker than ever. Time to go for her, then.

The uneven squiggle on the steps rises before him. Ahead, just beyond the turn to the third floor, he catches the faint overspill of milky glow.

That's her. Around the twist of the stairs—just ahead.

Drew pauses a second or two longer before rounding the angle, preparing himself to see the essence of an old woman, not too clever, but frightened and dangerous.

He ascends, turns the corner, stops. Stares. Disappointed.

Near the top. Not sharply delineated but merely a larger blob of energy spilling from one step to the next. The merest suggestion of a human form slumped against the wall.

Charlotte?

The crude head shape lifts itself at his warning. She drags herself to the top step.

Why can't I see you even now? Were you that weak all your life?

The guttering glow falters through the doorway at the top of the flight. Drew lunges upward, hears her high, thin, terrified cry. The last strands of his controlling will snap. All sense leaving him, Drew is propelled at incalculable speed through a kind of portal and as the soft borders at the edges of life buckle, he feels himself hurtling upward toward an infinity of cryptic design, larger shells in smaller chambers housing tiny echoed rooms, then—

Slowing—

Stopping.

Perimeters resolve, the cataract of chaos mutes. The stairs again. Silence. Wholeness. Not even the vague memory of pain. No trace of any energy trail.

How far?

Drew Beltane opens his eyes at the pitiable weeping, raises his head to look at her.

You're not—

His own pride again, and the answer so obvious. *Of course* Charlotte never went near Shipperton's third-floor room. *Charlie read it right, why wouldn't I accept it?*

Huddling in the doorway, clear as himself at last, tiny and terrified in her shapeless smock, no more than seven years old, she hunches forward and sideways from the rachitic deformation of her spine. Strings of pale, matted hair hang over eyes in which fright can only kindle the dullest hint of expression but which nevertheless are still the mirror of her mother's.

Frozen in horror, her mouth with its cleft palate quavers into a travesty of speech.

Uml.

Whatever it means, Drew understands that he was her special terror, a huge thing invading her secret place where loneliness at least held safety for her until he came.

With a whining moan, she scuttles away toward her old third-floor prison.

It's a new game, Rich. I've got no answer for it, but maybe I'm beginning to understand.

The upper halls were all the reality she ever knew. *No wonder the id's the only level she can be approached on.* One of the major stages in any child's early development is the capacity to conquer language. Charlotte's child, mentally and physically unable, never managed to think in words. *Deny that, and any seven-year-old is mostly id, all need and fear.*

Shipperton's old room is dim gray and as clear as the stairs. The little girl cowers against the low window. Drew pauses, not wanting to frighten her further. He kneels, holds out his arms, but edging sideways, she scurries around him. Strangely, though he cannot feel the floor beneath, his outstretched hand brushes the very tangible cloth of her smock.

Uml!

She calls frantically again and again, hobbling away down the hall. Drew is not surprised to see her wind from one room to another, putting up both arms to push open doors she cannot feel. She ferrets every chamber, each closet, then out again, calling, mouthing the same frustrated approximation of a name, searching the narrow limits of her remembered world—

Uml!

—for Emily! Who left her alone to wake in darkness. *Eternity reduced to that. She doesn't know she's dead, couldn't have had any conception of death, only that Emily never came back.*

The speechless child twists around to see Drew still following her, scuttles down the dark stairs to the second floor—*when was she allowed that far?*—and her movements are now less habitual and certain. She tries none of these rooms; very likely they don't exist for her. But she halts by the dim but recognizable perfection of Charlotte's photograph. A small hand lifts toward the picture frame far out of reach, her blunt little face screws up with the effort to connect vestigial memories of fading voices.

Mm . . . muh?

The inarticulate longing for the beautiful, empty woman in the picture lances Drew's heart.

Muh-muh.

The little girl's face contorts with the rage of her unsatisfied id.

Muh-muh!

A howl of fury as her tiny fists try to batter the picture that remains as untouchable as the original was. Forgetting all about Drew, she crumples into a silent ball of misery.

Drew waits just beyond arm's length, saddened by the inexpressible cruelty of Aubrey's cold blue light. *Charlie's got a book, right enough. When I get back—*

When I—

How odd: one more anomaly on this new and unexplored level of existence. The thought of return brings Drew no automatic mental picture of his room or his body. He knows precisely where Vita's bedroom is, and Creighton's and the others, but can't remember or picture his own at all. The harder he tries, the more it eludes him. He runs his thoughts backward to no avail. He has no memory of the room or how he came from it.

The child warily lifts her head and sees him. She squirms to a sitting position under the picture. Beyond a smile, he makes no move toward her, waiting for her fear to change into natural curiosity. Soon it does and he opens his arms to her, inviting her to come close.

But at the gentle movement, she lurches to her feet and presses against a wall neither one of them can feel.

Will you help me, lass? I'm lost, too.

More fascinated than frightened now. One little hand sweeps up awkwardly to brush the strings of hair back from her eyes.

Come on.

She takes a small, tentative step toward him.

That's it.

Another step. Drew allows her to come well within reach before resting his hands on her frail shoulders. No longer taut with terror, her features more than ever mark her Charlotte's daughter: the brow, the delicate nose and chin framing the malformed mouth. With an equal wonder, she explores the novelties of his own face and hair, his close-trimmed beard. Making a face, Drew sticks out his tongue.

Boo.

The action mystifies her at first. The next time he does it, though, she mimics him. He laughs gently, and his arms encircle her tiny waist, lifting her high. Her laughter tinkles like a tiny, distant bell.

And then she points to Vita's room.

Guh-dee.

It seems urgent to her. She points again, squirming to be set down. He does so, and she hobbles directly to Vita's room and into the closet. Only one object stands out sharply, the old rag doll perched where Drew returned it, on top of the dim bulk of the doll boxes. The child reaches for it, quite unable to understand why she can't get it.

Nearly seventy years she's wanted it. That's why it read so high: it was hers.

Drew tries to lift it down for her, but the doll is no longer real for him, only a remembered image. His solid hand grasps nothing.

Rich, at this level, I can't even feel the floor under me. Nothing's real but me and the child.

He lifts her again, high enough for her to reach the doll, watches the bafflement as she tries to touch it and can't. Venting a little mew of impatience, she flails her hands at it, then looks to Drew for an explanation.

Guh-dee?

Raggedy's not real any more. You have to be a big girl and find something new.

Another clumsy attempt to clutch the doll; a whimper of frustration, then she gives it up. Drew puts her down and she shambles out into the hall once more. He hesitates, musing over the vague shape of the doll, the vaguer contours of the house around him. Each new insight he has on this level is automatically addressed to Richard Creighton and is accompanied by the urge to get back and tell it. *But how? Where?* His own room, his own body, are a black hole in his memory. *They don't exist.*

Moving from the gray of the closet to the paler gray of Vita's room, Drew finds it all pallid. *Reality fading.* He gazes through the windows in Vita's octagonal sitting room at the bare suggestion of a world beyond. The realization gradually dawns on him, wrapping him in a moment's panic before he ultimately accepts it. All those years of wanting to be free evidently built up quite a deposit in his will, eventually overbalancing the instinct for survival. A slow accretion till that moment on the stairs when he lunged upwards after her and part of him must have known what it was doing. The heart, blood and damaged muscle and nerve sprang open like a time lock.

You've made it, Beltane. Escape velocity.

Drew laughs softly with genuine amusement. So much for observed empiricals and questing intelligence. There'd be no revised notes to Rich Creighton, no compliments to Charlie, no matter how well-deserved. *And I won't tell them a bloody thing about the way it actually is: very few clear answers, but a whole new world of questions.*

He hears her weeping again as he climbs up the back stairs. Finds her hunched on the top step, face hidden in her hands. Drew sits beside her, and the child automatically cradles herself inside his arm. She points down the steps.

Foh...

What?

Wiping away the dim recollection of tears, she points downward again, looking up at him to make it right again.

Father? Did Derek sometimes visit her surreptitiously by way of these—

Foh.

No. Something bad.

Foh.

And then Drew understands.

A fall. That's how she died.

Yes, of course. He almost broke his own neck on the damned back stairs. Perhaps Emily left the door open for a short errand. *Or—*

Somewhere in the darkness, it happened, and afterwards there was only loneliness and Emily never came back.

Uml?

Rising, the child starts to repeat her endless search in familiar rooms, stopping at a picture to cry and howl with rage, yearning for a doll she can never hug again . . . but mercifully, Drew stops her. *That much I can do, anyway.* Like the child, he has forgotten his way back. Logical perhaps, but no longer important. More to the point—and tremendously exciting—he *does* remember the way out of Aubrey House.

Once more, Drew lifts the little girl. In the sure strength of his arms, her weight is slight and precious.

Miss Aubrey, I think it's time to go.

Uml?

We'll see.

He carries her downstairs at long last, all the way to the first floor.

That's the front door, lass. Not sure what we'll find on the other side . . .

But the possibilities fascinate Drew Beltane.

CHARLOTTE'S KIN

■

Because it was Sunday, Charles only succeeded in reaching Dr. Lichinsky's message pickup service, but they reassured him they'd get through to the psychiatrist as soon as possible. He hung up and checked the time: one-thirty. He hoped Sam wasn't just about to sit down to a big family dinner.

Feeling flushed and a trifle gouty from his overindulgence of wine, Singleton wobbled and puffed his way upstairs. Though there was a water closet on the first floor off the mud room, it was chilly out there, and he preferred to relieve his overtaxed bladder in his own bathroom. *Odd how territorial one becomes about one's toilet when away from home*. He did his ponderous best to tread softly past Drew's closed door. *Let him sleep*. He wondered again what, if anything, had passed between Beltane and Vita. *The numb way he just looked at her there on the bed*. He himself had shed tears, though a small part of him wondered whether that wasn't too facile and convenient an outlet. It would be long weeks and months of little pangs before he fully comprehended how sad life would be without Vita. *They say a friend's death is the most forceful way to be reminded of one's own mortality. You really mourn the loss of part of yourself.*

Downstairs, the telephone rang. Cursing Merlyn's differential frugality that limited Aubrey House to a single phone without extensions, Charles hurried out of his room. Just before he reached the head of the stairs, a peculiar sense of presence momentarily stopped him—as if Drew were in the hall with him, and not asleep in his room. Then the phone rang again, and Charles lurched downstairs with an alarming lack of coordination. Somehow he managed to reach the living room in one working piece.

"Sam? Bless you for calling back so quickly."

239

"Charles, my service says you told them it's an emergency." Lichinsky sounded drily skeptical.

"It's not me, Sam, it's Merlyn."

A sharp intake of breath. "What's wrong with her? What did she do?"

Strange thing to ask. Charles related the grim events of the past two days. Judging by the exclamation he heard, Lichinsky was shocked by the news of Vita's mental collapse and death. When Singleton was finished, the doctor said, "Look, I'm going to get into my car and start right now for Bucks County General. Call them so they'll know I'm coming, and for God's sake, Charles, don't let them release Merlyn before I arrive."

"Thanks, Sam. I'll call them immediately." Charles rang off, got the number from Information, and soon was talking to the same nurse who'd phoned him shortly before. She assured Singleton that Lichinsky's wishes would be respected.

"Good," Charles said. "Dick Creighton ought to be arriving there any minute. Will you apprise him of the situation?"

"Certainly."

Charles put down the receiver. Feeling short of breath, he unbuttoned his collar as he slowly remounted the stairs. Lack of sleep was catching up with him. *Drew had the right idea: mere oblivion*. Which, after all, wasn't so very far removed from what Richard advocated: expunging the past entirely. The difference was purely quantitative—either a few hours of rest while the body repaired large and small agglomerations of cells of cryptic design, *health the ultimate opiate*, or the lifelong policy of obliterating crippling memories. It had a seductive allure, hamstrung as he was between horrors he could not change, sorrows that sooner or later were bound to come. *Bracketed by ghosts*.

He pushed the door to his bedroom open and entered the tapestry-shrouded chamber. Time to lie down when he began to feel his convictions slipping—an all-too-familiar sensation. Charles had a propensity for being swayed by authority figures. *Ironic when that's what I'm supposed to be, Oracle of the Great Beyond.*

Charles kicked off his shoes, plucked the burgundy quilt free of the bolster and slid between the sheets, still tormented by what Richard had said. He could not help envying Creighton's absolute self-assurance . . . every abstruse fragment fitted into a philosophic mosaic whose design Charles could only dimly intuit. Not that he could for a moment seriously accept the cold geometry of the other's cosmology, but at least Richard had reached his conclusions without the intermediary interpretation of an unfeeling orthodoxy.

What a blessing it must be to be sure of things, like Dick. An end to posing. Or just an end.

When the doorbell rang, Singleton had been asleep for nearly two-and-a-half hours. He woke with a dull headache. Glaring groggily at his watch, he saw it was twenty past four. Probably too soon for Richard or Sam.

He shuffled stocking-footed downstairs, his clothes rumpled from sleeping in them. Whoever was outside had stopped ringing the bell in favor of pounding on the door. The noise aggravated Charles' headache. He flung the door wide, prepared to utter a tart comment, but his indignation died when he saw two strangers on the porch. One was a uniformed policeman well over six feet tall. The other—a large, burly man in brown suit, vest and wide tie—had a pair of ice-cold gray eyes, a squashed nose mottled with small red veins, jowls and a pair of moist, everted lips that reminded Singleton of a person eating a piece of fresh fruit.

The plainclothesman flashed an open billfold containing an ID card, photograph and badge. He was certainly far different from any sheriff Charles might have conjured up in his imagination, stocked as it was by leftover images from films and televison. His name was Harry Armbruster.

"Mr. Singleton," he said, "I need to ask you a few questions concerning the late Mrs. Henry."

"Very well. Come in, please."

Charles took them to the salon. He sat, but the sheriff

stood by the piano. The uniformed officer took up a position in the entrance arch, legs widespread, arms akimbo.

"Mr. Singleton," said Armbruster, flipping open a small notepad, "this is more or less a routine inquiry. Any case involving an unusual death comes under my purview. Now according to my information, you were the first to find Mrs. Henry last night." His voice was midway between wheedling and a whine, but Charles did not for a moment believe the sheriff's visit to be a casual one.

Singleton explained about Merlyn's accident. "I drove her to the hospital. Dr. Creighton—he's another one of Miss Aubrey's guests—was with us. The emergency room was very busy because of the storm and all the accidents. The three of us didn't get back till very late."

Pencil poised, Armbruster asked Singleton if he could fix the time precisely.

"About one a.m. Perhaps two or three minutes before the hour."

"Go on."

"Dr. Creighton came into this room with Miss Aubrey to have a drink. I went upstairs, passed Mrs. Henry's room and noticed her door slightly ajar. I decided to look in on her, and . . . well, I found her."

"How long was that after you entered the house?"

"No more than a minute or two." Charles shuddered. "I'm afraid I screamed. That's when the others came."

"What others? Miss Aubrey and Dr. Creighton?"

"Also Mr. Beltane."

"That would be Mr. Drew Beltane?"

Charles nodded, disturbed that the sheriff already seemed to know their names. *Why?*

Armbruster's thick lips compressed. Charles wished he would avail himself of a handkerchief and blot them. "Mr. Singleton, was Beltane in the house with Mrs. Henry while the three of you were at the hospital?"

"Well, yes, he was," he reluctantly replied, realizing it was Drew that Armbruster was most interested in, "however—"

"Where was he when you returned at one a.m.?"

"Presumably in bed."

"Presumably?"

"Well, when I cried out, he came from his bedroom. I don't know if he was asleep at the time."

"Now let me understand this," the sheriff persisted. "You say he came from his bedroom. You mean, you looked into the hall and saw Beltane emerging from his room?"

Charles cursed himself. *Right into the trap.* "No," he said unwillingly, "Drew entered Mrs. Henry's bedroom by way of a connecting door. Their rooms adjoin."

Armbruster closed his notebook. "Right. Is Beltane here now?"

"He's upstairs sleeping."

"You'd better wake him."

"Can't it wait till this evening? We're all quite exhausted. I might add that Mr. Beltane's health is rather frail."

"Get him down here."

"But it's preposterous to suspect Drew of anything."

"Did I say anything about him being under suspicion?"

"One needn't be an intellectual giant to see you want to blame him for that dreadful thing that happened to Vita. Believe me, it's really quite impossible."

"Is it?" Armbruster wet his flabby lips. "Maybe you can offer me another explanation for an apparently normal, healthy woman dying of shock? She was alone in the house with only one man, and the autopsy shows traces of semen in her vagina. Now, Mr. Singleton, if you'd rather not disturb Beltane, I'll go up and get him myself."

"N-no," Charles stammered, "I . . . I'll get him for you."

o thank you god
Silence.
A horrible rattling in her throat.
And Charlotte's eyes glaze over.
yes child
no god no i want to be me make me be
beautiful, child, you'll be beautiful like me
Her fierce eyes.
you
Laboring breath, sucking in just enough life to make the
old machinery spin one more revolution.
you
Fierce eyes, like an angry owl's, fixing her. Suffers the
pain, Merlyn, wincing, says nothing, cutting her skin, nails,
fingers gripping her thin wrist, frail hand surprisingly strong.
come closer
yes, gramma
merlyn?
Only the idea of her, not seeing her, uncomprehending,
they turn full on her.
here, gramma
where? can't see you
Old owl eyes stare emptily at the ceiling.
yes'm
you, child?
Alluring, calling only eyes, faces bashful insincere over
held fans Japanese like room Charlotte's windows obscure
curtains lace semiparted streams sun morning.

please go see her now right away
but daddy

Through her closed eyelids, Merlyn sensed the dim glow
of the bedside lamp. She rose gradually through deep layers

of semiconsciousness, the purposeful hushed activities in the hall outside nudging her this way and that like warm surf gently lapping the salt-caked shingle of her life.

When she opened her eyes and adjusted to the soft light, Merlyn remembered everything: Vita's death, her own uncontrollable rage, the screams of the man she attacked, hands prizing hers away from his head, the stab of the sedating needle and all things slowing down to a lugubrious parody of life, asking for Richard to come, and that was all she remembered till now.

"Welcome back, Merlyn."

It was an effort even to think about turning her head. There was an ache in her temples, and her cheek itched where the broken jug had cut it. But the sound of Richard's voice near her made Merlyn feel better. She wanted to rest on its comforting masculinity, wrapping it round her like a warm robe.

"H-hello." Her throat felt clogged. "Have I been out long?"

"A while. It's nearly five o'clock. How do you feel?"

"Probably only twice as bad as I look."

"You look only half as lovely as usual."

"Don't, Richard. What I really want is . . . to be like St. Bridget."

"Who?"

"The one who disfigured herself."

"Merlyn, please. Life's not quite that bleak."

"You're an odd one to say so." With an effort of will, she wearily shifted her head so she could see him. There was something subtly different in the way he looked back at her; his long angular face, usually so grave, reflected an unfamiliar composure.

you must be very quiet and very polite and don't say anything unless she asks you to

  but daddy

"I stayed with her, Richard. With what was left of her."

"I know. The nurse told me."

"I made a decision then, while I was sitting by her bed-

side. I'm going to sell the house. I want nothing more to
do with it."

"But you've got people coming on Tuesday."

"Oh, shit, I forgot! Well, they're going to be the last.
The cleaning crew comes tomorrow. I'll deal with them,
and then that's it, we can all leave for New York by noon.
Wish I didn't have to spend another night there."

"Look, don't try to decide anything now, you're in no
shape to make big decisions." He took her hand in his.
"Whether you stay at Aubrey or not, you have to consider
that it's a major portion of your income. Don't throw it
away on a whim."

"You call what happened to Vita a whim?"

"No, that was a tragedy. But we can't assume Aubrey
House made it happen."

"Oh, Christ, Richard, it's Charlotte, can't you understand
that *even now?* She's malignant, and I loathe her, and if I
have to, I'll burn the fucking place down—if it'll only get
that bitch out of my life once and for all."

"Merlyn, listen to me a minute. That's no way to destroy
Charlotte." He gently disengaged his hand. "I don't believe
there's anything intrinsically good or bad about a pile of
bricks, wood and stone. It's the memories your house holds
for you that are malignant. By all means, let's go back to
New York, but find a way to get rid of the past without—"

me?

she wants to talk to you right away

"—and I've been living in a vacuum for the past month,
paperwork piling up, insurance forms I couldn't face. I
couldn't even go to the garage and look at the car, let alone
drive it. But when the nurse called and Charlie was too
drunk, I had to get behind the wheel."

thank you god

very soon

thank you god

"—sn't easy. Toughest five miles I've—"

very soon

thank you god

Richard rose to his feet. "There's someone outside who wants to see you, Merlyn. Are you up to a visitor?"

"Who? Charlie?"

"No. It's a friend who drove in all the way from New York. Charlie called him."

A wan smile. "Sam Lichinsky?"

"Uh-huh. Do you mind?"

yes daddy

"No. I need to talk to him."

5:07 p.m.

Back and forth, back and forth, Richard Creighton paces the confines of the hospital waiting room, 20 by 30. Drab pale-green walls, plastic green chairs, green ashtrays, tattered out-of-date periodicals bound in green leatherette holders. Nothing to delight the eye, engage the mind. Limbo. An antechamber for the anxious, depot for depressing news.

Lighting the last of a pack of cigarettes he purchased barely an hour earlier, Creighton inhales deeply, breathes smoke as he flicks away the match and continues his aimless prowling.

—Lichinsky's likable enough.

Minimally competent?

—Too soon for a verdict. Condition of the patient not necessarily prejudicial to the caliber of the physician. At least he cares enough to drive out of state on a Sunday.

A stout nurse enters the room and beckons to Creighton.

"Yes?" he asks, approaching her. "Is Dr. Lichinsky done already?"

"No. You have a phone call."

He follows her out of the waiting room and across the hall to the nurses' station. Promising her that he won't tie up the line too long, he picks up the receiver and discovers an agitated Charles Singleton on the other end.

"Dick, it's me. How . . . how's Merlyn?"

"All right, I suppose. Lichinsky's in with her now. I expect we'll be here a while longer. How's Drew? Still sleeping?"

An unaccountable silence. Creighton experiences a sudden awful premonition.

"Richard," Charles says at last, "I . . . I have bad news about Drew."

Creighton forgets to breathe. "Drew?" he repeats in a husky whisper. "What's the matter?"

248

"He's dead."

A long pause.

"Dick . . . are you there?"

An even longer pause while Creighton clamps his customary iron control over his deepest feelings.

"Dick?"

"Yes, I'm still on the line, Charlie. How did he die? Like Vita?"

"No. He looked quite peaceful, actually. At first, I thought he was still asleep."

A sudden flare of hope. "Charlie, could you be mistaken? I mean, if Drew were in a deep trance or a coma—"

"No, Richard, he's gone," Singleton answers with leaden finality. "But that's not all I have to tell you."

—Jesus, there's *more?*

"A short while ago, Dick, a rather brusque sheriff named Armbruster arrived at the house."

"I've met him."

"You have? How?"

"He was here at the hospital trying to bull his way into Merlyn's room. When that didn't work, he badgered me for ten or fifteen minutes, trying to make some kind of a case out of Drew raping Vita. The man's an ass."

"Or thereabouts," Singleton sourly agrees. "I thought that once he met Drew, he'd realize just how absurd it was to imagine him overpowering Vita. So I went upstairs to fetch him, and . . . well, that's when I found him."

"How did Armbruster react?"

"The bloody fool's convinced that Drew committed suicide, presumably out of remorse or perhaps shame."

"He said that?"

"No, Richard, he didn't have to. I overheard the sheriff on the telephone instructing his forensic people to come for Drew's body. I imagine he expects they'll discover poison in his stomach or something similarly Florentine. My God, Richard, what if the newspapers pick up on this? They'll positively ruin Drew's reputation."

—You mean his memory.

"Charlie, calm yourself. It won't help any if you get sick over this. We'll have to find some way to take care of Armbruster. Look, did he give you any kind of clue as to what he's trying to base his case on?"

"Yes, he did. I'm reluctant to repeat it. It was their business, no one else's. Do you recall that I speculated on whether or not Vita and Drew had become lovers?"

"Yes."

"Well, the autopsy confirmed it."

Creighton is surprised to find he can still be shocked.

—Well, Charlie can't always be wrong. Law of averages.

"There's one other thing," Singleton adds. "Armbruster had his man poke into Drew's things and Vita's room . . ."

"And you just *let* him?"

"Richard, we're talking about a policeman the size of a Watusi warrior! And what could I have done to prevent it? I'm only a house guest, after all."

"Sorry. You're right, of course. Odds'll get you he didn't have a search warrant. Well, go on."

"They found Drew's missing cane in Vita's closet—you know, the storage space with the old dolls in it."

"Yes. So what in hell does *that* prove?"

"I can only guess that our Sherlockian sheriff thinks Drew used his cane to inflict the cuts Vita had on her thighs."

"Bullshit. He would've fallen on his face trying. And anyway, her nails were bloody. Those wounds were obviously self-inflicted."

"Yes, well, at any rate, Armbruster took the cane along with him."

"Hm. Anything else?"

"No. Fortunately, I wasn't altogether without my wits."

"Meaning what?"

"After I tried to waken Drew and couldn't, I admit I panicked and called for help. But before Armbruster got there, I noticed a pile of notepaper that Drew had written on. The top sheet indicated it was a letter to you. I had a sudden mental flash that Armbruster would confiscate it, thinking it some kind of suicide note. Not that I supposed he'd find anything in it, but I didn't want him carrying it off before we'd had a chance to read it. I just had time before he came into the room to fold up the papers and stuff them in my jacket pocket."

"Good for you. What does it say?"

"I haven't had the opportunity yet to look it over. They only just drove off with Drew's body, and I wanted to call you right away. Should I read it to you now?"

"Better not. One of the nurses is giving me impatient looks to get off this line. I'll see it when I get back to the house—unless you want to take a taxi over to the hospital?"

"I don't feel up to it, Dick. But would you mind if *I* read the letter? I mean, I know it's addressed to you, but—"

"Charlie, it's all right. Go ahead."

"Thank you."

"Look," Creighton says, "I've been thinking . . . maybe we'd better not say anything about Drew to Merlyn, at least not just yet."

"How do you propose to keep it from her? She's going to wonder where he is."

"Maybe we can pretend he got a telegram from overseas and had to go back home on an emergency."

"But Richard, surely that clod Armbruster will spill it when he talks to her."

"Not if Lichinsky forbids him to bother her."

"But by tomorrow, the story is likely to be in the local papers."

"By tomorrow, Charlie, we're going to have Merlyn back in New York. I just don't want her to learn the truth about Drew till she's put distance between herself and that damned house."

Blaming the house?

—The house. Her parents. Charlotte. Especially Charlotte.

Finally subscribing to the theory that it's haunted?

—For Merlyn, it is.

And objectively? After two deaths?

Nothing.

"Well," Singleton dubiously remarks. "I'll certainly co-operate in keeping it from Merlee, but—as Maria Ouspen-skaya might have put it, Dick—'I vish you luck...'"

Hanging up, Creighton bleakly regards the phone, thinks about Drew Beltane, who, five days earlier, he regarded as nothing more than a brilliant if slightly wrongheaded Scottish elf.

And now? Hypocrite lecteur...mon frère?

—Christ, they've all become family. Even poor Charlie.

The heart abhors a vacuum.

Forcing himself away from the subject, Creighton considers Vita's autopsy. It strikes him that Armbruster hurried it along, considering that she died less than four hours earlier.

—Not that it'd take that long to find what he was looking for. But maybe there's something else worth knowing.

Lightning usually leaves scars.

—Pretty unlikely, though, that I could get my hands on the report.

What about Lichinsky?

—True. Vita was his patient, too.

Creighton once more looks at Merlyn's door, wondering how much longer her session with the analyst will go on.

Aubrey House is charged with expectation as young Merlyn wakes that sunny morning in July. Her humid room is already bright with promise. Putting her skinny legs over the side of the bed, she bounces to her feet, heart full of hope. Summer flutters the curtains through her open window. She examines her slim profile wistfully in the looking glass, wondering when her breasts will begin to grow. *Gonna be soon, Lizzy says*.

Already sticky with sweat, Merlyn quickly showers, then dresses in her favorite blue and white frock *just like Dorothy Gale* and hurries downstairs, hoping that the Great Day has at long last arrived. The very air in the front alcove, she thinks, is waiting, suspended, for the Moment of Moments.

In the salon, her mother converses in low tones with an elderly man and woman whom Merlyn thinks she knows, though their backs are turned so she cannot see their faces. She slips quietly past the archway and continues along the hall to the back of the house.

In the kitchen, Liza dishes up her favorite breakfast, shirred eggs in buttered breadcrumb cups, meaty bacon strips curled round each orange yolk, every slice sizzled so long over a low heat that there are hardly any crimps. Merlyn is sure her daddy is in the breakfast nook, but she prefers eating at the kitchen counter on a high stool with Liza to talk to her. Sometimes the large dusky-skinned cook treats her like her own daughter, cradling the twelve-year-old in her arms, crooning about the way it's gonna be when her buds sprout and little boys start to notice how pretty she is, and even though Merlyn finds it hard to believe that any man will ever want to look at her twice, she loves the warm feeling that wraps her like a blanket when Liza cuddles her. Other times, though—when Mama or Charlotte are about— Liza is all business, fretting Merlyn's pleas for attention with stiffly remote frowns.

What's she gonna be today?

"Is gramma getting better?" she asks the cook.

"She's gonna do fine, Little Miss Dollytop. Whether God say come or go, she's gonna do fine. Drink your milk."

"Can't I have chocolate?"

"Your daddy emptied the quart last night. You drink your milk now, you gotta grow strong bones."

"Lizzy, I don't want my bones getting any bigger, my hands are already way too large!"

"Hush now, baby, God don't make mistakes. He give you nice big fingers so's you can do Good Works."

"But are you sure, Lizzy?"

"Sure about what?"

"That God never makes mistakes?"

Waggling her head disapprovingly, Liza begins to frame a reply, but then a footstep sounds in the pantry, and the cook reverts to her expected status of employee. She finds an excuse to go into the sewing room, leaving the kitchen free for Jason Aubrey to talk to his daughter.

Merlyn bends her attention to her food, pretending not to hear her father walking toward her. But when he is directly behind, she turns on her stool and gives him a big smile.

"Are you almost finished your breakfast?" he asks in the soft, expressionless voice he never raises for any reason whatever.

"Yes, daddy."

"Merlyn, you know my mother is very ill."

She tries to keep any trace of betraying emotion from the tone she uses. "Is gramma gonna die, daddy?"

"Well, she's very old."

"But she's sick, too, daddy. I heard the doctor telling Mama it'd only be a matter of time."

"That wasn't meant for your ears, Merlyn."

"I didn't listen on purpose, daddy. But is it true?"

Jason Aubrey sighs. "I'm afraid it is. Your grandmother will die very soon."

O thank you, God!

"She wants to talk to you right away."

"To *me*, daddy?"

"Yes. You must be very quiet and very polite and don't say anything unless she asks you to. Now hurry on up to her room."

"But, daddy—"

"Not now, Merlyn, there isn't enough time. Go on."

but daddy i'm afraid i don't want to die too

Morning sun streams through the semiparted lace curtains that obscure the windows of Charlotte's room like Japanese fans held over insincere bashful faces.

"You . . . child?"

"Yes'm."

The old eyes stare emptily at the ceiling.

"Where? Can't . . . see . . ."

"Here, gramma."

"Mer . . . lyn . . ."

"Yes, gramma."

Charlotte's fierce owl-eyes turn toward Merlyn, but do not see her, only a distorted caricature *not me at all*. Her shriveled parchment hand possesses surprising strength as her bony fingers clasp Merlyn's thin wrist, long nails cutting her skin, bruising tender flesh. The child winces but tries to tolerate the pain *you must be very quiet and very polite and don't say anything unless she asks you to*.

"Growing . . . child?" Charlotte labors to speak but is too weak to do more than gasp isolated syllables. Merlyn begins to feel giddy, her grandmother's intent stare whirling her down to places she never dreamed existed before, while overhead the walls seem to shoot up around her, almost as if she could wear the whole house like a cloak.

A coughing fit racks the old woman. It subsides; she fights to draw in just enough life to force the worn machinery of her body through a few more cycles. Only her grip on Merlyn's wrist remains strong.

i didn't do anything wrong, i didn't go near her dolls again, what does she want, she looks hungry

Thoughts echoing cavernously in the unexplored void of Merlyn's skull. Charlotte's eyes burning like high desert sun.

"You'll . . ."

"What, gramma?"

A ragged exhalation.

". . . beautiful . . ." A whisper, almost an accusation. ". . . beautiful . . . me . . ."

Merlyn suddenly understands. Her lips draw back in protest, but her father's admonition freezes it there. *NO, gramma, me! Merlyn! ME!*

Charlotte's cracked lipstick-crimsoned mouth spreads in a grimace meant to be a smile. The movement causes bits of dry rouge to flake from her hollow cheeks. She tries to speak again, but the only sound to emerge is a faint guttural rattle.

Silence.

Please, God, is she dead now? But how can she be? Her waxy fingers still clutch tighter and tighter; her vacant stare holds the child's fear-filled eyes transfixed; the corded muscles of her stringy throat stretch laterally, widening her mouth to shape the words once more *just like me child just like me.*

Minutes tick sluggishly past. A fly batters itself against the windowscreen, trying to escape into hot July sunlight. The air is thick with lavender. Charlotte's fingers pinch so hard that Merlyn's small hand feels numb *but daddy wants me to be quiet 'cause it's his mama and he hardly ever asks me to do anything but daddy i can't help it daddy too hard i can't help it*

Merlyn whimpers, "Gramma, please let me go, you're hurting me!" But the old woman neither answers nor releases her. The little girl begins to cry, but her tears dry up in sudden terror when Charlotte lifts her head off her pillow and, with a convulsive shudder, jerks hard at Merlyn's trapped hand, yanking the child toward her. Again. Again. Tottering off balance, Merlyn struggles desperately to move back from the wrinkled yawning mouth, now only inches away from hers. The walls surge over them both, impelling Merlyn down, down into the depths of Aubrey House. She shrieks once as she falls, then Charlotte's bloodless gaping lips cover hers.

"And then?" Lichinsky gently prompted. "What happened afterwards?"

"And then I blacked out, Sam, and didn't wake up for a long time. Not for six months. They took me to Europe for treatment." The blonde stared at the ceiling of her room in Bucks County General Hospital. "I didn't learn what happened till a long time later. Jason found me on the floor with my wrist broken, but my grandmother still had hold of me. The handyman had to bring pliers and break four of Charlotte's fingers to get me loose."

click

Resting on the semielliptical side table, the cassette machine began to revolve. From its input socket, the microphone cord trailed along the floor to Charles Singleton's hand. The pudgy medium lay across Richard Creighton's bed with loosened belt and collar, his vest and top trouser button undone. He felt ill with clogged sinuses, a knot in his stomach and a sour taste in his mouth from a recent bout of sickness. He suspected he was running a slight temperature, but his glazed eyes burned with a feverish light as he held the microphone close to his lips and spoke into it.

"Richard, I've taken one of the new, unopened tapes, so don't worry that I've erased anything you need. I'm sorry to enter your room unbidden and use your recorder without first asking permission, but I've had a terrible new insight into Aubrey House and I feel I must share it with you. I . . . I simply haven't the stamina to write it all out on paper. Nor the time." He checked his watch. "Right now, it's shortly before six, not even an hour since I called and told you that Drew died. I don't suppose you'll be getting back here for a while yet, but just to be sure, as soon as I'm finished taping, I intend to run an experiment upstairs in Shipperton's old room. In order for it to be valid, I must be alone in the house while doing it.

"Frankly, Dick, I hope it fails. Had Drew proposed this theory to me a few days ago, I'm sure I should have swiftly rejected it. But in this dreadful place, the most godless things begin to seem possible to me."

Singleton paused to reach for the newly opened quart of sherry on the floor next to his legs. Puffing with the effort, he took a long drink directly from the bottle, smacked his lips and continued.

"I've left Drew's memoranda for you on the top of your

dresser. When I stuck them in my pocket, I didn't realize there were actually a few things in the pile. There's a ghastly little footnote to the Charlotte-Emily problem, but I leave that for you without comment, and then there's the letter he meant for you. It states that he utilized the out-of-body experience to track down the cold blue light. He claims it's Charlotte. There's also a brilliant suggestion concerning Phyllis Burton's last diary entry. Drew says the spirit is 'lower' and 'deeper' because it exists at the id level. Interesting inasmuch as the presence may be that of a child who probably did not live long enough to develop much of a superego.

"But what chiefly triggered me was the sheaf of notes I read concerning Vita. Drew had a long talk with her the other night and learned she'd been seeing and hearing things at Aubrey vastly different from what anyone else ever reported.

"According to Drew's notes, Vita repeatedly heard the phone ringing and saw the unknown spirit intercepting calls she felt sure were meant for her. Now Vita told me on several occasions about a young man with whom she had been in love many years ago. Her parents disapproved of the match, but he asked Vita to run away and marry him. She almost did, but in the end her parents browbeat her into saying no. He telephoned her several times one night, but her entire family was on hand 'to keep her from making a great mistake.' Anyway, you see the parallel? Drew speculated that whatever psychic energies Vita sensed at Aubrey House were distorted by the memories, wishes and fears of her psyche."

Charles paused for another sip of sherry.

"I find this enormously suggestive, Richard. The thing which has puzzled me the most about Aubrey is the disparity of experiences the five of us have undergone. Vita's catastrophe, Drew's struggle on the rear stairs, the two sides of Merlyn's personality flickering in and out of focus . . . and hardly anything for you or me.

"However, Richard, if one expands on Drew's thesis

concerning Vita, this problem begins to sort itself out. Look at it this way: a nine-volt battery may be employed to operate a portable radio or tape recorder or one of those handheld computer games. The application may differ, yet the source of energy remains . . . constant.

"What if Aubrey House is like that? An enormous psychic battery that may not only be drawn upon by the spirit or spirits that dwell here but by certain living people as well. People whose auras—to use Drew's musical analogy—most closely approximate the house's dominant chord or its harmonics. Who? Merlyn, surely. Olive Masconi. The Falzer team to a lesser extent. Drew and Vita and the Burtons.

"But why did the last ones I mentioned die? If Drew is correct, Vita's mind distorted the energy and magnified her own subconscious needs till her brain short-circuited. How do we know a variation on the same thing didn't happen to Drew? Perhaps Aubrey's like a giant Rorschach, an inkblot rendering back precisely what the investigator thinks he's going to see.

"This is a horrifying notion to me, Dick, contrary to all I've ever believed, yet you suggested something not dissimilar when you spoke at church and said that the people interviewed by Perry were subconsciously programmed by their churches and families and the media to witness the terminal visions they said they experienced beyond clinical death."

Rising unsteadily to his feet, Singleton wiped his florid face with a soiled handkerchief and buttoned his trousers. "Dick," he said into the microphone, "I don't even want to go into the monstrous corollaries that this theory suggests to me. I fervently hope I'll wake up tomorrow and view it as a wild fantasy compounded of grief, shock and too much wine. Meanwhile, however, I plan to conduct the experiment I mentioned. Of course, if I'm not on the house's hypothetical frequency, it will fail. But perhaps my séance did not succeed only because I held it too far away from the part of the house where the energy is strongest . . . where the Aubrey spirit is confined.

"The nature of this experiment, Dick, is that I expect to find Charlotte's daughter in Emily's old room. If I do, it may be because she's really there, or it might be entirely a product of my preconception. The thing is, it would be an entirely different result than what Drew came up with.

"Drew was a brilliant investigator, Dick, but he had flaws. Such as inflexibility on the subject of technique. Going OBE is a dangerous method for probing the spirit world. Not only does it put one on the ghost's own turf, so to speak, but the nature of astral projection is inescapably subjective. Like your hypnagogic state. One leaves the body from a condition of sleep/waking during which ideation grows rather internalized.

"Now who did Drew say he saw in that room? Charlotte Aubrey. He himself admitted puzzlement at finding her in a place that she surely avoided while she was alive. Well he should have been puzzled! Because the only spirit one could possibly expect to find in that room is the remnant of that sad little girl exiled there by Merlyn's wretched grandmother. My guess is that since Drew knew I supported that contention, something inside him wouldn't permit him to accept it, too. He *had* to be the ultimate authority on Aubrey House and its mysteries, and that need may have transformed what he actually saw up there into what his ego *wanted* him to see.

"I'm going upstairs now, Dick. I have to do it alone. The presence of someone else in the house might warp the energy source and make it unavailable to me. All my life I've had difficulty asserting myself in the presence of any really forceful personality. Perhaps the only way Aubrey will speak to me is now while I'm here by myself.

"Tomorrow I may test the house differently, but tonight when I open myself to the presence on the third floor, I fully expect it to be Charlotte's child."

His thumb flicked the remote button on the microphone.
click

* * *

Head reeling, Singleton lurches to the second-floor landing and peers upward, dismayed at the steepness of the
ascent. He sucks in air through pursed lips. His heart pounds
rapidly.

*Steady on now, Charlie. You always fancied yourself an
actor. Remember what they taught you: a good actor must
achieve a certain neutrality.*

With one hand gripping the railing and the other grasping
the thick branch he found that morning in the woods, using
it as a makeshift crutch, Singleton starts up the stairs but
after five steps, slumps winded onto one of the treads. Pulse
pounding in the prominent veins to either side and just above
his eyes, Charles attempts to call up strength from some
distant inner landscape and as he does, a cold blue mist at
the foot of the flight twists like a phantom glimpsed in the
skyward-curling smoke of an opium pipe.

And where are you going, Charlie, boyo?

—Drew?

Perhaps.

—I'm going up to Emily's room to hold a séance.

*Why? Didn't you read the notes? It's Charlotte. No one
else.*

—I might see her. But I don't think so. I expect it will
be that poor child. And tomorrow, I might summon the
Ghost of Christmas Past.

Tch. Such a bleak notion, Charlie. Sterile. Agnostic.

—I can't understand why God permits the things that
happen in this house.

Call up your mythical roommate Angelo and ask him.

—Angelo? He doesn't exist. And no one knows that but
me.

Right, Charlie.

Silence. Fingers of mist trail up the staircase, shaping
nothing but themselves.

Face flushed and feeling giddy, Charles hauls himself
up two more steps, then two more. His temples throb. He
wants to stop and rest again, but forces himself to peg the
final distance to the landing and across the hall in search
of Charlotte's kin.

Singleton enters the old room, puts down the stick and squats by it, assuming a semi-Lotus posture on the floor. A moment of deep breathing.

"Charlotte Aubrey's child? Let me help you."

As his chin sinks onto his breast and he slips from calm consciousness to trance, the chamber grows colder. The small half-circular window is nearly dark. The faint blue afterglow seems to thicken as Charles thinks about the sad little child whose own mother was incapable of offering needed security and love *but Papa was hardly ever home* and it was so hard to remember what he looked like—a short, trim man with a fierce mustache—but Mama was large and vivid with that white-hot glowing V slashing a double angle down her forehead just before she smacked him when he made any of a million mistakes, he couldn't help doing wrong, Mama's rules changed with her moods, but when Papa comes home he'll punish Mama, he always does, and so will I, I'll go downstairs and hurt her, no I mustn't Emily says no I can't go downstairs not ever no but yes I'll hurt Mama I will downstairs yes downstairs yes downstairs hurt Mama downstairs *yes*

Rising from the floor, fists choking the shaft of the gnarled branch, the inner child lurches through the door, face mottled with primal rage.

The thick acrid odor of institutional cooking assailed Sam Lichinsky's nostrils as he emerged from his session with Merlyn and crossed the hospital corridor to the drab waiting room. Upon seeing him, Richard Creighton rose, but the doctor gestured for him to resume his seat and took the chair beside him.

"Merlyn's getting dressed now," Lichinsky said. "I'd rather she remain here tonight, but she says no, she wants to be ready for the cleaning people tomorrow. She can be quite a strong-willed young woman when she wants to be."

"*Les mots justes,*" Creighton nodded. "What about a motel?"

"She vetoed that suggestion too."

"Well, how do you feel about her returning to Aubrey House tonight? Is it really dangerous for her, do you think?"

Lichinsky's homely features drew downward. "I'd just as soon see her out of there altogether. I've been worried about her. I didn't want her coming here in the first place. It's no pleasure to find out my fears were justified."

"Fears about what? The house?"

Lichinsky wearily nodded. "It seems to kick off everything destructive within her. But since she won't have it otherwise, I'll come along with you and make sure she's settled in peacefully for the night. I may sedate her. Then I've got to drive home myself. I have a full caseload tomorrow."

"It was good of you," said Creighton, "to come all this distance, especially on your day off."

"Day off?" The doctor laughed ruefully. "That's an occupational illusion."

"Look, Sam, before Merlyn comes out here, there's some bad news I'd better tell you. And I've got a favor to ask . . ."

* * *

On his way down in the elevator by himself, Lichinsky mused over his breakthrough with Merlyn. Though her hatred and horror of her grandmother Charlotte undoubtedly went farther back than the hideous morning of the old woman's death, the trauma of twelve-year-old Merlyn's experience that day made things immeasurably worse. It defined those contradictory personality swings she was subject to: by becoming a little girl, she escaped that empty womanhood she equated with her useless beautiful grandmother, but the regression interfered with her sense of Self, engendering the need for an opposite move toward accepting her role as a lovely, eligible young woman. Which in turn brought her too near Charlotte . . . and the pendulum swept back in the other direction. Along the way she encountered a succession of older lovers, men most likely unaware of their need for emotional scourging, something Merlyn was only too ready to satisfy—wanting daddy to protect her but determined to punish him for sending her off to her ordeal with her dying grandmother.

And behind it all loomed the house itself, a symbol of haunted, inescapable Fate. Charlotte's grisly death-kiss surely was caused by an early onset of *rigor mortis,* the condition hastened by the heat of that long-ago July morning. Merlyn even admitted that explanation occurred to her in the intervening years, and yet she still believed Charlotte's ghost waited for her in her childhood home. And somehow caused Vita Henry's death. *Creighton's right, she'll be better off if we can avoid telling her about the Beltane chap.*

The elevator car jerked to a halt at the basement level. Lichinsky got out and followed the directions the nurse had given him: left along the hall through an unmarked double steel door. The temperature suddenly grew perceptibly colder.

He found the office he was looking for and made his request.

After a subdued dinner in town with Merlyn and Richard, Lichinsky followed them as they drove in the rented Rolls a few miles into the country. It wasn't long before both vehicles pulled up in the driveway of Aubrey House.

It was too dark for him to get more than the vaguest impression of great size surrounded by rolling lawn, but when he entered the foyer, Lichinsky was impressed by the sheer scale of the house.

His blonde patient invited her analyst into the living room and somewhat shyly offered him coffee and brandy. *Disconcerted with having to deal with me socially*, he thought. *Especially here in the eye of the storm.*

"Coffee will be fine," he told her, "but I'd better skip the brandy. I've a long drive ahead. May I use your phone?"

"Help yourself, Sam. It's on the piano."

She exited toward the rear of the house and Lichinsky made a call to his wife, assuring her he ought to be home around 11 p.m. He hung up and waited for the operator to call back with the charges.

Creighton murmured, "Were you able to get a look at Vita's autopsy report?"

"A hurried glance, yes. She suffered a devastating systemic shock. As violent as if she'd been struck by lightning. Massive cortical damage—"

The telephone rang. Excusing himself, Lichinsky picked it up, listened, made a note of the cost of his long-distance call so he could deduct the amount from Merlyn's next bill.

As he was hanging up, Merlyn reappeared with a silver tray laden with linen napkins, silverware, matching coffee pot, cream and sugar containers, all of the most exquisite craftsmanship. She poured coffee for the two men and set down a snifter of cognac for Creighton but took nothing for herself.

"Sam," she said, "if you'll excuse me, I'm going to get comfortable in a robe and slippers. Also, I thought I'd check in on Charles and Drew, they may want to come down and say hello."

Creighton, exchanging a glance with the doctor, stammered, "Uh, Merlyn, I . . . uh, I didn't have time to tell you . . . Drew had to leave . . ."

She frowned. "Just like that? Why?"

"I...I don't know the details. I was at the hospital. Charlie mentioned Drew got a telegram, sent his regrets and split."

"Must've been an emergency to get him away from here," Merlyn observed. "Well, he always was abrupt...Sam, you will wait till I come back downstairs, won't you?"

Lichinsky nodded. "You won't be long?"

"Ten minutes." She left the room and started toward the second floor. As soon as she was out of earshot, Creighton urged the doctor to continue.

"The autopsy? Right. As I said, there was tremendous cortical damage, practically total disintegration. A complete absence of amino acids in her brain cells, and the medulla— *good God!*" Almost dropping his coffee cup, Lichinsky spun toward the stairs and the howl of dismay and anger coming from the top of the flight.

"Merlyn!" Creighton shouted, dashing out of the room. Lichinsky hurried behind as the other took the steps two at a time.

Merlyn stood at the rear of the second-floor corridor wringing her hands by the large photograph of her grandmother. The girl's face was wax-white. Tears streamed down her cheeks as she clawed back a lock of hair with a convulsive motion of her hand.

"Look what he did!" she moaned. *"Look what he did!"*

The facing of Charlotte's picture was shattered and sharp fragments of glass lay strewn on the carpet. The photo itself was puckered and torn from a series of savage blows and there was one great lateral slash across the temples. The enigmatic expression in Charlotte Aubrey's eyes would never again puzzle anyone.

In her grief, Merlyn paid no attention at all to the crumpled figure of Charles Singleton sprawled on the rug near the photo. One of his hands still clutched the broken shaft of the tree branch. The upper portion lay a few feet off.

"Get her out of here," Lichinsky ordered, kneeling down beside Singleton, reaching for his pulse.

Creighton obeyed, struggling Merlyn away from the damaged picture. Just before he entered her bedroom with her, he looked back and saw Lichinsky raising one of Charles' legs in the air. It fell limply to the floor.

A little less than ten minutes later, Merlyn Aubrey lay on top of her silken bedspread, head propped up by several soft pillows. She stared vacantly into space.

Oh God, let it end. Burn down this fucking place and end it.

Richard Creighton opened the door and came in. Placing a hypodermic and a small packet of pills on the nightstand, he sat on the bed next to Merlyn and gently stroked her uninjured cheek with the back of his hand.

"Sam took Charlie to the hospital. Faster than waiting for an ambulance. I called ahead and alerted emergency and the ICU. Sam thinks it's a stroke."

"He'll die, too," she murmured apathetically. "I killed my two best friends, bringing them here."

"That's not true, Merlyn. You had nothing to do with Vita's death. And Sam says Charlie has a fighting chance."

A flicker of interest. "How soon will there be any word?"

"Not long," Creighton replied. "Sam said he'd call as soon as he knows something. He left you a sedative. If you don't know how to inject yourself, I can do it for you. There are also a couple of tranquilizers for tomorrow."

"Tomorrow?"

"When we go back to Manhattan. I told Sam I'd take you straight to his office."

The father figures are out in force.

"I'm not at all sure I'm going to leave, Richard."

"You've *got* to be kidding!"

"If I'd only done what Charlotte wanted me to in the first place and stayed here where I belong, maybe none of this would have happened. This *is* my home."

"It's just a house," he argued, pressing one of her hands between his. "Listen to me, Merlyn. Charlotte's dead, and so's your past. You can't touch yesterday or make any piece of it return. I finally reminded myself of that when I drove to the hospital to be with you. I mean, it doesn't matter a whole lot whether or not I feel guilty about my family's death, it still won't bring them back."

A sardonic smile tugged at her lips. "'The moving finger writes, and having writ, moves on and does not give a shit.'"

Creighton couldn't help chuckling. "One way to sum up the workings of Fate. Anyway, tomorrow I'll take you back to New York and we can try to put our lives together again."

She shrugged. "Mine was never together in the first place. Maybe I'd better come with you, though . . . someone ought to get Vita's cat out of the kennel."

"Cut it out," he snapped. "I'm really tired of your elaborate defeatism. It's a convenient copout. If you want things to matter, you have to work at it."

"Says the expert. Look, Dr. C., you can spare me the 'life is worth living' bullshit. Such as it is, dear heart, I've tried to make my life work, as you put it, but all I've ever done is screw up royally. I flunked out of grad school, lost every job I landed. Never met a man I didn't end up hurting. You can't convince me that the world's a better place because I'm in it."

Still holding her hand, Creighton gave Merlyn a wintry smile. "I wouldn't even try to. The world could care less. But there's always a choice—only you have to supply your own reasons."

She took away her hand and abruptly changed the subject. "What really happened to Drew, Richard?"

He hesitated one telltale second. "I . . . I told you all I know about it."

"You're not telling me the truth. I saw the way you and Sam looked at each other when I mentioned Drew's name earlier."

Creighton tenderly pushed away a strand of yellow hair from her forehead. "I thought you weren't going to call me a liar any more."

Before she could respond, the phone rang.

"I'll be right back," he said, quickly retreating.

Merlyn waited for his footsteps to die away down the stairs. Then she got out of bed and, slipping into the hall, turned right and entered Drew's room.

At first glance, it seemed empty, vacated. And then she noticed his shoes peeking out partway beneath the bed. She opened the armoire and saw his clothing hanging up. In the drawers were extra socks, shirts, handkerchiefs.

My God, he's dead, too.

She returned to her room, angry at Richard for trying to "protect" her. For a moment, she thought about locking both her doors, but then another idea occurred to her.

Picking up the hypodermic from her nightstand, she took it into the bathroom and emptied its contents down the toilet.

"Hello?"

"Richard, it's Sam Lichinsky. I got Charles into the hands of the ICU staff."

"What are his chances? Or is it too soon to tell?"

"Yes, it's a little early, though the feeling here is fairly optimistic that he'll come to in a few hours."

"Was it a stroke?"

"I'd say so. On the right side of his brain, so there'll be paralysis on his left side—impossible to tell at this stage to what extent—but his speech won't be affected. Naturally, there'll be the prospect of therapy, but again it's speculation at this point. The next few hours are crucial."

"Are you going to wait there till he comes to?"

"I really can't, Dick—I've got to get on the road. But as soon as Charles is up to it, if he wants I could have him transferred to Doctors Hospital on East End."

"You mean he's your patient, too?"

"Privileged information, Dick. Don't mention anything to Merlyn about what I just said, all right?"

"I won't say a word."

"Speaking of Merlyn, how's she holding up?"

"Not as good as she might. She's asking questions about Drew."

"Have you sedated her?"

"Not yet."

"Do it at once. Stay with her till you're sure she's asleep. I'll expect her in my office tomorrow."

"She'll be there, Sam. Good night."

Hanging up the phone, Creighton thinks about what he has heard as he returns to the second floor. Singleton, with his excess weight and nervousness and the way he was drinking that afternoon surely was headed toward trouble, but what ever possessed him to smash the picture of Charlotte Aubrey? The exertion probably was the last link in the chain of circumstances leading to his stroke. Had he begun to succumb to whatever killed Drew and Vita?

Coming around to the opinion that there's something here to succumb to?

—Nothing so positive as that. Just wondering.

?

—Whether Charlie's stroke actually saved his life. Assuming there *is* a force at Aubrey inimical to certain mental states—capable of eradicating cognition—maybe the immediate catastrophe of apoplectic hemorrhage served Charlie as a cut-off.

Equating Aubrey energy with electrochemical imprint of individual brain patterns?

—Negative to positive. Aubrey may beam opposite frequency, invoking morbid electrolysis.

Basis?

—Vita's state of shock. Absence of amino acids in her brain. Devastating protein decomposition.

But Charlie claimed Drew looked peaceful.

—Two possibilities: A. Gradual onset of Aubrey effect reduces extent of trauma, or B. Drew blocked out total impact by some form of overriding natural death-wish.

Corollaries?

—Not now. Look at Merlyn.

He stares through the open doorway at the young woman, now undressed and prone upon her bed. She wears nothing but a filmy blue robe that covers without concealing the graceful contours of her naked flesh.

"Merlyn?"

No answer. Approaching, he sees that her eyes are closed. Merlyn's breath is deep and regular. Resting at her side on the silk coverlet is the hypodermic. Creighton picks it up. Empty.

—Powerful dose Lichinsky concocted.

He tosses the used needle in the wastebasket and switches off Merlyn's table lamp. The room goes dark, save for the spill of light through the open hall door.

Her uninjured cheek presses into the pile of downy pillows, her scarred side exposed to Creighton's stare. He savors the dim silhouette of her features, exquisite to him even in disfigurement. His eyes linger on the smooth, inviting curves of her neck and back and hips. The illumination from the corridor slants across her legs and buttocks, more effectively concealed now by the refraction of the thin garment resting lightly over them. Hesitantly, against his own will, his hand reaches out as if empowered with a separate intelligence; his warm palm gently brushes the hollow of her back and finds it cold.

Afraid to disturb her by working the covers out from under her, he goes to the other side of the bed and, grasping the far edges of the spread and blanket beneath, folds them over Merlyn to roll her in their warmth. She sighs and seems to snuggle deeper into slumber.

Creighton stands a moment more by her side then, leaning over to kiss her forehead, goes out and closes the door behind him.

In his own room, the first thing he sees is the rumpled state of bedclothes he automatically straightened that morning while pursuing Routine amidst tragedy. Then Creighton notices a pile of papers on his dresser.

—Must be Drew's notes. Wonder whether Charlie left any of his own?

On his way to find out, he nearly trips over the microphone cord extending from the bed to the table with the semielliptical top. Creighton snaps open the tape-feed aperture and finds a partially-used cassette inside. He pushes the Rewind button, but nothing happens.

—Damn! The battery's dead again.

Picking up the machine, he carries it into the hall and down the corridor to Drew's room. He enters, finds a socket and plugs it in. Rewind. Play.

click

He hears Singleton's voice. "Richard, I've taken one of the new, unopened tapes, so don't worry..."

—Sounds like he's laboring for breath.

Probably was.

"—what chiefly triggered me was the sheaf of notes I read concerning Vita . . . unknown spirit intercepting the calls she felt sure were meant for her . . . telephoned her several times one night, but her entire family was on hand 'to keep her from making a great mistake.' Anyway, you see the parallel? Drew speculated . . ."

—A crucial parallel. Positively mechanistic mental breakdown. Metaphysical solutions need not apply, after all.

But what kind of breakdown results in such cataclysmic damage?

—I don't know. Not my field.

"I find this enormously suggestive, Richard," Singleton says on the tape. "The thing which has puzzled me the most about Aubrey is the disparity of experiences the five of us have undergone. Vita's catastrophe, Drew's struggle on the rear stairs, the two sides of Merlyn's personality flickering in and out of focus . . . and hardly anything for you or me."

—That's an easy one to explain, Charlie.

But not in mechanistic terms.

—Singleton's dearth of imagination, my lack of involvement.

Either you believe energy field theory or you don't. See-sawing back and forth—

—Only proves I don't know what to think.

The sound of Singleton's taped message begins to fade. Creighton glances at the monitor light, but it still glows. Nothing the matter with the machine.

"However, Richard," Singleton seems to whisper, "if one expands on Drew's thesis concerning Vita, this problem begins to sort itself out. Look at it this way: a nine-volt battery may . . ."

—May *what?*

But the voice merges into the tape surface's background hiss, then disappears altogether. Creighton runs the cassette forward, stops it and presses Play, but hears nothing. He repeats the process several times, but only the soft monotonous whisper emerges from the speaker.

The battery must have gone dead, the way it did before.

—Maybe.

What other explanation?

—The stroke.

Absurd. He never would've made it to Charlotte's picture. And his voice wouldn't've faded out.

—Wonder what Charlie thought he'd hit on and how he hoped to test it?

Drew's notes might suggest something.

—Maybe.

Back in his own room, Creighton takes off shoes, shirt, trousers and dons a dressing gown. He stretches out on top of the bedclothes and, by the light of a reading lamp above his pillow, begins to shuffle through the thick pile of handwritten papers. The chamber is dark, save for the dim bulb just over his head. The connecting door to Merlyn's quarters is, as usual, closed and locked.

He reads the letter Drew addressed to him and finds it both touching and maddening; the former because it brings forcefully home to him how swiftly a deep bond of friendship was forged between him and Drew Beltane; the latter because of the uncritical trust the Scot placed in the so-called out-of-body experience.

—Perfectly exasperating. Granting the possibility of there even being such a thing as genuine "astral projection," how could he hope to be an objective observer during such an event?

He claims it enabled him to find Charlotte.

—It probably enabled him to undergo a fantasy of that character.

Hypnagogia?

—That and a touch of ESP and you probably have the whole OBE phenomenon that mystics gabble about.

A phrase at the end of the letter puzzles him, but he

peruses the Emily Shipperton note next, and the passage becomes clear.

> Now I'm on my way down to meet Charlotte on her own ground, the id level. I have the advantage this time. I've run her energy very low and she won't be able to siphon mine because we'll be on the same plane. By now, she must be scared out of her vacant little mind, probably thinks it's Judgment Day, and she has good reason to fear that event, I'm afraid.

—So Drew thought that Charlotte was capable of murder. Of giving the order to Emily, at least.

Likely?

—No. I see the logic, of course: Charlotte and Derek go away till she has her new baby. Little Jason is mercifully normal. Mama begins to fear for him with a retarded sibling hidden away. Maybe the little girl already showed evidence of a destructive spirit. Shipperton does Madame's will, perhaps an "accident" is arranged. Suddenly Emily moves down to the second floor at an astounding increase in salary.

Objections?

—Charlotte too simpleminded.

Speculation.

—No: Merlyn's testimony. Eyewitness. And Emily never could have done it. Not after raising the child for seven years, virtually its mother.

Maybe she needed the money. Ailing relatives to support?

—Groundless theorizing.

But why did Charlotte move her downstairs?

—Who knows? Perhaps Emily was blackmailing her to keep her first child a secret. Maybe she and Charlotte were lovers. That would fit what we know about Charlotte—not letting her husband near her bed, locking the door, hating men.

Are we discussing Charlotte? Or Merlyn?

—Pure woolgathering. No way of ever knowing the truth about that poor little girl's death.

True. But Emily's move downstairs might've been motivated by something else entirely.

—?
To protect Charlotte from her daughter's ghost.
—Ridiculous.
Then why are you still here at Aubrey House?
—Merlyn.
Ridiculous.
—Sure about that?
Nothing.

Yawning, Creighton turns to the final stack of papers, Drew's report on Vita's midnight caller and its parallel to her lost love. Combined with what he has already heard Singleton say on the tape, the implications of what he is reading dawn on him and Creighton feels a too-familiar leadenness settle on his spirit. He drops the last leaf to the floor with the rest of the papers. His eyes race over the tortuous patterns of garish wallpaper in the small patch revealed by the feeble glow of the reading lamp.

—Ironic. Vita. First to die and yet the first to perceive the possibility. How'd she put it? "Maybe we're all seeing and hearing different things." Charlie probably conceived it, too; must be the idea he hoped would prove incorrect once he ran his test . . . or no, maybe he only caught a piece of it. Hard to imagine him getting it all. Too radical for a man craving the reassurance of godhead.

Specifically?
—That there are no ghosts. Only a need for them.
Just here at Aubrey? Or—
But his weary brain can no longer cope with the problem. Creighton closes his eyes, and the twisted ambiguities of the Aubrey equation vanish down the firetrails of thought. Only the burning image of Merlyn's unclad form lingers, a shadow-puppet flickering on the retina of memory.

Merlyn. In the room with him. No lights left to brighten Aubrey House, but he had no trouble seeing her there, small breasts tipped toward his mouth, the eagerness in her eyes as her tongue licked along lips shaping words he could not make out because the other voice would not stop calling.

daddy . . . daddy . . . I can't find you . . . daddy . . .

Over him, suspended in air, too far away to fold in his arms, the perfect blush of her young skin, the blonde delta of her sex *I shouldn't look* opening for him if he could only reach, but he had to answer someone *who?* I can't come, not now. Errands. Miles to go.

busy Creighton time valuable

Always the same illogical road: what maniac engineer designed it? A steep-banked dirt track hanging precariously over the lip of a ravine, a descending C along the ridge's edge, curving down around a colossal reservoir filling with a storm-lashed flood and only if he could drive fast enough might he clear the valley floor, escape the churning waters threatening to engulf him, truck and all. But to dare the embankment courted almost certain death, plunging over the slope, the sheer weight of the canted rig toppling him into the V-gorge. No time for sober judgment: the dark valley rapidly disappeared beneath the angry deluge. He disengaged the clutch, starting *down all?* wheels spinning in muddy earth, at first slowly then building speed *too fast daddy*

———

Washington Lane was always dangerous in winter. A precipitous hill, worse when frozen over, a car might hurtle to the bottom and straight across the intersection, jumping the traffic light and the way had better be clear in case you couldn't stop, you don't argue with a truck as big as a diesel went from warning to danger to death as Lana frantically pressed the unresponsive brake harder and harder and then the impact as her blood gushed but didn't puddle and his daughter's small head smashed into the windshield creating an abstract spider pattern of shatter waves.

The web broke. Reshifted.

—Now I'm there. Really.

Marla and Lana, daughter-wife, emerge from the car. No blood. Not a scratch on either one. Frozen parody of death. The old familiar accusation on her lips: *you never had time for us, Rich, and now look what you've done.*

"Not me, Lana. I didn't really hit you. I wasn't driving."

oh yes you were daddy

"No, baby. I wasn't driving."

yes you were daddy all the way to the hospital

Richard Creighton wakes. Immediately aware of the different atmosphere, reality versus false waking. His red eyes try to focus on the blotch of hideous tan and yellow wallpaper. He hears a muted hiss, groggily wonders whether he left the tape recorder running, then remembers the battery is dead.

Creighton sits up, sleep suddenly ebbing from his limbs and brain. He blinks his eyes at the wash of light coming through the wide-flung door to Merlyn's bedroom. Turning his head, he stares through the gaping portal but does not see her, not even the flicker of her shadow.

He swings his feet over the side and stands on the cold floorboards in stocking feet. The distant whisper grows slightly louder, resolves into the gurgling of running water.

A moment of hesitation, then Creighton pads softly into Merlyn's room. The gentle glow of the table lamp shows him she is not there. The scent of lavender is stronger than ever.

The *sssss* of flowing water dies away but is immediately replaced by the sound of splashing and the delighted giggles of a happy child. At the far side of the chamber, Merlyn's bathroom door stands ajar. Creighton takes a step toward it. The laughter grows louder.

"*I* know you're out there," she calls, a teasing note in her voice. "Why don't you come on in and play?"

A tingling prickles his spine, but Creighton is too entranced to pay heed. Merlyn calls him again to come in and be with her. He takes one uncertain step at a time, the yellow oblong of the portal beckoning him closer, closer, until at last he stands in the doorway and sees an immense bathroom, easily 20 by 20.

Clouds of steam fill the air, but he is still able to make out the pink and white mosaic of the tiled walls and floor, the translucent rectangle of a stall shower, the gleaming fixtures of washstand, toilet and bidet. His own bathroom has an old-fashioned ball-and-claw tub, but sunken into the floor of Merlyn's is a giant whirlpool, filled now with a rich lather of soap bubbles.

Merlyn splashes suds gleefully into the air. Her bare breasts glisten just above the water line; the rest of her is concealed by the foam. Her hair hangs loosely about her shining, merry face; Creighton sees dimples he never knew she had in her cheeks.

"Doesn't this look like fun?" she asks in high, piping tones.

Mesmerized, he walks into the room and over to the tub. The damp floor soaks through his socks. He peels them off and tosses them negligently aside. Perspiration spangles his forehead as he stands above her amidst the hot vapors.

"You'll get your robe all wet." Chin on hand, Merlyn stares saucily up at him. "You don't need it. Why don't you take it off, then you can sit down next to me and say how pretty I am."

He lays the robe upon a hamper and, wearing nothing now but shorts, curls up on the tiled floor at the rim of the tub. She sprinkles him with hot water, giggling.

"You're wearing your underwear inside out! How silly!"

Creighton grins. "I have to. The elastic band irritates me." His eyes wander over the surfaces of her small body that the suds reveal one moment, hide the next. Merlyn dimples up at him, then turns her mouth into a moue of mock-disapproval.

"Mustn't look at me. Naughty." She scoops up handfuls of lather and decorously forms them around the contours of her breasts. "Am I *really* pretty?"

"Yes, Merlyn, you are." Running his fingers lightly over her unscarred cheek, Creighton leans over and absently kisses the top of her head, but as he does he notices on the other side of the tub, perched on the marble washstand, the grinning rag doll that once was the only toy of Charlotte's unwanted little girl.

daddy pick me up carry me home I don't like it here

Steam wafts ceilingward from the sunken bath. Hunching over, Merlyn hugs her knees together, pinioning them. Her chin rests on her breast as she peers sidewards at Richard. A cunning smile plays upon her lips as she finds an oval cake of soap in the tub. Drawing it slowly between her thighs and over her tummy and around each erect nipple, she holds it on her open palm for him to take.

"Wash my back—please?" she whispers, her tongue flicking in and out of her parted lips as he accepts the smooth moist oval. Her heavy-lidded eyes seek his once more, then she turns her back on him, arching it sensually.

Hot water spills over the rim of the tub, wetting him. He dips the soap beneath the bubble-covered surface, then begins to stroke it over the long undulating S of her spine, up along her back, circling her glistening shoulders and neck and down again to the top of the sparkling froth.

Merlyn's chest rapidly rises and falls. She stands up in the tub, her back toward him. Miniature globes of suds cling to her hips and the tapering of her thin, girlish thighs. "Come into the tub," she murmurs, her voice deeper, huskier than before. "Don't stop."

He steps in. Hot water laps his ankles, bubbles tingle boldly on his naked legs. Merlyn's shoulders arch till they rest against his chest, then she bends back the other way, molding her curves to his. Spellbound by the warmth of her, he lets out his breath in a long, slow sigh as he glides the bar of soap down her backbone, over the swelling rise of her buttocks and along their declivity.

Reaching around behind her, Merlyn captures his hand and guides it to her breasts. He caresses them with the slippery soap, and then she urges his hand downward, her voice a throaty chuckle not at all like a little girl's. "Lower, Richard. Deeper."

The bar slides from his fingers and into the water, but she holds him fast and draws his hand nearer to the center of herself. A long breathless moment, then Merlyn turns and looks mistily into his eyes, her mouth slack with desire. She lowers her gaze and sees the outline of his erection through damp shorts.

An instantaneous change comes over her. With a sudden laugh, the blonde drops playfully to her knees, a grin on her face like some knowing child trembling on the cleft of puberty.

"I've got a secret," she whispers. "Want to guess it?"

He shakes his head. His knees are suddenly feeling weak. One of his arms trembles of its own volition. "Why don't you just tell me what it is, Merlyn?"

She nods mischievously. "You won't repeat it to anyone?"

"Of course not."

"Once I did a bad thing. I took my gramma's dolls out of the closet."

—What's happening to her?

"Merlyn, you told me all about that. You didn't know they were hers."

"No, no, this was another time. I got all of them and lined them up on my gramma's bed. It was a real bad thing. She screamed a lot when she saw them. I swore on her Bible—she made me do it—that it wasn't me."

"And then what happened?"

"Emily put them all back and nailed up the closet. But gramma got real sick. Then they took Emily and she died in a home, daddy told me, and my grandmother went away for a while, too. But she never really got better after that."

Creighton stares at her in mingled horror and compassion. "Merlyn, did you ever tell this to Sam Lichinsky?"

"No. Only to you and once, years after it happened, to my father." With drooping spirits, she slumps into the water till the foam nearly covers her shoulders. "Jason never raised his voice about it, only said very softly that I ought to be ashamed of myself. He hardly ever spoke harshly to me, never spanked me for anything. He just didn't care."

"Maybe he did but had a hard time showing it." Creighton

wades to her side, his passion gone. He draws her head to his chest and fondly strokes her blonde tresses. "Some men can't manage to reconcile their feelings for the ones they love."

"Are you talking about yourself now, Richard? Did you ever let your daughter know how important she was to you? Did you love her enough to spank her?"

"Once or twice."

She brushes her lips against his jaw. "What about me? Do you care enough for me to punish me?"

"I don't think you've done anything wrong."

"Oh, Charlotte would disagree. She knew I did it that morning she died. So now she expects me to replace her."

"Merlyn, cut it out. She's dead. She can't do anything to you."

"Yes, she can. She will."

"No. Tomorrow I'm taking you home to New York and you won't ever have to set foot in Aubrey House any more."

A hopeful light enters her eyes. "Can you *really* make that come true? I want it to happen."

"I promise."

Her sudden laughter is high and shrill as Merlyn abruptly straddles Richard's thighs. She covers his mouth with hers while the rag doll leers down on them sardonically. Creighton does not respond at first, but her darting tongue re-awakens his desire and sheer physical need confuses him as Merlyn fumbles at his shorts, freeing his erect member. With a girlish giggle, she touches the lips of her vagina to the engorged tip of his penis, gently rubs it, then rises from the water, her hips swaying in teasing circles. She repeats the tormenting cycle again and again, bringing their organs into brief contact only to separate them. He raises his hips to meet her downward stroke, but she is too swift for him. Merlyn laughs at his efforts as if they were playing for points and she was winning.

"Merlyn," he begs, feeling giddy, *"please..."*

But she does not tire of the delicious torture. Cheeks flushed, tongue licking the corners of her mouth, Merlyn lowers herself onto him time and again only to move away whenever he thinks he will at last be granted entry. His senses blur into a single mindless need, his pulse is a tide that will not be denied. With one hoarse cough, he grasps her tightly and forces her down onto his straining member. Merlyn utters a single cry of humiliation and rage, then is still. He clutches her buttocks in a paroxysm of lust but ultimately cannot ignore her motionless contempt. His anguished passion dies away within her.

—Where are you, Merlyn?

Where?

She stands up and walks away from him, stepping out of the tub. She drapes a thirsty towel about her body, then turns upon him, her face contorted with an ugly sneer. *"Vite, vite, mes petits poissons!* You . . . dirty . . . *man!"*

"Merlyn!"

"You can't have Merlyn!" she retorts.

She exits through the bathroom door. Creighton sloshes out of the tub and follows. The weight of his damp shorts drag at him. He strips them off and tosses them away, grabbing for his robe at the same time.

Merlyn is not in her bedroom. He stumbles into his own quarters, but she is not there, so he wobbles weak-kneed to the hall door and through it.

"Merlyn!"

He finds her standing at the far end of the corridor, looking up at the maimed photograph of her grandmother. Creighton hurries to her side, but she spins away from him, hands upraised as if to ward off evil.

"Don't touch me!" she commands. "Keep your hands off!"

"Merlyn, calm down, you're overwrought. Come to bed, I'll—"

"What? You can't give me a sedative, you don't have any more hypodermics. Or isn't that the way you want to inject me?" She laughs hysterically. "What do you want from me *now?* I'm ugly! Can't you see I'm ugly?" She claws away her soap-stringy hair from the cut and torn contusions she sustained in the preserved-food room. "Ugly! Go push your dirty thing in someone else!"

"Merlyn," he tries to reason with her, "I won't touch you any more. Just come to bed."

"So you can crawl over me? Look at me! *Ugly!*"

"No, Merlyn, you're a beautiful young woman."

Eyes wide with fright, she shakes her head in violent denial, flailing her arms in the direction of Charlotte's slashed picture. *"She's* beautiful, not me!"

"Why? Because of those wounds? They'll heal. You'll be more lovely than Charlotte ever—"

"Oh, no I won't!" Turning once more to the picture, she laughs mockingly. "Grandma, you win! I'm going to be *just like you!"* When she lifts her strong, sculptor's hands to her eyes, Creighton thinks Merlyn is weeping, but then she faces him again and he sees the blood streaming down her fingers and out of gouged, empty sockets.

"MERLYN!"

Aubrey House rocks dizzily about him. Sick with nausea and horror, Creighton lurches forward. His foot slips on one of Merlyn's ruined eyes and he skids to a jarring crash beneath Charlotte's sightless picture. A pain rips across his bare arm.

Backing away from his blundering approach, Merlyn screams for him to leave her alone. She smashes into a wall she cannot see, reels, totters away from where she hears him groaning from another sudden shooting stab of pain.

Fleeing from the sound, Merlyn touches the surface of an unlocked, knobless door. In her fright she hurls herself through. Creighton yells a desperate warning to her, but it is drowned out by Merlyn's mortal howl of terror.

Merlyn Aubrey lay moaning at the foot of the dark, steep servants' staircase, her neck broken.

Oh God, Richard...where are you? I need you...I hurt.

Soft footsteps descend toward her.

St. Bridget, Richard...see? Now she'll never never want me.

But peering up into the gloom, Merlyn realizes the dusky figure standing on the steps above her is not Richard.

"Little Miss Dollytop, you better get up from there."

"Lizzy? That really *you?*"

"Mm-hmm. Here, baby, let me help you."

Merlyn whimpers. "But it hurts me to move."

Paying her no mind, the other lifts Merlyn by the shoulders and steadies her onto her feet.

"Lizzy, how'd you *do* that? I don't hurt any more!"

"That's 'cause you're dead, honey."

Merlyn stands very still, hardly daring to believe her good fortune. "Oh, Lizzy, *am* I? Really and truly?"

"Really-truly."

A bright smile breaks out on Merlyn's face. She feels like laughing, singing. With a wonderful new sense of freedom, she starts off down the stairs, passing by the broken shell that was once herself.

But the old woman puts a restraining hand on Merlyn's arm.

"What is it, Lizzy?"

"You gotta come upstairs with me."

Merlyn pouts. "How come?"

"Your gramma's waiting for you."

CREIGHTON'S CHOICES

■

On the steps not far above Merlyn Aubrey's stiffening corpse sits Richard Creighton, cinching the sash of his dressing gown around his left arm, which was deeply sliced when he fell into the large fragments of glass that dropped from the frame of Charlotte's picture when Charles Singleton shattered it. He has already lost a considerable quantity of blood.

Feeling weak and rather lightheaded, the philosopher wearily cudgels his brain into considering the options of his plight.

—Not much farther to the first floor. Struggle down the stairs. Through the laundry room, kitchen, pantry, main hall to the living room. Piano bench, telephone. Dial Operator. Emergency. Still another disaster at Aubrey House.

Or

—Let it end.

Arguments pro vita?

—Imagine: Creighton, Richard Alan, B.A., M.S., Ph.D., authority: metaphysics, epistemology, interdisciplinary convergence. Latest work explores further reaches of relativism as applied to paranormal experience, specific application— survival. Experimental model: Aubrey House, R.D.1, Doylestown, Pennsylvania.

Needed?

—Charles will live and write his book and get things all wrong. Close, but reinterpreted for the acolytes.

Whereas?

—?

Imagine: Creighton, R.A., definitive word on events at Aubrey House!

—Irrelevant personal desire to be final arbiter.

Yes: a rush to interpret, just like Charlie. Drew. Merlyn. Vita.

291

—But Singletonian opus will mislead.

Sure about that?

—No.

Therefore ... other arguments?

Creighton muses on the Aubrey paradox, unable to sort the conflicting strains of logic and intuition as his brain labors from lack of oxygen.

—No answers. Only questions, suppositions, probabilities. Striking theory of psychic energy.

Untested.

—Testable. But only if I live.

Fallacious. Cf. CREIGHTON, R. & KORR, S.E., (1978), Mental Efficiency and Waste: *"Nothing is ever lost. In a world surfeited with talent, an idea ripe for the times will repeatedly and often simultaneously resurface. It is a natural process of cognitive evolution."*

Silence. Creighton struggles for air.

—In that case, some value to practical personal observation of Aubrey effect *in extremis.*

Lana? Marla?

—Every death. All the murdered seconds of my past.

Living: desirable a priori?

—Paradox of beauty and horror. Mahler craving Heaven on the brink of godlessness. Nietzsche dancing over old terrors while his mind and body and nation all decayed from within.

Conclusion?

—Decision to ... endure: arbitrary product of individual's ... given circumstances ... moment to moment ...

A far-off shrilling from below. Lichinsky calling? Singleton? Armbruster at the door? Or just the chimelike sounds too often heard when the human mind descends into trance?

Logy and cold, Creighton makes a token effort to rise and go answer the phone, is surprised to learn he cannot move his limbs. His mind dimly perceives the new wetness trickling down his slashed arm.

—Funny ...

?

—Didn't . . . tie sash tight enough . . . no need . . . no need to choose . . . after all . . .

His own voice. Garbled. What words?

". . . Perry's subjects passed beyond clinical . . ."

—?

". . . but what does that mean? Only that their hearts were not . . ."

?

". . . not functioning. However . . ."

However?

". . . blood in . . . skulls not totally dysfunctional . . ."

—Yes, but where *am* I?

Outside Aubrey House. The road beyond the driveway absolutely deserted. Dark Pennsylvania woods, fields extending to an empty horizon. Stars sparkling in moonless September sky. The silence of a total vacuum, save for a cutting night wind.

—Dead?

Reasonable assumption. Bled to death.

A pall of loneliness and cold.

—This the traditional Afterlife? Where's Marla? Merlyn? Anyone?

Several ways of interpreting.

—?

World of night = custom-tailored punishment. Torment designed specially for soul in spiritual limbo.

—Or?

Not punishment. Afterlife as accidental byproduct of happenstance universe.

—Or?

Aubrey House reproducing both *conditions from the building blocks of your ambivalence toward survival beyond death, plus guilt vis-à-vis Marla/Lana/Merlyn.*

—No.

A reverse Rorschach, an inkblot that interprets the patient: Aubrey's energy pool refracting what the subcon-

*scious mind most wants and/or fears—for you, an eternity
of solitude to wander in...*

—No!

...and Dr. Richard Creighton the very first and only
ghost *ever to exist.*

—*NO!*

The echo of his own words suspended in time.

"...oxygen flowing across their brain cells..."

—Yes, let *that* be it: my body really slumped on the rear
staircase, my dying brain hallucinating this whole irrelevant
horror.

But still—the dark Pennsylvania road before him un-
wavering, unchanging, a problem without a solution like
the squaring of a circle or trying to find the law of succession
of prime numbers.

Silence. The surface of the distant lake shadowy and
motionless.

Shivering at the keen slice of the wind's blade, the lonely
man trudged wearily into darkness. Overhead, the night sky,
pinpricked with a thousand glinting stars, shone down on
him and the fear-shot work of the Seven Days with a cold
blue indifferent light.